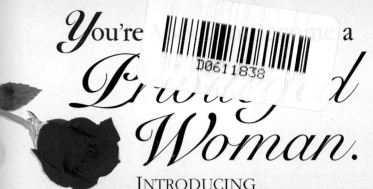

You're a

Privileged

Woman.

INTRODUCING
PAGES & PRIVILEGES™.

It's our way of thanking you for buying
our books at your favorite retail store.

Get all this Free
WITH JUST ONE PROOF OF PURCHASE:

◆ **Hotel Discounts** up
to 60% at home and
abroad ◆ **Travel Service**
- Guaranteed lowest
published airfares
plus 5% cash back

$50 VALUE

on tickets ◆ **$25 Travel Voucher**

◆ **Sensuous Petite Parfumerie** collection

◆ **Insider Tips Letter**
with sneak previews
of upcoming books

You'll get a FREE personal card, too.
It's your passport to all these benefits– and to
even more great gifts & benefits to come!

There's no club to join. No purchase commitment. No obligation.

Enrollment Form

☐ *Yes!* I WANT TO BE A *Privileged Woman.*

Enclosed is one *PAGES & PRIVILEGES*™ Proof of Purchase from any Harlequin or Silhouette book currently for sale in stores (Proofs of Purchase are found on the back pages of books) and the store cash register receipt. Please enroll me in *PAGES & PRIVILEGES*™. Send my Welcome Kit and FREE Gifts -- and activate my FREE benefits -- immediately.

More great gifts and benefits to come like these luxurious Truly Lace and L'Effleur gift baskets.

▶ DETACH HERE AND MAIL TODAY!

NAME (please print)
_____

ADDRESS _____ APT. NO _____

CITY _____ STATE _____ ZIP/POSTAL CODE _____

☐📖 **PROOF OF PURCHASE**
Pages & Privileges™
SAMPLE ONLY

Please allow 6-8 weeks for delivery. Quantities are limited. We reserve the right to substitute items. Enroll before October 31, 1995 and receive one full year of benefits.

NO CLUB! NO COMMITMENT!
*Just one purchase brings you great **Free Gifts** and **Benefits!***
(More details in back of this book.)

Name of store where this book was purchased_____

Date of purchase_____

Type of store:

☐ Bookstore   ☐ Supermarket   ☐ Drugstore

☐ Dept. or discount store (e.g. K-Mart or Walmart)

☐ Other (specify)_____

Which Harlequin or Silhouette series do you usually read?
_____

Complete and mail with one Proof of Purchase and store receipt to:

U.S.: *PAGES & PRIVILEGES*™, P.O. Box 1960, Danbury, CT 06813-1960

Canada: *PAGES & PRIVILEGES*™, 49-6A The Donway West, P.O. 813, North York, ON M3C 2E8

PRINTED IN U.S.A

"I'm far from perfect,"

Fiona said quietly.

"So am I."

He leaned forward and kissed the corner of her lips. Her mouth was ripe, and as enticing as forbidden fruit. He could feel the warmth of her breath as she sighed, but she didn't pull away. He enclosed her in his arms, a safe warm harbor, and took her lips fully. There was such a sweetness, such innocent seduction, in the way she yielded, a sigh, a gradual melting of her body into his, slowly, ever so slowly.

He had never been one to play games with women, to pressure or even to woo. Women had come to him, women with no thoughts of commitment. Women who liked his warm smile and the touch of his strong, wide hands. Women who had remained friends when they were no longer lovers.

Women so different from the one he held in his arms.

Now he saw how dangerous the most honorable intentions could be.

Dear Reader,

Welcome once again to a month of excitingly romantic reading from Silhouette Intimate Moments. We have all sorts of goodies for you, including the final installment of one miniseries and the first book of another. That final installment is *MacDougall's Darling,* the story of the last of The Men of Midnight, Emilie Richards's latest trilogy. The promised first installment is Alicia Scott's *At the Midnight Hour,* beginning her family-themed miniseries, The Guiness Gang. And don't forget *The Cowboy and the Cossack,* the second book of Merline Lovelace's Code Name: Danger miniseries.

There's another special treat this month, too: *The Bachelor Party,* by Paula Detmer Riggs. For those of you who have been following the Always a Bridesmaid! continuity series from line to line, here is the awaited Intimate Moments chapter. And next month, check out Silhouette Shadows!

Finish off the month with new books by Jo Leigh and Ingrid Weaver. And then come back next month and every month for more romance, Intimate Moments style.

Enjoy!

Yours,

Leslie Wainger
Senior Editor and Editorial Coordinator

Please address questions and book requests to:
Silhouette Reader Service
U.S.: 3010 Walden Ave., P.O. Box 1325, Buffalo, NY 14269
Canadian: P.O. Box 609, Fort Erie, Ont. L2A 5X3

HEARTBREAKERS

Emilie Richards

MacDougall's Darling

THE MEN OF MIDNIGHT

RITA
—Award—
Winning
Author

Silhouette®
INTIMATE™MOMENTS®

Published by Silhouette Books

America's Publisher of Contemporary Romance

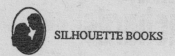 SILHOUETTE BOOKS

ISBN 0-373-07655-X

MACDOUGALL'S DARLING

Copyright © 1995 by Emilie Richards McGee

This edition published by arrangement with Harlequin Books S.A.

® and TM are trademarks of Harlequin Books S.A., used under license. Trademarks indicated with ® are registered in the United States Patent and Trademark Office, the Canadian Trade Marks Office and in other countries.

Printed in U.S.A.

EMILIE RICHARDS

Award-winning author Emilie Richards believes that opposites attract, and her marriage is vivid proof. "When we met," the author says, "the only thing my husband and I could agree on was that we were very much in love. Fortunately, we haven't changed our minds about that in all the years we've been together." The couple has lived in eight states—as well as a brief, beloved sojourn in Australia—and now resides in Ohio.

Though her first book was written in snatches with an infant on her lap, Emilie now writes full-time—unless the infant, now twelve, reminds her that it's her turn to do car pool. She loves writing about complex characters who make significant, positive changes in their lives. And she's a sucker for happy endings.

For Linda and Bruce Beebe,
who made it easy to go to Scotland, and for
Emily Jarvis, who made it easy to be there.

Prologue

1965

There were few stars visible. Those that were streaked through the inky night sky each time Terence MacDougall narrowed his eyes and tilted his head to peer at them.

"Falling to the earth, they are! All the stars in the bloody sky falling to the earth, and no' a thing to be done about it!"

With the last word he stumbled over a stone and sprawled facedown, sinking inches into the peaty soil before he could determine exactly what had happened. With a supreme effort he rolled to his back and faced the sky again. When his head was cradled securely the stars no longer blazed across the sky. They danced a flirty Highland fling, winking their wee starry eyes and twitching their wee starry bottoms. He crooned a tune in encouragement.

"O' the Highland lass will love all day and niver ask yer pardon. But the Lowland lass niver loves a'tall. She'd rather be yer warden...."

Terence could keep a pub full of brawny Highlanders enthralled with his fine tenor voice and colorful lyrics. But he wasn't at his best sprawling fifteen yards from Loch Ceo's shore without an audience. He cleared his throat to try again, but no tunes came to mind. He stared at the sky, and the stars rearranged themselves again, spelling out a message like a glittering theater marquee in far-off Edinburgh.

He pointed his index finger and read the words out loud. "Terence MacDougall, Esquire, requests the pleasure of yer attendance at the christening of his firstborn son..."

His voice trailed off. He couldn't remember what Jane planned to name the bairn. He would have no say in the matter at all, of course. Jane was a strong-willed woman, given to fits of stubbornness and red-haired fury.

Had it been his fault that she'd gone into labor a week ahead of schedule so he hadn't been home to help? Had it been *his* fault that Jane's own granny, who had agreed to assist with the delivery, had fallen sound asleep and couldn't be wakened when the pains got sharper?

No, nothing was Terence's fault, except planting the braw laddie inside Jane, of course. And hadn't it turned out all right, anyway? Jane had found her way to the wee cottage hospital and borne their new son in one of its sterile rooms. And she'd had plenty of company.

Plenty of company.

He crooned a new tune. "O' the laird and lady came to town in shoes of Spanish leather. Old MacDougall came to town arrayed in heath and heather...."

Aye, *his* son, Terence MacDougall's own son, had been born at the same moment as the laird's. Right beside him...or nearly so. Old Dr. Sutherland had caught the laird's heir, while Jane had delivered Terence's by herself in the next room.

And there was the wee matter of the other babe, the third male bairn who had been born at exactly the same moment in the bed beside Lady Ross's. The son of the innkeeper, Donald Sinclair, caught just in the nick of time by Dr. Sutherland's nurse, Jeanne.

Three laddies, born exactly at midnight on Hallowe'en. And no one who had been in the hospital that night could testify which had come first or last.

Gingerly Terence sat up. The effects of a night of whisky were beginning to weigh on him. He had promised Jane that once she'd given him a son, he would stop his drinking and look for a steady job. He had every intention of keeping his word, but even Jane couldn't expect him to stay sober before the lad came home from the hospital. He was a father now. There was much to consider.

He stood on wobbly legs and squinted into the darkness. Just ahead, the silver gleam of the loch beckoned to him. He lived on the loch, just around the bend, but he had chosen this place on the shore for its unobstructed view and isolation. No one was about.

He stumbled forward and thought not a whit about the other stones that were conspiring to trip him. The loch belonged to Terence. Loch Ceo's waters ran through his veins; her waves beat against the shore in the precise rhythms of his heart. He was as shallow as her shoals and as profound as her uncharted depths. He was wed to her in a way that he would never be wed to Jane.

"I've a son now," he shouted when at last the icy water lapped at his shoeless feet. He had lost his shoes somewhere on the journey here from the village—it was not the first pair. He waded deeper, ignoring the shock. "I've a son, darling! A wee laddie with hair as red as his mum's and eyes like autumn heather. Did you hear me, darling?"

The waves picked up, as if in answer. But it was not the loch to whom Terence spoke.

"I dinna know what we'll call him. Fergus, perhaps. Or Geddes. Geddes MacDougall. Do you like that, darling? Does that suit you?"

His words echoed back to him in spurts and wisps. He knew immediately that neither name suited. He tried again to remember what Jane had wanted to name the bairn if it was a lad. He regretted for an instant that he hadn't listened harder. Jane was a good lass. She deserved better than he gave her. Was it her fault that his loyalty, his deepest love, was reserved for another?

"Andrew!" The name came to him in a flash. Aye, he and Jane had discussed names one night before he wandered into the village for his nightly rounds at the hotel pub. Now it popped into his whisky-sodden brain. "Andrew Mac-Dougall. Do you like that, darling? Does that suit you better?"

There was no movement on the loch, but he knew that Andrew would suit, and well. "There were two others born this night," he shouted. "But our lad was the brawniest, darling. There's some who are saying already that the births are an omen, it being Hallowe'en night and all. That the three laddies' destinies are entwined. Do you think so?"

The picture of the three infants formed in Terence's head. When he had arrived at the hospital, they had already been laid out side by side in three wee cradles, and even the laird had not dared to make a fuss. In the presence of the others, each babe had quieted, as if the laddies belonged together and knew it somehow. They were uncommonly handsome weans, not a puny one among them.

He didn't know he was weeping until the tears frosted against his cheeks. Only then did he realize that his feet were numb and the numbness was creeping toward his knees.

"Show yerself, darling," he crooned. "Show me ye're happy, too."

A large part of Terence's life had been spent staring at the loch. Had he pursued his studies with half as much concentrated zeal, he would possess a university degree. Had he spent his energies on a job, he would possess a country estate and a braw house somewhere north of Princes Street in Edinburgh.

"Show yerself, and let me see how happy ye are for me!"

He stood motionless and waited on legs that had lost all feeling. A cloud crossed over the crescent moon, and the loch was a shrouded mirror. Then, as the cloud passed, the loch shone clearly again, an undisturbed stretch of water that passed seamlessly into the horizon, undisturbed except for a large ripple in the center, widening and dipping and lapping its way toward the shore.

"Darling," Terence breathed. "My very own darling."

He shaded his eyes, although there was no glare. He wished for field glasses, for the crystal clear vision of his youth, for a head unclouded by the pub's best whisky. A shape appeared, a silhouette as graceful, as proud as a beautiful woman. "Mercy." But he needed no mercy, no rescue, no explanation.

"Mercy, darling. At last! And what a night ye've chosen."

He stared for what seemed like forever, until the loch was once again as still as the moment before dawn. His legs were numb clear to his hips when he finally turned away. He stumbled, but he had expected to, and he caught himself as he fell. The icy waters washing his hips and chest chilled him to the core, but they were no match for the warmth blazing inside him.

He was Terence MacDougall, husband of Jane, and now, father of Andrew. He was a failure in all the ways that the world counted success. He was a drunken fisherman and tour boat guide, a worthless storyteller and composer of bawdy songs.

He was the man who had just witnessed a miracle.

He clawed his way to the shore and slapped and rubbed his legs until feeling began to return. Then he stood gingerly and headed around the bend in the direction of the lochside cottage that had always been his home. At the precise point where his view would become obscured by trees, he turned. His voice was choked with emotion.

"Farewell, darling."

There was no answer, but Terence hadn't expected one. Miracles neither spoke nor showed themselves twice. He would live the rest of his life on the strength of this one. He would teach his son about miracles.

"Farewell, darling. And remember the lad's name is Andrew. Just so's ye'll know when you meet him. He'll be a fine laddie, our Andrew. I promise. A fine, fine lad."

There was no answering ripple, but Terence knew his darling had heard. He had lost his hat along with his shoes, but he tipped it anyway before he disappeared into the trees.

Chapter 1

Not too far away, in a lake so deep that its waters lap at the very center of the earth, there lived a young water dragon named Stardust. Perhaps that seems like an odd name for a dragon, but even on nights when the stars shine their brightest over Serenity Lake, they are only twinkling, shifting specks of dust to the creatures who live beneath the surface. On such a night, Stardust was born.

Fiona Sinclair looked down at the hint of green peeking through an eternity of cotton candy clouds. To anyone gazing skyward from that lush landscape, the plane on which she traveled would be a tiny speck, a silver daylight star. She had gazed at the skies often enough in her twenty-five years, gazed and dreamed and made a wish on every passing plane that she would be on the next one.

It was a cliché, but too true, anyway. She should have been more careful about what she wished for.

"Do you have a little girl?"

Fiona turned her gaze to the dark-haired child seated at the end of the opposite aisle. She hadn't really noticed her before. Fiona hadn't noticed much of anything since boarding the plane except the fear generating and regenerating inside her. Now she summoned a smile. "No."

"Then who's that for?" The little girl, dressed in a red skirt, red tights and a red T-shirt swirling with silver and gold pinwheels, pointed to the book in Fiona's lap.

"My niece. Her name's April, and she's almost eight. How old are you?"

"Oh, much older," the little girl said with a world-weary sigh. "Nearly ten."

Fiona nodded gravely. "Then I suppose you're too old for picture books."

"Definitely. But I read the Stardust books. When I was a kid."

Yesterday, Fiona translated silently. "And what did you think of them? Did I make a good choice?"

"She'll probably like it okay. Is that a new one?"

High, high praise. Fiona surprised herself with a genuine smile—the kind she thought she'd left somewhere back on the ground. "Yes. The newest." As a matter of fact, the book wasn't even in the stores yet. Fiona was the author, and her advance copies had come as she was gathering her luggage for the trip to the airport.

The little girl leaned across the aisle and squinted at the cover. "It looks like Stardust has a new friend."

"I think she finally decides she has to swim to the other side of the lake and look for another family of water dragons."

"But she was scared to leave her cove. She was scared to go anywhere else."

Fiona silently handed the book across the aisle.

The little girl took it with naked enthusiasm. She was halfway through the first page when she looked up. She struggled to look bored again. "I'll just read it and tell you how it is, in case it's no good."

"I know you'll be honest." Fiona sat back and closed her eyes.

There were so many routes to those dragons across the lake, and so many ways to get there. Swimming was only one.

She heard a giggle across the aisle, and the rustle of a page. She wondered—as she had every minute of every day since she had begun to plan her own escape—if she would survive this taste of the world beyond her own cove.

It was not Andrew's fault that his clothes smelled of smoke and his fingernails were imbedded with ashes. Nor was it his fault that his hands weren't quite steady. He had scrubbed them repeatedly, blistered skin and all, at a cottage near the scene of the accident, scrubbed them with soap designed to dissolve everything it touched, including a layer or more of skin. But the ashes and the blisters would remain for a long time still.

So would the memories.

He was not a man to be easily shaken. He had worked on North Sea oil rigs since the day he graduated from university, and he had seen his fair share of disasters. In his days as a diver he had discovered the body of a comrade wedged between two pieces of pipe, deep in Davy Jones' locker. As a drilling engineer on a control platform he had watched a ninety-knot wind sweep a pair of Norwegian roughnecks to Valhalla. He had volunteered for rescue missions on land and sea and never flinched when called upon.

But the tragedy he'd witnessed this afternoon was enough to make him wish he could pull over to the side of the road and have a good cry.

He couldn't pull over. He was already late, despite his promise to Duncan Sinclair that he would not leave Duncan's sister Fiona waiting at Prestwick Airport. He had been entrusted with Fiona's safety, fragile, frightened Fiona, who had rarely been away from her home in New York. Fiona, who at twenty-five was beginning a journey that might lead straight back home if Andrew didn't get to the airport soon.

For a man in a hurry, his driving was nothing short of pitiful. In the past hour he hadn't come close to the speed limit. Each time his foot pressed the accelerator, he saw twisted metal and clouds of poisonous, choking smoke.

And he heard the cries of a child.

The surrounding traffic slowed to his speed as he neared Prestwick. Now there was nothing he could do except pull into line at the motorway exit and follow the stream of cars to the airport car park. It was an hour beyond Fiona's arrival time when he locked his door and started toward the terminal.

Prestwick was a maze of airline counters and waiting areas. He scanned computer monitors, but he was so late that Fiona's flight was no longer listed. He stood in an interminable line to find out where her plane had landed, then jogged toward the appropriate gate, weaving his way through crowds colorfully dressed in saris and turbans, Savile Row business suits and skimpy resort wear. He asked for directions from a teenager whose pale green hair clashed with a plaid kilt worn above knee-high cowboy boots. But only when the young man pointed at the gate just behind him did he spot the woman sitting in a remote corner.

Andrew stood absolutely still as he gazed at her. Fiona had been three at their last meeting. He had been eight. She was the wee sister he'd never had, the sister torn from him by tragedy and the manipulation of unfeeling adults. In the years since, he had tried more than once to imagine her growing up. Through Duncan's eyes he had followed her progress, even gazed at rare photographs. But nothing had prepared him.

Nothing.

Fiona looked up, and her eyes met his. He was not a man to wax poetic. Gold was gold, and brown was brown. But as he walked toward her, he could see that Fiona's eyes were a glorious combination, butterscotch sunshine, molasses moonlight, vibrant, courageous beacons in a face fast giving way to terror.

"Andrew?"

"Aye." He approached her slowly, carefully, as he would approach a wild creature. "Aye, I'm Andrew. And it's glad I am you're still here, Fiona."

Her lips curved into a forced smile. Her words emerged one at a time, as if each took great fortitude. "Where would I have gone?"

Gingerly he took the seat beside her. They were the only people at the gate. A sign explained that the next flight scheduled to use this area wasn't due to arrive for another two hours. "I was afraid you might turn around and go home."

She looked away, presenting him with a snub-nosed profile and clouds of pale red-gold hair. "Well, I thought about it. But it's a very long trip."

"I left in plenty of time this morning. I truly did. It's just that there was an accident...." He didn't want to go on.

Curls whirled in disarray as she faced him. "Oh, I'm so sorry. Are you all right? You weren't hurt?"

"No, I came along afterward."

"Then the road was blocked?"

That had been the least of it. "Aye."

"Do you know...? Was anyone...?"

"It was a bad crash." He looked down at his blistered hands, still red from their scrubbing, still imbedded with ashes. He clasped them behind him so that he wouldn't have to look at them and remember. "So, tell me about your flight. Was it comfortable? Did they feed you well?"

"I didn't eat."

"And why was that?"

"My heart took up all the room in my throat."

He surprised himself with a laugh. If he'd thought about it, he wouldn't have dared. He knew Fiona was deadly serious, that the flight here had probably cost her every ounce of courage she'd ever hoarded. But at his laughter, she smiled again. And this time the smile—a Mona Lisa beauty—was almost genuine.

"I know it sounds funny." She made a wry face, and soft ginger-colored freckles danced along her nose and cheeks. "I'm afraid you're about to find out what a barrel of laughs I am."

"Never." He sobered. "Have I told you how glad I am to see you?"

"Are you?"

"You've changed a bit. Grown a foot or three, but you're still our Fiona."

"Am I?" She shrugged, and the movement sent the collar of her long-sleeved blouse sliding up her neck before it settled against her throat again. Only then did he notice the scars that her hair and collar had hidden.

His gaze wandered with studied casualness back to her face. "Aye. Welcome home, darling. It's been far too long."

Color washed her cheeks, a pale apricot hue that warmed her fair skin. "Maybe not long enough."

He reached for her hand. Like his father before him, he was a man who touched easily. For all Terence Mac-Dougall's faults, he had taught his only son there was no shame in touching. Andrew wove his thick, ash-darkened fingers through Fiona's slender ones, ignoring her when she tried to pull away. Her hand was as soft as he had expected against the raw skin of his. He felt it tremble.

"Far too long," he said again. "This is where you belong, Fiona. It always will be. You have more family here than just Duncan, Mara and April. You've Iain and me, too, and Iain's wife, Billie. There's nowt that any of us would no' do for you."

"That's very kind, but—"

He squeezed her hand before he withdrew his. "Now we'll get you a bite to eat before we're on our way back to Druid-heachd. Have you talked to Duncan?"

"I phoned him. He told me that two different inspectors had shown up at the hotel unexpectedly last night, and both insisted on his undivided attention today. He said that you had volunteered to come here instead, and that you're a man of your word." She looked up at him through gold-tipped lashes. "If a bit slow about it."

He laughed. "Well, he's right, for all that. Let's find some food, then I'll ring him and explain."

She made a soft sound of protest, but he ignored it. He stood. "What about your bags?"

"A man from the airlines promised to store them for me at the baggage claim. I gave him my tickets."

"Then we'll eat first."

She stood, too. "I can easily wait, Andrew."

"Then you've more self-control than I do." He took her elbow as if he had been guiding her through crowds all his life. The gesture seemed to surprise her, but she didn't pull away. "I saw a café with sandwiches and coffee no' too far away. Will that be good enough?"

"Plenty good enough."

He walked slowly, purposely shortening his long stride. Duncan had told him once that Fiona limped. He noted now that there was an artfully feminine swish of her hips each time she stepped forward with her right foot, but nothing like he had expected. It did slow her pace a little, and he compensated easily.

He made conversation as much to put her at ease as to put the accident out of his mind. "Did you get any sleep on the plane?"

"Not a bit."

"I know your heart was in your throat, but what kept your eyes from closing?"

"I propped them open with my fingers so I wouldn't be sleeping when we crashed."

He groaned. "I was the same way the first time I flew."

"I don't believe it."

"It's true. But I was in a helicopter flying out to my first job as a diver off an oil platform, and I was supposed to be fearless. My job depended on it. So I whistled as loud as I could until the gent beside me threatened to loosen a few of my teeth."

"Not good for whistling."

He was already charmed by the sweetly serious way that she joked. She wasn't a bit sure of herself, but she wasn't so shy or retiring that he had to work to draw her out. From everything he had been told, he'd expected a woman who wouldn't meet his eyes. A floor watcher. Instead, the woman beside him was gazing avidly at everything and everyone that passed. She stayed close beside him, as if she were glad for his sheer masculine bulk, but as they walked, her eyes drank in every airport detail.

"Here we go." He abandoned her elbow and grabbed a door instead. "It's casual and quiet inside. You can eat and rest a few minutes before we start back."

There was an empty table near the door, and he took it, seating her where she could gaze through the glass partition at the passing crowds. She sank into her chair as if she had found a permanent home. Her eyes were grateful, but her lips were drawn in a thin, tight line. For the first time he clearly saw what her decision to come back to Scotland had cost her.

"You'll feel fit and ready for anything after you've had a bit to eat." He signaled a gray-haired woman in a white apron lounging against the front counter, and after she had uncurled herself one millimeter at a time, she ambled their way. Fast service was obviously not the motto here. Andrew wondered how many flights had been missed while passengers waited for a cup of coffee. "Do you know what you'd like? It looks as if you'll have plenty of time to decide."

"Soup, if they have it."

They settled on two bowls of beef and barley soup and a pot of hot tea. Andrew planned to sneak six lumps of sugar and half a liter of cream into Fiona's cup. He wished he could lace it with whisky, as well.

She spoke after their server ambled away. "Andrew, do you know that your hand is bleeding?"

He looked down. His hands throbbed, but that was no surprise. He had ignored the pain, even welcomed it as his due, an easily borne, infinitesimal particle of the human misery he had witnessed earlier. Now he saw that the skin along the heel of his right hand was cracked and swollen. And there was blood.

"I'm sorry. Did I get it on your shirt?"

"I don't know. That's hardly the issue, is it?" She took her napkin and dipped it in the ice water that had been set before her. Then she dabbed it against Andrew's hand. Gently. More gently than anyone had ever touched him.

He had been fine until that simple kindness. He had been fine, but now, suddenly, he wasn't.

He got to his feet, but he couldn't think of an explanation he wanted her to hear. "I'm going to ring Duncan now. Will you be all right?"

"Of course. Go ahead." She looked as if she wanted to say more, but thankfully, she didn't.

He had to exit the restaurant and walk a distance to locate a telephone, but he wasn't sorry. Fiona didn't need to hear what he had to tell Duncan. As he waited to be connected, he stood with his back to the passing foot traffic and his hand cupped over his ear. When Duncan came on the line, he wasted no time on formalities.

"I'm here, Dunc. Fiona's fine, and we'll be on our way soon. We're just having something to eat first."

He waited for Duncan's anger to blow itself out before he spoke again. He registered but didn't really hear the scorching lecture on the other end. When Duncan fell silent, Andrew spoke. "There was a three-car pileup on A82. I was the first car on the scene. One of the cars ignited, Dunc. There were people inside."

Suddenly he couldn't say anything else. Until the moment Fiona had sponged his hand he had successfully pushed the worst of the accident out of his mind. Now, safely away from her, he relived it, in all its horror. He swallowed once. Twice. He still couldn't speak.

"Jeez, Andrew. I'm sorry." Duncan's tone was tortured with guilt. "Why didn't you tell me that right away? I should have known you'd have a good reason for keeping Fiona waiting."

"I would no' have come at all, if it was anyone but Fiona here waiting for me."

"Did you tell her?"

"None of the details. God, no. What could I say? It was a wee girl in the car, Duncan, and her parents. I was able to get the bairn out, but not her mum and dad. They're...no' with us anymore."

"Is the little girl going to be all right?"

"No." Andrew ran his hand through his hair. "They were taking her to Glasgow, to a hospital with a special burn unit, the same one where Fiona was taken...."

Duncan was silent, too.

"What could I say to Fiona?" Andrew asked. "What could I possibly tell her?"

He felt a hand on his shoulder, the faint pressure of a woman's fingers. He turned and saw Fiona gazing at him.

"You could have told Fiona the truth," she said. Her eyes gleamed with reproach. "Exactly the way you just told it to her brother."

Chapter 2

"I did no' want to upset you," Andrew said, when he and Fiona were on the motorway to Druidheachd. "I did no' want your first day back in Scotland to remind you of your own days in hospital."

"There's nothing you could say or not say that would make me forget them. I grew up in hospitals." Or maybe she hadn't grown up. Sometimes Fiona wasn't sure. "Pretending I was never hospitalized doesn't help me. Tiptoeing around the truth doesn't help, either."

"Do you want to hear all of it, then?"

Gazing at Andrew's profile as the motorway flashed by outside the window, Fiona considered. Neither of them had felt like eating after he'd finished his phone call with Duncan. They had gathered her luggage and started toward Druidheachd. But until now, they hadn't really talked.

Her memories of Andrew were hazy and childish. Fire-engine red hair. Being lifted to sit on shoulders that were sturdier than Duncan's and considerably lower to the ground than her own father's. A loud laugh. A bright smile. And stories coming so thick and fast that she could hardly savor one before another had begun.

That boy, the hero of her early childhood, was now a man. And what a man he was. The sturdy youthful shoulders were as broad as an oxen yoke. The hair had ripened to a darker shade, a rich shining auburn that fell in a thick shock across his forehead. His hands—now she understood why they were sore and bleeding—were a giant's hands. Andrew was everything she wasn't—brash, strong, fearless. He was exactly the kind of man who had always frightened her the most.

She stared ahead of her. "I think you should tell me. Yes."

He began, but his reluctance was obvious. "I left my house early this morning. I did no' want you to be forced to wait for me. I knew..."

She saved him from further explanation. He had understood how frightened she might be of coming to Scotland, frightened of the things that everyone else took for granted. "Thanks for that."

He continued. "It's been so long since you've been here. I'm certain you can no' remember the roads near the village. They've changed hardly at all since you were a wee lass. They're as narrow, as curved and treacherous, as they were in our grandparents' time. In *their* grandparents' time."

"And if drivers take them half as fast as you take this motorway, then there's bound to be trouble."

He tapped the brake immediately. "I normally travel at twice this speed."

"Maybe it seems fast to me because you insist on driving on the wrong side of the road." He glanced at her, and she forced a smile.

"There were few cars on the road at that hour." His hands gripped the wheel. "I was planning what I would do when I got to the airport. How I would spend the time before your flight. I calculated that I'd have to wait at least an hour. So I decided to take the longer way there. It's a bit more scenic, and it seemed a fair way to waste time. I was between two villages, on a stretch in the mountains, when I saw smoke rising from somewhere beyond. I thought perhaps someone was burning strips of moorland. It's done to encourage certain types of undergrowth for game birds, and this is the proper time of year. I thought it might be interesting to watch."

"I wish it had been that innocent." Fiona could see from Andrew's expression that he wished the same.

"When I got on a straight bit of road, the smoke thickened. I could see cars ahead of me. For a moment I thought they had stopped to watch the fire, too. Then I realized they *were* the fire, that there had been an accident, a pileup. I still dinna know how it happened. Who was going in which direction, or why they collided. The road was steep. Perhaps brakes failed. Someone panicked. But the three cars were at angles across the road, two of them folded together as if they'd come off a line just that way. I got as close as I dared—there was more and more smoke every moment. I was afraid of an explosion. I pulled off the road and began to run...."

Fiona sat quietly, her hands clenched together. He was much too good a storyteller. She could see the accident unfolding before her. She didn't prod him to continue. She heard him fighting his emotions, trying to tame them to spare her his misery.

But they would not be tamed. He spoke faster, as if to finish sooner. "There was a man in a business suit slumped over the steering wheel of the car that was closest to me. His car seemed to be the least damaged, and when I started toward him, he waved me on and opened his door. He managed to get himself out and away from the fire. There was an old woman collapsed against the door of the next car. The door was hardly that anymore. There was no way to open it, but I was able to reach her from the other side and drag her free. I carried her away from the crash. She revived as I carried her, and I laid her on the side of the road beside the man from the first car."

"You probably saved her life."

Andrew didn't acknowledge Fiona's statement, as if it were too insignificant to comment on. "Another car had arrived and stopped by then, full of half-grown lads. One of them ran with me back to the wreck. The smoke was thicker, and I could see flames licking at the interior of the first car.

I knew there was no one else inside, and we went straight to the third. There was a man at the wheel—or what had been the wheel—and a woman beside him. They were already dead." He slammed his palm against the steering wheel. "I hope to God they were already dead, Fiona."

She rested her hand on his shoulder for a moment. She didn't know what else to do. Her eyes filled with tears, which were infinitely preferable to the vision that filled his.

"The flames were fast growing thicker. I knew it would only be seconds at best before the petrol blew. I shouted to the lad to get away, and I started to back away, too. Then I heard a child screaming. I shielded my face and leaned forward, and I saw what I'd missed. Right in the midst of the smoke and flames there was a child strapped into the back seat. And she was..."

"Don't!" She took a deep breath. For a moment the world grew dark. She took another, and another, until the darkness receded. "I'm sorry. I..."

"You dinna need to apologize."

Minutes passed before she spoke again. "You got her out?"

"Aye. And the tank blew just after."

"Oh, Andrew."

"A crofter had seen the flames, and it was no' long before assistance arrived. We did what we could for the wee lass until they took her away. But she was badly injured."

She heard the truth in his voice, not his words. He didn't expect the child to survive. "There've been so many advances, so many new ways to care for...burned children. It may not be as terrible as you think."

"I dinna even know her name. If I ring them, they'll tell me that I've no right to know her condition."

Fiona was silent. She replayed his words in her head. She measured her own fears, a lifetime of living as a recluse, the insecurities that had kept her a child for twenty-five years. When she spoke, her voice was firm. Confidence that she didn't feel buoyed it. "Then we'll go to the hospital, and we'll insist that they tell us."

"I'll no' drag you there, Fiona. If I go, I'll go alone. Later, when—"

"We'll go now, Andrew. Right now. And we'll make them tell us how she is. Because you won't sleep tonight, and you won't think about anything else until you know. And neither will I."

Andrew's doubts were as thick as the smoke at the scene of the accident. What odd hand of fate had drawn Fiona into this tragedy in her first hours on Scottish soil in more than twenty years? For all her brave talk, she looked as if a breeze would send her spinning. She had neither eaten nor slept since leaving New York. Even if he discounted how difficult it had been for her to come to Scotland at all, the picture was still of a woman using up her last reserves of strength.

He still had time to skirt Glasgow and continue toward Druidheachd. There was still time to alter their plan. "You're certain you want to do this?" he asked. "There's no shame in changing your mind."

"I would like to see how she is."

"I should no' have burdened you with any of this."

She was silent for so long that he thought she wasn't going to answer. "I've spent a lifetime not being burdened," she said at last. "I've been protected and sheltered until I'm not sure who or what I am. I had hoped it might be different here."

He had been chastised. There was no doubt. "It's just that—"

"It's just that I was burned as a child myself, and I was taken to the very same hospital. And because you're a kind man, you want to spare me those memories. Nothing can spare me, Andrew. I haven't forgotten any of it. I won't suddenly remember the horror of it when I walk through the door. It's with me always. I can face this."

There was nothing else he could say.

He knew Glasgow well. Almost no one would say it was Scotland's most picturesque city, although it was the largest. But there was an energy here that he found satisfying, a spirit of renewal that had transformed some of the city's worst defects. He came to Glasgow when he wanted to lose himself in her theaters or pubs, or just in her exuberant bustle. But today there was no joy in his drive through the city. He pointed out no landmarks or monuments. And when he finally parked his car in front of an imposing Victorian era building, he still couldn't find anything to say.

"We'll go in together," Fiona said. She didn't look at him.

"Aye."

"Andrew, whatever has happened to her, you did your best. How many men would have risked their life the way you did?"

"If I had found her first, she would no' have been so badly burned." He heard her quick intake of breath. Misery filled him. He had not meant to admit that.

"You rescued the survivors as you came to them! Anyone would have done the same. If you'd taken the time to survey the scene and make choices about who to rescue first, you might not have had the time to rescue anyone."

"I almost missed her completely. I panicked. I overlooked her at first. If I'd been more careful . . ."

"How can you be so hard on yourself?"

He got out of the car and came around to open her door. "It should never have happened."

"Now you're making sense. It shouldn't have." She stood to face him. "But unfortunately, nobody consulted you or me. And all we can do now is make the best of it."

Her chin was raised so high he almost didn't notice the slight wobble. Shame filled him. He was leaning on her, burdening her with his own misery. He had been sent to take care of her. Duncan had trusted him to take care of Fiona, and she was taking care of him.

"I'm sorry. I dinna know what's wrong with me. You're right. I'm no' God. I know that. It's just that . . ."

"You wish it could be different. I know. I understand that."

Andrew studied her face. She wasn't pretty. He decided that now. Her face was too sharp, too intense for so predictable a word. With her pale curry-colored hair, her ginger freckles and thin, turned-up nose, she might have been merely adorable—if her life had been different. But so much was written on Fiona's face, so much pain and longing and hope—especially hope—that no one would think her adorable again. Her amber eyes devoured everything in her path; they smoked with emotion. Her mouth was soft and vulnerable. And expressive. She was so obviously a woman who had never learned the art of letting any moment pass without wringing something from it or without letting her reaction show.

"Let's go," she said.

"Thank you."

"What are friends for?"

Not for what he wanted from Fiona. The realization came as an unwelcome surprise. Andrew thought of himself as a simple man. His taste in women had always been simple, too. He appreciated laughter, energy, buoyant good humor. He had looked for women who didn't take life seriously, and, most especially, who didn't take him seriously. Fiona was none of those things. She was a rare butterfly, slowly, so slowly, emerging from a dark, cramped cocoon. She could so easily be frightened away or, worse, injured. She was not for Andrew MacDougall, nor should he even want her to be.

And yet already he felt a pull toward her that went beyond anything as ordinary as friendship.

"We will no' stay long. I promise." He started toward the hospital entrance. He didn't want to think about his feelings anymore. He'd never thought of himself as a man who was capable of so many confusing emotions.

She fell into step beside him, and he slowed to accommodate her. They didn't speak again, not even when they were inside. They wound their way through the hospital maze, through nurses and desks and explanations of why no one could tell them anything. They moved steadily onward, but as they conquered each new hurdle, Andrew watched Fiona's skin grow paler and her step less confident.

"I want you to sit here and wait," he said at last, pointing to chairs outside the swinging doors that led to the sixth floor burn unit. It was the last place they could try, and a sympathetic nurse had suggested they come up and attempt to speak directly to someone on the floor. "There's nowt to be gained by going inside." When she started to protest, he held up his hand. "We might have better luck if I go by myself, Fiona. They might be less intimidated and more inclined to give me information."

She appeared to consider, then she nodded. "I'll wait."

He watched until she was seated before he pushed open the doors to continue his search for information. The unit was a long narrow hallway with a dozen rooms on either side and corridors leading in both directions. Personnel scurried from room to room, but no one was on duty at the central desk to help him. He knew better than to stop the nurses and doctors in the midst of their activity. Life and death were precariously balanced in this ward, and he remained out of the way, impatiently waiting until an older man in a white uniform stopped to ask if he needed help.

He explained as succinctly as he could. "I can no' get her face from my mind," he said, after he'd told his story. "I have to know if she made it, if she's going to be all right."

The man patted his shoulder. "I just came on duty. I'll check the records and see what I can find."

Andrew felt such a rush of gratitude, he couldn't speak. He nodded.

"Wait outside," the man said. "I'll get back to you as soon as I can."

Andrew went to wait with Fiona. He was encouraged for the first time. He strode out to tell her that they would know something soon, but Fiona wasn't there.

"She's so tiny. You're sure this is the right child?"

The nurse standing beside Fiona nodded solemnly. She was a young woman, not much older than Fiona, with a plain, sturdy face dominated by compassionate blue eyes. "Aye. This is the one that was brought in from the accident your friend described. We think she's not more than three."

Fiona stared through the glass at the dark hair spread across the white pillowcase, the pale heart-shaped face. There were tubes and machines and monitors. A nurse bent over the bed and adjusted the IV. "What are her chances?"

"Fair, I think. The moment she's out of recovery they'll take her up to the unit where you were waiting. She survived the surgery, and the burns aren't as extensive as your friend feared. Sometimes these injuries appear to be worse than they are."

"And sometimes they're worse than they appear."

"Her name is Hume, we think. The car was registered to a Robert Hume in Woodstock, England. The police are trying to trace her relatives now."

"The poor baby."

The nurse was silent for a moment. "I've seen far worse cases walk out of here and go on to lead normal lives."

"I was one of the ones who didn't walk out of here," Fiona said.

"Pardon?"

"I was a patient in this hospital when I was three. In the burn unit. And it was a long time before I walked."

"I'm sorry. I had no idea. Actually, I thought you were an American. From the accent."

"I was born in Scotland. After I was burned, I went to the States for rehabilitation. My mother was an American, and she insisted. I . . . I haven't been back until now."

"Then I'd say you have a natural bond with Miss Hume."

"I guess I do." Fiona wished she could go to the sleeping child and comfort her. She would need much comfort in the days to follow, and the people who could have offered it were dead.

"We have to go now. I really shouldn't have brought you up here. It's against all the rules."

Fiona summoned her dwindling resources to smile her appreciation. The nurse was the same one who had recommended that she and Andrew go directly to the burn unit for information. She had found Fiona there and reported that the child was in recovery after emergency surgery. She had offered to take Fiona to peek through the window in the door, but only if they went immediately. There had been no time to wait for Andrew to return.

Now they walked down the hall together and waited for the elevator that would take Fiona back upstairs to find Andrew. "Will they let us visit her, do you think? When she's able to have visitors? We're not family, but Andrew saved her life, and I . . ."

"I'll speak to her doctor. I'll tell him you were here and ask him to make a note in her chart."

The elevator door opened, and Fiona stepped inside. "You've been so kind."

"I feel so sorry for her, the poor wee dearie. If those were her parents in the car, then she'll be so alone through this. It seemed that since you were so concerned..."

"I appreciate it. Andrew will, too." She waved goodbye as the elevator closed its doors.

Andrew was pacing the sixth floor waiting room when she arrived.

"Are you all right?" He pushed his hair off his forehead, a useless gesture that was completely endearing.

"I'm just fine, and I think your friend is going to be, too."

"What do you mean?"

"I just saw her. I'm sorry you weren't with us, but there wasn't time to find you." She explained what had happened.

"She's in fair condition?"

"I think that was an educated guess. I'm not sure they're issuing any evaluations yet. But the nurse felt she has a good chance. She's burned over thirty to forty percent of her body, not all third degree. There was some internal bleeding. They had to do surgery, but it turned out to be relatively minor. The nurse couldn't be more specific than that. It was a miracle she told me that much."

Andrew sat down and rested his head in his hands. Fiona sat beside him. She focused on his hands, which looked swollen now, which they hadn't earlier. "Andrew, we're going to stop by the emergency room, or whatever you call it here, and get them to treat your hands. You're risking infection."

"You think she's going to be all right?"

"I think so. And she's being well cared for. They're searching for relatives now. They've traced the car to a Robert Hume in England."

He looked up. "There was a moment, just after I got her out, when I wondered if I'd done the right thing to try and save her. Did I do the right thing, Fiona? Now, with everything she has to go through, all the pain and sadness, did I do the right thing?''

She knew why he asked *her.* The answer was a gift that only she, or someone who had gone through the same terrible experiences, could give him. She had survived a fire, too. Had she wished sometimes that she hadn't? Did she wish it now, when she looked back at everything that was behind her?

"You did the right thing." She took a deep breath. She had said the words because they were the ones he most needed to hear. But they were true. She realized it with a new and profound relief. "You did the right thing, Andrew. And someday she'll be as happy as I am to be alive and to have a full life ahead of her."

His eyes glistened. He nodded.

Her heart turned over slowly. In that moment he was as vulnerable as she had been all the days of her life. She guessed that much of what he'd felt today was new to him. He was a strong man, a good man. But today he had needed strength. *Her* strength.

"Thanks," he said. His voice was husky.

"I think I'm ready to face Druidheachd."

"I think you're more than ready." He leaned over and kissed her cheek. His lips were warm, and the intimacy, the rare feeling of being cherished and accepted, was a streak of sunshine through her exhausted body.

"Let's go home, Andrew," she said, when he moved away.

"Aye, Fiona. Let's go home."

Chapter 3

The old gray stone building was not a prison. It was the first home Fiona had known as a child, the village hotel and pub that had been run for generations by her ancestors. The Sinclair Hotel was the rink where she had skated in wool socks across slate floors, the sanctuary where she had been wrapped snugly in the love of her family.

Until the night when the fires of hell had nearly consumed her.

"You were so young, no more than a wee girlie. Does it seem familiar?"

Fiona stared at the hotel from the passenger seat of Andrew's car. "I don't know what I remember or just what I've been told over the years."

"You were happy here. Always smiling, laughing. And dancing. I would sing, and you would dance."

"You remember that? You were only a little boy yourself."

"Aye, I remember."

She switched her gaze to Andrew. "Did you carry me on your shoulders?"

"Aye. Have you been told that?"

"No."

A smile peeked through the layers of exhaustion on his face. The smile seemed natural; the haggard lines of fatigue did not. "You would kick, and I would tell you to stop. Then you would pat my hair and tell me you were sorry. Just when I believed you'd learned your lesson, the exact moment I relaxed, you would kick me again."

"It seems a little late for an apology." She smiled, too.

"Let's go inside. Duncan and Mara will be waiting."

"You'll come, too?"

"Aye. There's nowt you can do to stop me." He opened his door and came around to open hers.

Fiona wasn't sure that she wanted Andrew to stay. He needed rest. The strain of the accident and its aftermath was clear, and she knew that his hands throbbed, although he hadn't complained. He had submitted to having his hands dressed and bandaged at the hospital, but he hadn't taken the painkillers issued to him, because he had needed a clear head to drive the rest of the way home. She wondered, too, if on some dark, unconscious level he welcomed the pain as his punishment for not rescuing the Hume child sooner.

There was a selfish reason for wanting him to leave, as well as one for wanting him to stay. Fiona was filled with pride, if not with courage, and she did not want Andrew to witness how difficult it would be for her to walk through the hotel's front door for the first time in twenty-two years.

Then there was the part of her that wanted to lean on him, the part that yearned to have him beside her. The part that was willing to sacrifice all her considerable pride for the strength and comfort of his presence.

He opened her door, and she knew the moment had come. He held out his hand. She took it gently, and her own hand was swallowed and cradled. "Duncan and Mara have made changes in the place," he said. "Mara appreciates everything old, and Dunc wants all the old swept away and replaced. Between them, they've struck a balance. It's cleaner, brighter. More welcoming. But it's still the same hotel."

Old. *Auld.* Something wept inside Fiona. Andrew's accent, thicker and more musical even than Mara's, connected with wisps of memory inside her. It was the sound of home, denied to her for twenty-two years. The sound of love and acceptance and the life that had been cruelly taken from her. She stood and looked up at him. Her throat was tight, and her heart swelled against her rib cage until it had no room to beat.

"You have only to walk through the front door," he said. "And it will be better."

She nodded. Denying her fear was futile. The blood had drained from her cheeks, and the hand enclosed in his was shaking.

They walked up a cobblestone path, past shrubs just on the verge of bloom. A sweet fragrance teased the air, and she saw rows of purple hyacinths outlining the border that circled the hotel.

"Aunt Fiona!" The door flew open, a massive wooden door that had creaked and groaned for centuries, and a child flew toward them. "Aunt Fiona!"

Andrew dropped her hand just in time for Fiona to fling open her arms. April fell into them. "Aunt Fiona!"

Fiona clasped her niece and held on for dear life. "You've grown. I can't believe it. You've grown again, and I just saw you."

"It's been months!"

"Too long."

"Welcome home, Fiona."

Fiona looked up and saw her brother standing in the doorway. For a moment there were only the two of them.

I'm back, Duncan, but I don't want to be here.

I know you don't, Fiona. I didn't expect you ever to find the courage to come home, but I'm glad you did.

She responded to the welcome he'd issued out loud. "Thank you," she said. She wanted to say more, but the words wouldn't come. His serious gray eyes didn't change as he smiled at her.

"Fiona." Mara pushed past her husband. Her blond hair fanned out behind her as she descended the steps. She seemed to float, as if she somehow had transcended the earth at her feet. Mara and Duncan had been married at Christmastime. Fiona had liked her new sister-in-law on sight. Mara was a large part of the reason she had come back to Scotland.

Fiona held out her arms, and they enveloped each other in warm hugs. Then Duncan was beside her, hugging her, too. She rested in the arc of his arms for a moment, Duncan, who had been the only true constant in a childhood gone berserk.

"Come on up to our apartment," he said. "We'll skip a tour for now. Mara will put on the kettle, and you can put your feet up. Then we'll have supper. I made linguine with clam sauce. Your favorite."

"You were always the best cook in our family."

"Andrew?" Duncan said. "We're expecting you, too. We've set a place for you."

"I dinna think so. I've—"

"Andrew, please come," Fiona said. She took a step toward him. Just one uncertain step. She extended her hand. "It will do you good. Please?"

He seemed torn and suddenly—terribly—alone. She took another step toward him. "Duncan really *can* cook. I promise."

He smiled at her. "Aye, I'll come."

"Goody!" April said. She flung herself at Andrew, and he caught her and swung her to his shoulders.

Fiona saw him grow paler, as if the little girl was the weight of the world. She knew the hands that had caught April must throb unmercifully, but when April was settled, he patted her legs. "Let's go, Springtime. You tell me where."

"Tell Uncle Andrew to take you straight to our apartment," Duncan said. "He's in no shape for a gallop through the hotel."

Fiona watched Andrew duck as he carried April through the doorway. She frowned and followed close behind, worried that he had taken on too much. She could almost feel the torment in his hands, the strain of every screaming muscle.

She was inside the hotel, walking beside Duncan and Mara through the reception area, before she realized that she was home. Finally and irrevocably home again.

* * *

The linguine was perfect, the sauce pungent with Mara's own herbs and mushrooms coaxed from the woods near the mountain cottage she had built with her own hands. April had made dessert, an apple cake studded with walnuts and raisins and topped with fresh, sweet cream.

Duncan and Mara's apartment was comfortable and homey, an airy, contemporary space carved from eighteenth century stone. The walls were cream-colored, the furniture light oak and beech. Muted abstract art adorned the walls, and tulips in hand-thrown pottery adorned the tables and shelves. April's toys nestled in corners and peeked from colorful chests. There was no attempt to hide the fact that a child lived here and was very much loved.

"You'll have more, Andrew?" Mara asked, as she passed the platter of apple cake in his direction.

Fiona watched Andrew from under her lashes. He had eaten little and spoken less. Her contribution to the dinner conversation had been even slighter. Duncan and Mara had covered their silences, and April had filled in cheerfully when no one else could think of anything to say.

"I could no' eat another bite, even though it is the best cake in the world," Andrew said, looking straight at April.

"Then you'll have some coffee?"

"I think I'd better be getting home to my dog." Andrew set his napkin on the table. "I left Poppy with a neighbor, and Mrs. Kent'll be ready to feed him to my darling if I dinna get home soon."

"You can't go," Duncan said. "Iain and Billie are on their way. At least stay until you've seen them."

"Your darling?" Fiona looked up at him. "Have I missed something, Andrew? Has the last man of midnight fallen?"

"Fallen?"

She had noticed his eyes before—she couldn't imagine how anyone would fail to notice them. They were a changeable hazel, nearly brown at times, but the green of a tropical sea when his emotions were aroused. Now they sparkled like sunlight on calm water, filled with the humor that she imagined was usually just under the surface.

"Yes, fallen," she repeated. "Married. Have you gotten married, too, Andrew?"

"Oh aye. I've been married since I was old enough to sit beside the loch and stare o'er the horizon."

Fiona had seldom been teased. Her life had been a serious business. Now she found that Andrew's teasing left a warm tingle inside her, as well as a trail of confusion. "I'm obviously the only person here who doesn't know what you mean."

"Andrew's darling is our resident loch monster," Duncan said. "I don't know why he's dragging this out."

She faced her brother and saw that his eyes weren't sparkling at all. He was staring at his childhood friend, the man who was closer to him than a brother, and Duncan's eyes were even more serious than usual.

"Fiona can take a bit of teasing," Andrew said.

"I suspect that Fiona's had a very rough day."

"Fiona is sitting right here and can speak for herself." Fiona said the words with a forced smile. "Fiona's a very big girl." She turned back to Andrew. "Tell me about this darling of yours."

"I dinna see why. You know the stories. I told you all about my darling when you were a bairn."

Not so far away, in a lake so deep...

"*You* were the one." She breathed the words. She leaned toward him. "You were the one who told me the stories about the water dragon?"

"I dinna know if I was the *only* one."

"All these years... I've wondered."

"It was the only way to keep you quiet. You were fair troublesome, Fiona, as apt to skreich as to tug at my hair."

"I didn't use the same stories, did I? The Stardust stories aren't the same—"

He shook his head decisively. "No' at all the same. I'm afraid *my* darling lives alone. I only wish she had so many friends."

"You've seen... your darling?"

He grinned. "No' a bit of her. No' a peek. No' a fin."

"But he will," April said. She got up from the table and circled it to climb up in Andrew's lap. He lifted her and set her in place as naturally as if she were his own child. "Uncle Andrew will see his darling," she continued. "Just once. That's all anybody's allowed. Right?"

"That's correct. One peek to a customer."

"Andrew has an imagination to rival yours, Fiona," Duncan said. "And he's not at all shy about sharing it with April."

"And you, my beloved husband, are in need of an imagination transplant." Mara kissed Duncan affectionately on the top of his head as she stood to begin clearing the table.

"If there was such a thing, Druidheachd would surely be the center where the transplants were performed. Never has there been a place with so many fanciful, impressionable, suggestible people!"

April wriggled down to help Mara, and Andrew leaned back in his chair, hands behind his head. He was obviously enjoying himself. "Dunc, correct me if I've my facts twisted, but do you no' make your living using what wee imagination you've been given to convince your fellow men and women to purchase what they never knew they needed?"

"Imagination's a completely different matter when it's used in the practice of free enterprise." Duncan allowed himself a smile.

Duncan had owned a successful advertising agency in Pasadena before his divorce from his first wife, but he had sold it, and the money had gone to her in exchange for custody of April. Fiona knew that her brother still missed the faster pace of the business world, despite his satisfaction with life in Druidheachd. "Duncan, have you started another agency?" she asked.

Duncan shrugged. "I'm doing some consulting. I commute twice a week and do the rest of the work from home."

"That's terrific."

"He'll no' be content until Glasgow is the Los Angeles of Great Britain," Andrew said. "And we are all awash in consumer values and valuables."

"I'm working with a tourist board, as well as several companies that export Scottish products," Duncan said. "And, as usual, Andrew is exaggerating."

"No' a bit of it. I'm telling the truth as I know it. You've plans to put your mark on Scotland. Before you know it, we'll be trading our shortbread and haggis for Save the Rain Forest ice cream and green algae sausages."

"I'll take the algae over haggis any day," Duncan said.

"Haggis?" Fiona asked.

"The intestines of sheep, stuffed like sausages. The intestines are the best part of it. It's downhill from there," Duncan said.

"You've truly a way with images, Dunc. I'm fain to see what you'll do to Scotland once you've had the opportunity."

"Are the two of you at it again? Shall I stand between you or let you slug it out?" The words sounded from the doorway. Fiona turned and saw a dark-haired man standing there. He was tall, almost regal, and at his side was a slender woman with brown hair and eyes that rivaled Andrew's for sparkle.

"Billie. Iain." Mara went to the doorway and kissed Iain's cheek. He embraced her before he passed her on to his wife.

Fiona watched with something like dread. She was exhausted. Jet lag and a wealth of new experiences and emotions had drained her of all reserves. Her life had been at best contemplative, at worst stultifying. But for a moment she wished for the peace of the familiar, for the boredom of seclusion.

Then she was swallowed in Iain Ross's arms, strong, confident arms holding her against a hard chest. "Ah, Fiona," he said. "You're every bit as lovely as I remembered."

She was at a loss for words. She was not lovely, nor would she ever be. She had been marked by fire, scarred by experiences that had made her a recluse for most of her life. Yet Iain told the truth as he saw it. She was beautiful to him. She was Duncan's sister, and for too short a time, she had practically been his.

She found herself embracing him, too. When he stepped back, she smiled up at him. "You're taller than I remember, Iain. But then, so am I."

His blue eyes were understanding, yet at the same time assessing. She had the strangest feeling that he completely comprehended what the day had done to her. "Come here, Billie, and meet the guest of honor," he said, without taking his eyes off Fiona.

Fiona found herself in another set of arms. Billie was wiry, and energy seemed to pulse in waves from her. Fiona guessed that Iain's wife was everything Fiona herself was not, lively, impulsive, courageous to a fault. Despite their differences, Fiona was drawn to her immediately.

"We've all been on pins and needles waiting for you," Billie said. "I wish you could have come for the wedding."

"I do, too." Fiona murmured the expected polite response before she realized that she really meant it. Billie and Iain had been married just three weeks ago. Fiona had been invited to the ceremony at Fearnshader, the manor home that had been in Iain's family for centuries, but she hadn't believed she was strong enough to make the trip. She had been told repeatedly that she wasn't.

Yet now she was here.

"Billie was the bonniest of brides," Andrew said. "The single lasses from six villages wept as she walked up the aisle."

Everyone laughed, except Iain, who narrowed his eyes. "And who are you to talk, Andrew? Is there a single woman in the north of Scotland who doesn't have you at the top of her list?"

"I suspect there are a few," Billie said dryly. "Though contrary to the utterly male perspective being expressed in this room, most women have better things to do than lay snares for recalcitrant bachelors or even to bother themselves with lists."

"Is that how you caught Iain, Billie?" Duncan asked. "You ignored him until he couldn't resist such a novel approach?"

"No, she nearly drowned herself right in front of me." Iain slung his arm over Billie's shoulder. "That caught my eye."

"Think what you will," Billie said, eyes shining. "But in my version of the story, *you* caught *me*."

Fiona was entranced by the interplay. The three men had been friends since infancy. They had been born together at the stroke of midnight on Hallowe'en in the tiny hospital that served the village of Druidheachd. The odd coincidence had been proclaimed an omen, and the babies had been raised to be as close as brothers. No parent, including the highly educated Malcolm Ross, tenth laird of Druidheachd, had dared to object.

Now two of the three men of midnight—as they were known in the village—were married, and their wives had been absorbed into the close circle of friends. Only Andrew remained alone. Fiona wondered why he had never taken the plunge.

She followed the stream of conversation, answering when spoken to but primarily enjoying the role of observer. Andrew gave a truncated version of the accident that morning and their visit to the hospital in Glasgow. Sympathy was expressed, but more important, it was apparent on the faces of everyone present.

They took coffee in the living room, and the talk turned to life at Fearnshader.

"Billie's having all the furnishings appraised and dated," Iain said. "Then we'll decide what to keep, what to donate to museums, and what to sell at auction."

"No one has thrown out anything at Fearnshader for centuries," Billie said. "It's less a home than a warehouse. If a piece isn't sturdy or useful enough to stand the rigors of real life, then I don't want it."

"I can see it now." Duncan held out his hands in the facsimile of a picture frame. "Fearnshader decked out in California contemporary."

"No chance of that," Billie said. "Just a Fearnshader you can walk through and furniture you can sit on. We'll keep the best pieces and the real heirlooms, the rest is history." Her smile was infectious. "Literally."

"As soon as you've settled in, Fiona," Iain said, "we'll have you for a visit."

Fiona smiled her thanks.

"We could use a visitor or two," Billie said. "There's been a noticeable lack of them since the wedding."

"Well, I've been there twice," Mara said. "And I know Duncan and Andrew have stopped by."

"I think what Billie's trying to say is that we've noticed a . . ." Iain shrugged. "A change? I don't know how else to put it, exactly, except that there's a new reserve in the way people in the village are treating us."

"Perhaps they're just keeping their distance for a time. They know that newlyweds have better things to do than entertain," Mara said.

"I'd like to think that's it." Iain didn't look convinced.

"I've wondered if it was me," Billie said. "If the fact that I'm from America, even though my family came from here originally, has upset people. But I was warmly welcomed when I first arrived, and even at the wedding, people seemed genuinely happy that Iain and I had found each other."

"It's only been a matter of weeks," Mara said. "Perhaps they're just adjusting to the change in your status. It's a wee village, and change comes slowly. It took more than a little time for me to be accepted."

Iain lifted one expressive hand. "Last week we decided to hire new staff to assist the gardener. We want to restore my mother's gardens."

"Lady Mary would be pleased," Duncan said.

"I asked the gardener to find helpers he would like to work with. I knew his judgment could be trusted. He came to me a few days later and told me that none of the village lads would come. He's had to go farther afield."

Mara frowned and turned to her husband. "Duncan, that sounds familiar."

"We've had a similar experience here," Duncan admitted. "I've had to advertise as far away as Fort William for new maids and a server for the dining room. And no one can explain why suddenly there's no help to be had in Druid-heachd."

"It's most certainly just a coincidence," Andrew said.

"Do you think so?" Iain turned to him. "Have you noticed anything odd yourself?"

"No' a thing. Duncan, has business dropped off at the hotel? The pub?"

"The daily receipts have been less at the pub, but not so much that I'd call it a trend. Business dips and soars on a regular basis, depending on the weather, the season...."

"Have either of you asked around? Have you questioned anyone?" Andrew asked.

"It's difficult to ask outright," Iain said. "But I'm keeping my eyes open."

"As am I," Duncan admitted. "And I'm listening."

"I think you'll find that it's nowt," Andrew said. "Just winter ending and the locals staying home and readying themselves for the occasional glimmer of bonny weather. The winter was worse than we've had in years. Perhaps our young people are all looking for positions in a better climate."

The talk drifted to other things. As if they were afraid they might wear out Fiona, Iain and Billie made excuses a few minutes later and left. Duncan went to help April get ready for bed, and Mara offered to help Fiona settle into her suite, which was just down the hall from their apartment.

Andrew stood as Fiona did. "I'll be saying good-night now."

Fiona didn't want Andrew to go. It was his strength that had gotten her so far today, and she didn't want to lose it. But there was more, an awareness of him that had sustained her, too. She had watched him throughout the evening, cataloging his responses, savoring his wit, basking in the warmth of his gaze when his eyes settled on her. She had a cloistered nun's experience with men, but she didn't need experience to know just how special Andrew was.

She held out her hand. "Good night, Andrew, and thank you for everything."

He took her hand in his bandaged one and held it for a moment. His hazel eyes glinted in the lamplight. "I'll see you soon, Fiona." He turned to Mara and kissed her cheek, then he was gone.

"The room always seems a bit dimmer when he leaves it, does it no'?" Mara put her arm around Fiona's shoulders. "Let's get you settled."

The suite Duncan and Mara had chosen for Fiona was huge, with a stove and refrigerator in one corner of the main room and a wide daybed, table and chairs along the other side. There were two multipaned windows that looked over the main street. The small connected sitting room had already been furnished with a magnificent old desk and a drawing table, and Mara told her that in the daylight the window there looked over an enclosed courtyard with neatly clipped boxwoods and beds of blooming bulbs.

"You know, of course, that any rooms in the hotel are yours for the taking," Mara said. "But I chose this for your first days here. It's close to us, but you'll have privacy, too. And it's one of the larger accommodations. Most of all, I thought you might like the views as much as I do."

"It's lovely. Perfect. I'm sure I'll be happy here."

"Will you?" Mara rested her hands on Fiona's shoulders. "That's all we want, Fiona. At any time . . . if there's anything we might do . . ."

"You've done enough just to let me come."

"This is your home."

There was nothing Fiona could say to that. She was about to be left alone with her ghosts, and she could feel them wrestling inside her already. Was home the place where you felt as if you were about to be torn to bits?

Fiona turned back to the windows after Mara had gone. Dark had settled in, along with a light rain, and only the occasional sloshing of a car on High Street was visible in the faded lamplight. Tomorrow the village green would be a bright emerald set amidst the gray stone of Druidheachd, but tonight there was only glistening cobblestone and the haze of drifting rain.

She sighed and turned away. Her suitcases had been unpacked by one of the hotel's maids and all her toiletries laid neatly in place. She could bathe and go to bed, as everyone expected.

Or she could not.

She stood, paralyzed. She was not used to being torn by indecision. There had been so few decisions to make in her life that choices had seemed exotic, heady things.

Now she must choose between courage and cowardice. Until now that choice wouldn't even have presented itself. Her life had been a study in cowardice. But she had altered that when she boarded the 747 to Prestwick.

The hotel had quieted considerably by the time she stepped outside her door. The old building seemed to settle as she listened. It stirred vague memories inside her. Had she really lain awake as a small child and listened to the hotel sigh softly as it readied itself for the stillness of night? It seemed so now. The sounds were so familiar and, best of all, calming.

She started down the corridor. She wasn't exactly certain of her destination. She thought the room she sought was on this floor somewhere, but she hadn't wanted to ask. Duncan might have persuaded her not to go there tonight, and if he had failed, he would have insisted on taking her there himself. She hadn't wanted company.

The room might be occupied tonight. She knew that was possible. If it wasn't occupied, the door would surely be closed and locked. It was foolishness to be wandering the halls of a hotel she hadn't lived in for twenty-two years, looking for memories that were best locked away. But even as she told herself to go back, she moved forward.

At the head of the stairs she turned and started up another hallway. With each step she grew more reluctant. Too many years had passed. She had been so young. Time guaranteed change. Even if she remembered the correct hallway, all vestiges of the fire would have been wiped away.

She stopped in front of the fourth door on the left and knew deep inside her that she had found her childhood room. Some memories were too powerful to be dissolved by time or will. She stood quietly and listened. There were no sounds from within.

No sounds.

She lifted her hand to knock softly. The woman whose knuckles rapped against dark wood seemed a stranger to her. What would she say if someone answered? She steeled herself and knocked again, this time louder.

When no one answered, she turned the handle slowly, cautiously. The door swung open, and even from the hallway she could see two freshly made beds waiting for guests who obviously would not be arriving that night.

She stepped inside before the voices in her head could stop her. Her skin was clammy, and her hands shook. Four steps inside, she leaned against the wall, hands behind her, and stared at her past.

"Good-night my dearie dearest. You'll be snug and safe here tonight, all warm in your wee bed. Nowt can harm you as long as we're next door. Your mum will come and tuck you in soon, and before you know it, it will be tomorrow and Duncan will be home again."

She closed her eyes, but the room was still before her. Her father's lean figure loomed above her. He bent to kiss her forehead, and she breathed in the faint scent of lime and pipe tobacco. She wrapped her arms around him, but already sleep weighted her eyelids.

The memories were as real as her own heartbeat. She had been nearly asleep when the door opened again.

"Fiona, you little rascal. Did you think I wouldn't find that picture you drew on the kitchen wall? What am I going to do with you? Never was there such a little girl."

The voice was female and, despite the scolding, indulgent. The scent this time was light and floral, the lips every bit as warm against Fiona's forehead.

"Are you cold, sweetheart? Would you like me to plug in your little heater?"

Her eyes flew open. There was no space heater in the room now, of course. Nothing in the room was the same as it had been twenty-two years ago. Fire had gutted everything along half the corridor, even the plastered walls. Had the building been anything but solid stone, it would not be standing now.

"I was afraid I'd find you here."

For a moment Fiona didn't know if the voice she heard was real or imagined. She turned her head toward the doorway and found Andrew standing there.

"I thought you might no' sleep until you'd faced this." He moved slowly toward her. "Were I you, I could no' have."

"It's madness." She turned away from him and stared out at the room again. "I found it. After all these years, I still knew exactly where to come.

"My bed was there, I think, and Duncan's over there. I was mad at him that night because he'd gone to spend the night with you and Iain. He always seemed to be gone, or you and Iain always seemed to be here. I didn't like being left out."

"Have you seen enough?"

Her eyelids drifted shut, and a moan, one helpless, futile moan, sounded from somewhere deep inside her. "I've seen it so often. In all of my dreams."

Strong arms came around her. She let him pull her against his chest. She could no more have resisted than run away. She wanted his arms around her. The soft cotton of his shirt brushed her cheek, but it was the only thing soft about Andrew. His chest was stone, as secure and solid as the hotel walls.

His hand stroked her hair. His fingers were trapped by a curl, then released. "You remember more?"

"I remember it all."

"Do you want to... tell me?"

She shook her head. She had no desire to share these memories out loud. She had learned long ago that no one could bear to listen.

"Then I'll tell you what I remember."

She lifted her head. The light was dim. Only a distant street lamp shadowed his face. "But you weren't here."

"No' that night. I came the next day, after I'd been told what had happened. You were in Glasgow, by then, of course. Your whole family was there with you. I'd been told no' to come to the hotel. Ordered, really. But as soon as my da's head was turned, I came anyway. It was a dark day, as if the sun had no interest in shining after what had occurred the night before. I walked the distance, because I was afraid my bicycle would make a fair bit of noise, and I did no' want to be caught. When I first glimpsed the hotel, I thought that I'd been lied to. Nowt seemed different. I expected to see you come bobbing through the front door."

Her face was so close to his that she could almost see his memories in his eyes. "I'm sorry you weren't right."

"Once I was inside, I knew it had no' been a lie at all. There were crews of men carrying out charred wood and water-soaked furniture. They passed close to me, carrying something long and narrow that still appeared to be smoking. I could no' tell what it was at first. Then I realized that it was your bed."

They were both silent for a moment. Fiona shuddered. Andrew drew his arms tighter around her. "And so I know," he said, "at least a bit. I know what you suffered that night, and I know how much of a miracle it was that you survived to come back here this night.''

"There were times when I wished I hadn't survived. I was too young to think of it that way, of course. I just knew that I wished it would all disappear, the pain, the skin grafts and surgeries. I would think of the pictures I'd seen of heaven, pictures in storybooks, and I'd wish I was there.''

"But it's different now?''

She thought of the little girl he had rescued and the conversation they'd had about it. "Yes, it's different.'' She turned, and he dropped his arms as she faced the room before her. It was a room, and there were no sinister presences here. It was simply a room.

She told him something she'd never told anyone. "The fire was caused by a space heater. When I began to think I'd need a passport, I went looking through some old papers to find my birth certificate. I came across the insurance report. I'll never know why my mother kept it. Maybe she thought that destroying it would compound her guilt somehow. But the report said that the heater was defective and it overheated. The cord shorted out and set fire to the rug beside my bed. Neither Duncan nor I was ever told that. The cause of the fire was supposed to be a mystery.''

"Her guilt, Fiona?''

"My mother believes she's responsible for . . . everything that happened.''

"I've never heard Duncan say so.''

"Duncan doesn't know, and I don't plan to tell him. Mother's kept it a secret all these years because she couldn't bear for us to know the truth. She was the one who pulled the heater from the closet and turned it on. She was the one who left it on that night.''

"Fiona, how can you know that?''

"I remember.'' She waited for him to dispute it. It seemed impossible that a child of three would know or that a woman of twenty-five would still remember. But he didn't dispute it.

"Do you blame her?''

"For that? No, of course not. She despised Scotland's climate. To her the hotel was always damp and cold, and she didn't want me to be uncomfortable. I can only guess, but I think she probably intended to come in a little later and turn off the heater. Instead she probably fell asleep or just forgot."

She turned again to face him. "But her guilt, Andrew, her guilt was more dangerous than any fire. Her guilt almost destroyed me."

He didn't ask how. He seemed to sense it, as if he could envision all the years since the fire when Melissa Sinclair had struggled to make life perfect—and out of reach—for her daughter. From guilt as much as from love.

Fiona didn't know why she had told Andrew all this. She had learned long ago to keep her thoughts and feelings silent inside her. She offered him a tremulous smile in apology. "It's the same room, but I'm not the same, am I? I had to come in here and walk out again on my own two legs. Time stopped for me after my father kissed me and put me to bed that night. And now I have to start it ticking again."

He rested his hands on her shoulders, bandaged hands that throbbed from another child's tragedy. He leaned toward her, and her eyelids drifted closed. He had kissed her cheek this morning. She expected, yearned, for the same, for the warmth of his lips, the cherished safety of his affection.

But his lips brushing hers were a surprise. They were warm and moist, and pleasure spiraled through her, entwined with surprise. He lingered, deepening the pressure until there was no mistaking the kiss for comfort. Her breath caught; her lips parted. A world of enchanted sensuality and black velvet nights seemed to hover within her reach.

She opened her eyes, and he lifted his head. "Time did no' quite stop, Fiona. You were a child then. Now you're a woman. And you have the rest of your life before you."

He touched her cheek with his fingertips, but he didn't smile. He left without another word, left her there to walk out of the room on her own.

He had been gone for a long time when she walked out into the hallway and closed the door quietly behind her.

Chapter 4

"It's enchanted." Fiona stepped over the ridge leading down to Mara's croft and stood staring at the view before her. "I can't believe you could bear to leave all this to live at the hotel."

"Your brother was an enticement," Mara said.

"Duncan?" Fiona raised a brow. "The same Duncan who plays rock music at top volume and never refolds a newspaper in the right direction?"

"I'd be the first to admit he's no' perfect. But he has a way about him you might no' ken, being his sister."

Billie crossed over the ridge to join them and the conversation. "I'm afraid she's right, Fiona. Every one of the men of midnight is irresistible."

It was a conversation Fiona might have enjoyed pursuing, except that she didn't know how to, exactly. The only man of midnight who had so far resisted his own irresistibility had been on an oil rig in the North Sea for the past two weeks as she slowly adjusted to living in Druidheachd. Andrew had dropped completely out of her life, and she missed him.

Mara put her arm around Fiona's shoulders. "Shall we explore?"

"I can't wait."

"You're certain you feel up to it?"

"I could walk a hundred miles." Fiona smiled. "Over the next year or so."

They took the gentle slope slowly, stopping to admire the thatched stone cottage that Mara had built with her own hands. Surrounded by the last stands of fading daffodils, sheep grazed behind a fence, several with lambs frolicking at their sides. "Once I bred all my ewes," Mara said, "but now I breed only as many as I'll need for my own spinning. I could no' bear to sell the young ones off each summer. Their mothers mourn them so."

Fiona had already seen the gorgeous yarn that Mara spun and dyed from the wool of her sheep. Mara had woven her a shawl for Christmas that was one of her most prized possessions. Now Mara had become the owner of a small shop in the village where she displayed her crafts and those of the other local artisans who staffed it. Mara was a woman of many talents. "Will you teach me to spin?" Fiona asked.

"Aye, and you'll be wonderful at it. Your fingers are nimble and your patience unending."

"Oh, it ends more often and a lot more abruptly than you might think."

"Billie, now..." Mara shook her head sadly, but her eyes danced. "Billie will never be a spinner. But I can see our Billie tramping the countryside, searching for plants to help me make my dyes."

"That's me, all right," Billie agreed. "Explorer and threat to all she surveys."

They petted and played with Guiser, Mara's border collie, as well as one of the sturdiest of the lambs. Fiona held the soft wiggling body against her own and was loath to give it up when it was time to put it back with its mother.

"We'll go have some tea now, if you're ready," Mara said. "I'm anxious to show you the cottage."

The cottage was charming from the outside, a fairy-tale residence. Fiona was awed as Mara explained how she had carried the stones for the cottage herself and set them in place in two parallel rows. The space between was packed with dirt for insulation. The roof was thatched with dried sedge in picturesque rippling whorls and webbed with wire mesh.

"In the old days," Mara said, "we would have held the thatch in place with hand-tied ropes made from straw or heath and weighted with stones. But I deviated a bit, like the lazy city dweller I am."

"The whole project definitely reeks of laziness," Billie said. "If you had even an ounce of ambition, you'd have built a whole settlement here."

"Ah, that comes next, and soon, I hope."

"What are you planning?" Fiona asked as she followed Mara and Billie inside.

The interior of the cottage was every bit as quaint and intriguing as the exterior. The rectangular space was divided by a bed raised off the stone floor on a platform. Fireplaces adorned each end of the room, one with iron kettles hanging from sturdy hooks and chains inside it. Rafters as thick as a ship's mast supported the roof above, as well as the dried flowers and herbs hung in colorful clusters below.

Mara gestured Fiona to a chair beside a gleaming walnut table. "I've no' told you my plans for the croft?"

"I don't think so." Fiona settled herself. The view out the small window just in front of her was more glorious than any artist's landscape.

Mara removed a kettle from the hearth and held it out to Billie. "Will you do the honors?"

Billie tucked the kettle under her arm and started for the door. "I think I've got the hang of your pump by now. I'll be back in a jiffy."

Mara struck matches to light a neatly laid pile of kindling. When it was blazing, she carefully introduced several small blocks of peat. By then Billie had returned, and Mara lowered a chain to set the kettle over the fire to heat. All three of the women wore sweaters and jeans, but Fiona was glad when the fire began to slowly warm the room.

Mara set out a teapot with delicate china cups. A tin of shortbread was next, followed by bannock and blackberry jam. "Well, I've plans to turn the croft into a school," she said, when she had completed preparations and joined them at the table. "It's been my dream for a time now. It will be a place for children to come and learn the skills of their ancestors. We'll construct more cottages like this one, raise animals and a garden together. I'll teach them to spin and dye and weave on hand looms.'' She tilted her head, as if she could see the entire picture. ''For a week or two at a time, of course. I've no plans for it to be large or important. Just a place to pass on the traditions and history of our Highlands.''

''It's a wonderful idea. When do you plan to start?''

''After Duncan and I have built our house.''

This, too, was a surprise. ''A house? Here?''

''I'll show you the site after tea. We've designed it already. And if it's done on time, then we can begin the school with a few children next summer.''

''You'll live here and not at the hotel?''

''I think we'll live in both places, most likely. Here in the summer and the village in the winter. But we can be flexible. As much as I like the hotel, I savor the privacy we have here, and I'm inclined to want to hole up in the country from time to time, even after winter's come.''

Fiona had already noticed that Mara retreated frequently to her apartment, particularly when the hotel was most crowded. ''You like the quiet, don't you?''

Mara didn't say anything for a moment, and Billie toyed with her cup. Finally Mara spoke. ''Fiona, there's something you ought to know about me. I've no' told you before this because it seems so...unlikely.''

''Unlikely?''

''I sometimes see the future.''

Fiona frowned, unsure what Mara meant.

''Sometimes?'' Billie said. ''Sometimes?''

''All right, then. Often.'' Mara smiled as Billie shook her head. ''Very well, Billie. Fair often. Is that better?''

''She sees the future as often as the rest of us remember yesterday,'' Billie said.

''And have you no' had your own brushes with things the rest of us can no' see?'' Mara chided Billie. ''Am I the only one whose sight has been extended?''

''I've never seen the future. Just...other things.''

"Other things from eight hundred years ago, to be exact. Other lives."

"Wait a minute." Fiona leaned forward. Her head was whirling. "Are you telling me that both of you have had, umm . . . psychic experiences?" She couldn't think of a better term, although that one seemed inordinately clinical.

"Put bluntly? Aye," Mara said. "And I know you must think we're both a wee bit gyte, at best."

"It does sound a bit . . . gyte, whatever that is."

"Daft . . . crazy. I've always seen bits of the future. I can no' explain it, nor do I want to particularly. But all too often I can sense what's going to happen to someone I meet. It's a fact of my life that I've learned to live with. And when it gets to be too daunting, I come here. I've never yet seen the fate of a sheep or songbird. I can rest here."

"And you, Billie?" Fiona said.

"Oh, nothing so exotic," Billie said. "Just a little brush with an ancestral curse. But it's all over now."

Fiona sat back and stared at them both. "Well." She didn't know what else to say.

"I felt I had to warn you," Mara said. "It seemed only right."

"Does this mean that when you look at me . . . ?"

"No. It's rare that I can see the future of those I love."

Fiona felt warmth radiate through her. "Thank you."

Mara got up to pour the water into the teapot, and Billie began to butter the bannock. "But I do have feelings about your future," Mara said. "No' predictions, mind you. But feelings."

"And?" Fiona asked.

"Billie and I have both put our pasts to rest since coming here. I think you will, too."

Fiona considered that. She had so often thought of herself as someone apart. Now, and as naturally as if it had always been so, she had been embraced and included in the friendship of two women she already admired immensely. Two strong women, secure in themselves, despite the trials they'd endured. "Well, that's why I came," she said at last.

"Then you came to the right place," Billie said, covering her hand. "And we're glad you're here."

* * *

Andrew stepped through the doorway of the hotel pub and paused to let his eyes adjust. He needed a wee taste and a bit of company before going home to sleep for a day and a night.

Andrew worked a fortnight at a time, and the work was constant and draining. He would work two more shifts before summer's onset; then he would be off until autumn. He had stipulated the odd schedule at the beginning of his employment, and although there were still grumbles from management when summer approached, there was never a threat of losing his job. He was talented at what he did and a hard worker with years of valuable experience. If his employers privately thought he was daft for trading his generous salary for the headaches of a tour boat, they kept their opinions to themselves.

The night was still early, and the pub was half-empty. As he stepped over the dog stretched across the threshold—a dog remarkably similar to the one waiting at a neighbor's house for him—he greeted men he had known all his life. Safely across he squatted and scratched Primrose behind his bedraggled ears until the dog rolled to his back, tongue lolling in total ecstasy. Primrose was April's dog, the brother of Andrew's, but at night, when April was in bed, Primrose appointed himself guardian of the pub doorway.

Andrew turned away and stood to find a hand stretched toward him, offering whisky. "Could you use this?"

"That I could." Andrew took the drink from Duncan's hand and held it out in the traditional Gaelic toast. "*Slainte mhah.*" Then he downed it in a single swallow.

"A bit dry, are we?"

"I dinna drink when I'm at work."

"Come over to the bar and I'll have Brian pour you another."

"And to what do we owe your generosity? Have you gone and sold Scotland to France while I was at work, Dunc?"

"Nothing quite so lucrative. I just want to talk to you."

Andrew had come for a few slaps on the back and the latest village gossip, not for anything serious. He thought longingly of his bed and the peace of the cottage where he had lived all his life. He lived there alone now. His father had been dead for more than a decade, and his mother had moved to Fife soon after, to rid herself of memories.

"Can we keep the conversation short, I hope? I've had just the barest wink of sleep in the past forty-eight hours."

"It won't take long, then you can go home and sleep straight through until your next shift if you want."

"I might well."

At the bar they both waited for a dram of the pub's finest, then took it to a table in the corner. Andrew leaned his chair back on two legs and watched his friend. Duncan seemed to be mentally sifting through openings, which was unusual. He had always been a blunt man who said exactly what he was thinking without preamble.

"It's about Fiona," Duncan said at last.

Andrew felt a thread of alarm. "Has something happened? She's no' gone back to America, has she?"

"No, nothing like that." Duncan sipped his whisky. Now that the opening was out of the way, he appeared to be planning what to say next.

Andrew was a patient man, but not tonight. "Would you get on with it, Dunc? It will be time for my next shift before you've made a start."

"Fiona's vulnerable, Andrew." Duncan cupped his glass in his hands and leaned forward so they were eye to eye. "I don't know what persuaded her to come back here after all these years. You know she never saw my father again after the fire, don't you? She never came to Scotland for visits, even when the doctors said she could. For a long time she wouldn't go anywhere, not even school. She was tutored at home for most of her childhood, then she went to a small, private academy for high school, and later, a local college. She'd leave in the morning and come back in the afternoon at exactly the same time every day. She wasn't involved in any activities. She didn't even have friends she spent time with."

"What has this to do with me?"

"I don't know what's made the change in Fiona. I never expected to see her here, but I can't tell you how glad I am that she's come. And I don't want anything to scare her away. She's still a three-year-old child emotionally, and anything, just about anything, could shove her straight back into her shell."

Andrew picked up his glass and sipped, but he watched Duncan over the rim as he did. He took his time, although until this moment he had been the one to hurry the conversation along. When he was finished, he carefully set down the glass. "And you think," he said, just as carefully, "that I might scare her, Dunc? You think that I might drive her all the way back to America?"

"To my knowledge, she's had no experience with men at all. Not one bit. And she doesn't know or understand you."

"What is there to understand?"

"Andrew, you're a man who likes women, really, genuinely likes them. Not all men do, and not all men understand women or even care to. But you do, and you're warm and affectionate toward every one you encounter, from Sheila MacClaskey's youngest baby girl to old Flora Daniels."

"What you're saying is that I'm indiscriminate?"

Duncan's eyes narrowed. "Fiona doesn't know you. She may not understand that you treat everyone the same way, and that even when you single someone out for special attention, it doesn't last."

"Indiscriminate and inconstant?"

"I'll put it right on the table. I watched you with Fiona the day she arrived, and I watched her reaction. She may expect more from you than you're willing to give. And I don't want her to get hurt again. I don't *ever* want her to be hurt again."

"Then I'd recommend you wrap her in some of Mara's thickest fleeces, for protection. Lock her in a room with no sharp objects, in a country with no threat of fire, flood or wind. Make certain she has no visitors, because visitors might bring disease or, worse, excitement into her life. And that might no' be good for her heart—"

Duncan thumped his glass on the table. "Cut it out!"

Andrew set all four legs of his chair on the floor. Quietly, carefully. "She is no' a three-year-old child, Dunc. She's a woman. And she's made that clear by coming here. I will no' ignore her to please or comfort you. I will no' do what the rest of you have done all her days. I will no' protect her from life. But you know, or you should, that I would no' hurt her, either. I can only imagine what turmoil you must be undergoing to suggest that I might!''

Duncan's jaw was rigid and his eyes the color of steel. ''I'm not suggesting you'd do it on purpose.''

''Then what are you suggesting? That I'm too clumsy or tactless to watch myself? That you're the only one in the village with her best interests in mind? Fiona's led the life of a nun—no, that's no' even true. A nun is surrounded by her sisters. Fiona's had only your mum, and from what I can tell, *she* sheltered and stifled her until Fiona had to run to the other side of the world to be free. Let her be free, Dunc. Let her make mistakes. Let her grow in all the ways she needs to. And give me credit for a wee bit of sense.''

Duncan was silent for a long time. When he spoke again, he only sounded weary. ''Do you know how badly she was burned, Andrew?''

''Do I have the medical report? No. Do I have the gist of it? Aye.''

''She came this close to dying.'' Duncan held up his thumb and forefinger. There wasn't enough space between them to pass a piece of paper. ''There's a lot that can be done now with plastic surgery, but there are things that still can't be. Sometimes there just isn't enough skin to go around.''

Andrew didn't wince. ''And?''

''Her face was spared, her hands, most of one leg . . . But her scars are extensive.''

''And if you dinna stop protecting her, there will be more scars inside than out.''

''I love you like a brother, Andrew, but Fiona *is* my sister.''

Andrew got to his feet. ''Then I hope you'll no' be called upon to choose between us.''

Outside, the cool nip of a Scottish spring day had thickened into the chill of night, but Andrew hardly noticed. He paused just beyond the hotel door and ran a hand through his hair. He no longer felt like sleeping. Adrenaline pumped through him, and he knew it would be hours before he could put his head to a pillow.

"Andrew, is that you?"

He recognized Fiona's voice immediately, but he wasn't sure from which direction it came. "Fiona?"

"Over here."

He gazed across the street to the village green, a rectangular slice of land shaded by ancient trees. He saw a woman's slender body silhouetted against gray sky, and he started toward her. Duncan's words rang in his head.

They were face-to-face before she spoke again. "I didn't know you were back." She smiled, and her eyes searched his face. "You look tired. Have you had any sleep since I saw you?"

"A bit here and there. What are you doing?"

"Just taking a walk. The air feels so luscious, I couldn't resist. It's so heavy, so soft, it almost feels like hands stroking my face."

The image did something odd to him. He felt it deep and warm inside him. But Fiona didn't seem to notice how sensuous her observation had been.

"I like the way everything smells this time of evening," she said. "There's peat smoke, but there's also a hint of flowers on the breeze. Winter and spring at war."

"Here in the Highlands we're never that certain which is winning."

"There are the sounds, too. Tires on slick cobblestone, now that's a wonderful sound. Night birds and children laughing. Music drifting from houses. I'm sure behind their curtains, people are dancing, slowly...." She laughed at herself. "My imagination knows no bounds."

"Nor should it."

"Don't you think so?" She made a wry face. "Sometimes I think it's supremely overdeveloped, but where would I be without it?"

He wondered if she was referring exclusively to her success with the Stardust books, or to something more. Had her imagination become a substitute for real life, and did she now wish to experience what she had only dreamed? "Your books are wonderful, Fiona. Glorious. I have them all."

"Do you?" She seemed surprised. "Really?"

"Shall I quote?"

"No!" She laughed. "Offering's good enough. I'm glad you like them."

"Would you enjoy some company? I think I need a walk, too."

"I'd love it. Usually April walks with me, but she's off with her friend Lolly tonight."

"Where shall we go?"

"I've found a favorite place. Do you want me to show you?"

"Aye."

She led him through the green, around a stone fountain that hadn't worked since his childhood and down a path still littered by winter's refuse. "Did you have a good two weeks?" she asked.

"Neither good nor bad. Busy. It still confounds me what a fuss and a mess we make to retrieve and sell the leaves and ferns of another age."

"Leaves and ferns? Oh, you're talking about oil. You think there's too much fuss?"

"When I was just out of university I found life on the platform exciting. Now it seems pointless. Man will wait until all the oil's finally gone before he looks for ways to live without it. We'd be better by far if we started looking harder now."

"I couldn't agree more."

"No?"

"I was at Mara's cottage today. And even though I'm not exactly equipped or ready to live that simply, it made me think how much we have that we don't really need."

"Are you certain you're Duncan's sister?"

She laughed. "I know you're teasing, but you're too hard on Duncan. It's not selling things that he enjoys particularly. It's the chance to exercise his creativity. And he's always found ways to take on projects he believes in. He'd never admit it, but he's really an idealist. Like you."

"Like me?"

"Aren't you?"

"It sounds bloody self-important and virtuous. And I've never stirred myself to be either."

"No, I think idealism just comes naturally to you. I think you live by your values."

"And how do you know so much about me?"

"I'm a great observer. When I was little, I learned how to judge people and what they said." She smiled up at him, and the rising moon caressed her cheeks and forehead with silver.

He was moved by the expression in her eyes. "What exactly did you learn?"

"When you're small, no one wants to tell you anything. They talk to each other, never to you. So I found out what I wanted to know by reading expressions and putting together all the things that adults didn't say to me."

"And now you think you know me?"

"I wouldn't go that far. I think I know some things about you."

"That I'm an idealist. What else?"

"That you're kind down to the bone. That you give everyone the benefit of the doubt and try not to judge. That you have a stubborn streak that gets you through the worst times in your life, but it probably also gets you in trouble."

He thought that her brother would certainly agree with the last. "I'm no' kind to the bone, Fiona. And there are people I dinna like, sometimes at first glance. And if I'm stubborn, it's often more for a lack of insight than idealism. Let's no' have any false ideas about who I am. I'm just a man like any other."

"Andrew, I never thought you were anything but a man."

She didn't sound hurt or dismayed. She sounded assured.

"Well, you dinna sound disappointed."

"You're a good man. If you weren't, *then* I'd be disappointed."

They stopped beneath a tree. He rested his hand against the trunk. "Why? What difference would it have made?"

"Well, I told you I have an overdeveloped imagination, right?"

"So you said."

"Well, I've imagined you all these years, and you're very much the way I imagined you. So I would have been disappointed if you'd turned out to be a scoundrel."

"Fiona, why would you imagine me at all? You were so young when . . . you left Scotland."

"It's simple, really. I held on to everything I did remember."

That, almost more than anything she'd ever said to him, made his heart turn over. She wasn't looking for sympathy. She had no idea how lonely she'd been, so lonely that she'd held on to the memories of a toddler. Loneliness seemed a natural state to her.

He thought about Duncan's warning. Andrew believed all his own logic, all his own replies, but he was struck with the basic truth behind everything his friend had said. Fiona could be hurt, and badly.

The first time he'd seen her he had noticed what beautiful hair she had. Now the wind bounced curls against her cheeks and neck as she stood looking up at him, and they were reminders of sunshine on a moonlit night. He remembered how her hair had felt the last time they'd been together. He had wanted to comfort her, but he had been struck then by how good it felt to touch her, to feel the silken, lively mass of her hair against his fingertips, the length of her body against his. Tonight he had denied his own power to hurt Fiona. Now he faced the fact that the possibility was there.

"Come on, I'll show you that special spot I was talking about." Before he could speak, she turned away from him and started away.

He wanted to call her back, to tell her that exhaustion had claimed him and he'd changed his mind about the walk, but it was too late. He followed behind her, crossing the road at the most secluded end of the green. They were heading for the loch.

She paused so he would catch up, then continued. "I'm sure this is a place you've been a million times, but I found it a few nights ago and fell in love."

"You give your heart easily."

"Not easily or often. But Loch Ceo is special."

"Aye. I've always thought so."

"I know. You take tourists out on the loch in the summer, don't you?"

"As many or few as want to go. We're no competition for Loch Ness here, and my darling's no public relations expert. She shows herself rarely. She's a shy lass and careful to whom she reveals a glimpse."

"Then it's not a thriving business?"

"No, for which I'm thankful. We're a wee clachan, off the tourist path, and we have just enough commerce to sustain us. Loch Ceo could no' handle a hundred tour boats with sonar and underwater cameras, and Druidheachd could no' handle an influx of tourists with cash to spend. Change comes slowly here, and we can incorporate new ideas and new ways of doing things if we have the time to plan for them. But I would hate to see what would happen if changes ever had to be made quickly."

"I like it the way it is."

"Aye, so do I."

Fiona parted overgrown shrubs and stepped through them, and Andrew followed. He took her arm when he realized where they were. There was a moderate grade dipping toward the shore, and he wanted to be sure that she didn't slip.

At the bottom he released her. The shore around the entire loch was narrow, but the spot where they stood was particularly so. A flat rock jutted into the water, and Fiona climbed up on it and beckoned for him to join her. A cold wind came sweeping over the water, and he was immediately chilled. From the rock above him she didn't even seem to notice.

"Look at this, Andrew. Have you ever seen anything so gorgeous? You can hardly see a house from this angle. I could almost believe we just discovered the loch ourselves and no one else has ever been here before."

There were a hundred views that were just as beautiful, and he suddenly yearned to show her every one. He climbed up beside her. "The moon loves the loch. She silvers every ripple."

"I've always liked moonlight the best. It's ... forgiving."

"Forgiving?"

"Moonlight softens and blends. It highlights only what it chooses. Sunlight exposes everything it touches."

Like fire. Andrew gazed over the water. "I saw Sara Hume today, Fiona."

"When?"

"I drove to Glasgow when my shift ended. Ordinarily I would have been back home this morning."

"I knew that they had verified her identity. I've called every day, but they wouldn't tell me much on the telephone except her name. Tell me how she is."

"Unbelievably tiny." And quiet. Far too quiet.

"Did she have anyone with her?"

"She has a granny who's come up from England to be with her. She's a kind woman, a very modern granny who watches everything carefully and has taken on as much of Sara's care as she's allowed. She insisted that they let me visit. We'll no' have trouble getting in to see Sara again."

"How is she really, Andrew?"

"They say she's responding well to treatment. But her spirits are low. She has an aunt who'll take her home when she's discharged, a young woman with two children of her own. She and Sara's mum were close, and she and her husband want Sara very much. But she can no' come to Glasgow for more than short visits, because she has her own children to care for. I think she needs more visitors, people who aren't there to hurt her—because that's the way she must view the doctors and nurses."

"That's exactly the way she views them. I remember hating everyone who walked through the door of my hospital room because inevitably they were going to cause me more pain. And I was too young to understand why."

"She responded to me. She listened to me talk. She even said a few words. Her granny said that Sara had been close to her father...."

"You'll be going to see her often, won't you?"

"Aye."

"May I come?"

He thought of everything that Duncan had said and all the things he himself had replied—and believed—in return.

"Aye," he said, after a hesitation. "If you want to come, Fiona, you're welcome."

She turned back to the loch. "I'll bring her my books. I know they're careful about most toys on the unit, because of germs, but they should let her have books."

"I planned to go day after tomorrow."

"I'll be ready."

Fiona was ready for everything. Ready to help, ready to embrace life, ready... Andrew put an end to that line of thought. "Are you ready to go back now?"

She opened her arms as if she wanted to take the loch back with her. "Do you suppose if I sat here and stared, didn't even blink, for a whole night, I'd see your darling?"

"She's been known to reward great patience."

"I'm not sure I have great patience anymore." She turned back to him. "Once that was about all I had."

Now her eyes were hungry for more. He could see that clearly, despite nothing except moonlight illuminating them. He wondered if she understood all that she hungered for, or if in the weeks to come, as her world expanded, she would begin to understand more clearly.

As they started back toward the village, he wondered if he would have the strength or clear judgment to walk the line between giving her the things she wanted and denying her those that would cause her more pain.

Chapter 5

Serenity Lake was a clear turquoise lake, with tall trees rising from its bank to shade the water from the eyes of curious creatures who lived on the land. Stardust loved the tree shadows as well as the sparkling sun-kissed water at the center of the lake. She loved the way water droplets showered the lake's still surface when she dipped low and flipped her slender tail. Best of all, she loved the reeds and rushes at the water's edge and the thick grasses along the lake's bottom, because she could nibble on them all day and never grow hungry. But as Stardust nibbled, she grew and grew and grew. Until one day she realized that she would not be just like all the other creatures in Serenity Lake. She would be much larger. So much larger that someday she might frighten her friends the fish, who now so cheerfully kept her company.

"She's asleep," Pamela Brownleigh whispered. "You've put her straight to sleep, Fiona. It's nothing short of a miracle."

Fiona closed her book quietly. She wasn't sure how miraculous it was to put a child to sleep with a book she'd written herself, but she was delighted for Sara's sake. She remembered too well how blessed sleep had been when she had been a patient here.

She stood and moved away from the bed. Sara was a tiny shape under a clear plastic tent and a heartbreaking array of dressings, but until she had fallen asleep, her dark eyes had followed Fiona everywhere. There were other children in the room, children who had been critically injured, too. Fiona had steeled herself for this, steeled herself for horror and the return of terrible memories. But all she had felt upon walking into the room was compassion and a desire to help.

"Did her mother read to her?" she asked softly as she gave the book to Pamela, Sara's grandmother, who was an attractive older woman with hair that was just beginning to gray. Fiona watched her tuck the book away in the drawer that held the few other toys the little girl was allowed to have.

"Yes, Penny was quite a reader. Sara could listen for hours."

"I'll come as often as I can."

"It will help. She has so little to look forward to." Pamela's expression was matter-of-fact. Whatever tears she had cried were past. Now her mission was to get her grandchild well enough to resume as normal a life as possible.

"She'll have a good life. You'll see. She has a wonderful grandmother to help her."

"And friends." Pamela allowed herself a rare smile. "I'm grateful to both you and Andrew." She looked up at the man who stood at the other side of Sara's bed, watching the little girl sleep. "There's little enough I can say to Andrew, isn't there? If it weren't for him . . ."

"He thinks that anybody would have done what he did."

"He's wrong, you know."

"Yes, I know."

"I can only be grateful that it was Andrew who came along that day."

Andrew came to join them. "I suppose we'd better go now, Pamela. But we'll be back."

"With more of your magic act?" Pamela asked.

"I'll make sure he practices," Fiona promised.

"It's a ween of blethers when a three-year-old child can see straight through every trick I do."

"A ween of what?" Fiona asked.

"A ween of blethers. It's nonsense, ridiculous." He shook his head. "You need educating, Fiona."

"It's nothing short of amazing I can understand you at all," she said, winking at Pamela as she spoke. "When the *r*'s are really rolling, I feel like I'm at the start-up of the Indy 500."

"His accent is music to my ears," Pamela said. "And will continue to be so forever."

In the hall, Fiona and Andrew removed the hospital gowns and masks they had been required to wear inside the ward and left them in a bin beside the door. Then they started down the corridor. Fiona watched more than one nurse—and a lovely young doctor—follow Andrew with their eyes after he'd nodded and spoken to them. Andrew had a way of making everyone his friend immediately, as well as attracting more than his share of feminine attention.

And he was such a vital, healthy presence on a ward where robust good health was a cherished dream.

"I'm hungry," he said when they'd reached the lobby. "How about you?"

It was well past lunchtime, but until that moment, Fiona hadn't thought about eating. She had been so engrossed in the unfolding drama upstairs. "Starved." And she was. She wondered how she had managed to suppress it for so long. "We could go back to Prestwick and see if the soup we ordered the afternoon that I flew in is ready by now."

Andrew looked at his watch. "No, it's still too soon. It'll be another week yet, at least. We'll have to take our chance on something here."

"Here?" She grimaced. She had been fine on the ward, but now she wanted to put the hospital and everything it stood for behind her.

"Here in Glasgow. No' here in hospital. I know a place close by. Shall we walk?"

She was already exhausted, and her hip and leg ached from standing for so long. But she didn't want to call attention to that. She nodded. "Sure, let's."

Four blocks from the hospital, she was sorry that she had been so agreeable. Andrew had shortened his stride for her, but his pace was still faster than she could comfortably walk. But again, she didn't want to admit that she had trouble keeping up.

"It's just at the end of this street," Andrew said, pointing to a stretch of several blocks. He hadn't spoken since leaving the hospital. Fiona knew that he was thinking of Sara and the other children in the ward. He had visited every one of them, told ridiculous jokes and spoken words of encouragement. His output of energy had been tremendous. Now he needed to readjust.

She kept pace with him at great effort. The street was completely ordinary, with small businesses interspersed with brick residences sporting small, perfectly tended gardens and neatly painted trim. They passed a tailor, a shop selling greeting cards and cheap souvenirs, a butcher with strings of rubber sausages looped in the window. She concentrated on everything except the growing agony in her leg and hip.

At the end of the street Andrew gestured to a narrow doorway. The acrid odor of smoking oil wafted from available cracks and crevices. Through the window Fiona could see several unadorned laminated plastic tables and a counter running the width of the room.

"Best fish and chips in Glasgow." Andrew opened the door and the smoke no longer wafted, it poured out to gleefully embrace the car exhaust that already perfumed the air.

Fiona preceded him. There was a menu of sorts posted above the counter. Fish and chips. Fish without chips. Chips without fish. "This is going to be a tough choice."

He looked at her for what she thought was the first time since leaving the hospital. "I did no' even think. Would you like to go somewhere with a bit more variety?"

"Are you kidding? My mouth is watering." And it was. In fact, she couldn't remember ever smelling anything more enticing. Eating had always been something she was required to do. For years she had been forced to consume calories as part of her rehabilitation. Everything she ate or drank had been carefully weighed and charted. By the time that regimen had been lifted, her interest in food had evaporated. She ate to survive.

Today she was going to eat for pleasure alone. The thought of that was almost pleasure enough.

"What kind of fish should I order?"

Andrew examined the menu. "I prefer the haddock."

"Good, I'll try it. And chips, too."

"Find a table and I'll wait for the food."

She didn't argue. She could hardly wait to get off her feet. Finding a table was a matter of choosing the best view out the grease-speckled windows. Only one table was occupied, and the couple sitting there sipping soft drinks looked as if they were about to take their final slurps.

She chose a booth in the corner and slid along the bench. It had been molded with the human form in mind, but the curves did nothing to ease the pain in her hip. She turned at an angle and propped her thigh along the bench's edge. The pain receded a little.

Andrew returned with drinks in tall paper cups. "I'll bet there's a country somewhere in the world without Coke on its menu," she said, as he set her drink in front of her.

"No' if Duncan and his kind have their way."

"Poor Duncan. You're never going to let up on him, are you?"

"Never." He slid into the seat across from her.

Fiona thought Andrew looked particularly charming today. He was wearing a hand-knit sweater of heathery gold, but as the day warmed, he had pushed up the sleeves to reveal wide, muscular forearms brushed with auburn hair. Casual clothing suited his wide-shouldered frame, but she could imagine him in something as formal as a tux, too. *Handsome* was too cultivated a word to describe him. But *rugged* or *appealing* were not.

She took a sip of her drink and hoped that the sugar and caffeine would restore some of her energy. "You were terrific with Sara. And with the other kids, too. You never let on how frightening they look. From your reaction, no one would ever have known they were any different from normal children."

"They *are* normal children."

She shook her head. "It doesn't do any good to pretend. They aren't normal. Not after what they've been through. They'll always be different, even if a miracle occurs and their bodies are perfectly restored. Every one of those kids has been to hell and back."

He didn't argue, which surprised her, because most people liked to keep up a pretense, if only to themselves. "I tell myself they're children, just like any others. I suppose that's just what I do to get through it."

"They have all the needs of other children. They need to be loved and accepted. You do a wonderful job of that."

"Sara may be discharged as early as next month."

"I know. Pamela told me. The sooner the better. As soon as she's out of danger she'll recover more quickly at home."

"How soon did you go home, Fiona?"

"I was in one hospital or another for most of five months. Then, later, there were other stays, for one problem or another. I used to think if I ever had a place of my own I'd decorate it in antiseptic white or insipid green and install loudspeakers in the hallway so I'd feel at home."

One side of his mouth turned up. "I was only in hospital once myself, just for a few days to have my appendix out. They swore I was the worst patient ever to darken their door."

"Come on, I bet the nurses adored you."

The other side of his mouth turned up, too. "Do you think so? Now that I ponder it, I received more back rubs than a pregnant mother of triplets."

She laughed. "I'll just bet." She sobered a little and spoke before she thought. "You know, that's the thing I missed most. I still remember just how terrible it was never to have anyone touch me. No one could give me a back rub, of course. They couldn't do anything except hold my hand sometimes. But even after I was out of the hospital..." She stopped. "I'm sorry. This is getting maudlin, isn't it?"

"No. What about after the hospital?"

"I guess people were still afraid they'd hurt me. And they were probably right. But I think it would have been worth it."

His eyes blazed with emotion. His voice deepened. "No one touched you?"

"That sounds crazy, doesn't it? They must have. I probably just don't remember very well." She said the lie with conviction and looked him straight in the eye as she did.

The clerk behind the counter gave a sharp whistle, and Andrew slid across his bench. "I'll be back."

She used his absence to stretch her leg out farther. It still throbbed, and she dreaded the onset of a serious cramp. She knew the signs, having experienced them for as long as she could remember. There was no real hope she would ever be without them. The last doctor she had complained to had simply said that she was lucky she had enough undamaged muscle to cramp at all.

Andrew returned with two gigantic bundles wrapped in white butcher's paper. "The portions are smaller than some, but the cooking's good enough to warrant eating here." He set one bundle in front of her, and she unwrapped it to find enough golden brown fish and french fries to feed the multitudes—without a noticeable miracle.

"I can't eat all this!" She leaned forward and inhaled, then closed her eyes in bliss. "But I'm sure going to try."

He unwrapped his and doused the contents indiscriminately with the bottle of vinegar at the table's edge. Then he sprinkled everything with salt and pepper. She was three delicate bites into hers before he started. He was done with his first piece before she'd finished half of hers.

She watched his strong, white teeth tearing into the second piece. "I can see why you were worried about the portions."

His eyes sparkled. "Have you never seen a man eat before?"

"Not with such a shameful lack of enthusiasm."

"Are you telling me that my manners need improving?"

"Your manners are perfect. It's your appetite that's exuberant."

"Is a man no' supposed to have an exuberant appetite?"

Unaccountably, she wondered about his appetite for other things. The night he kissed her came to mind. The kiss had been merely to comfort her. She knew that. He had not been moved to kiss her for any other reason. Yet now she wondered what it would be like to be kissed without reserve, to be stroked by his broad, rough hands, to be touched by the tips of his long, sturdy fingers. Would his lovemaking be as exuberant, as uninhibited? As soundly relished?

She looked down at her fish, hiding her thoughts. This was dangerous ground, forbidden to her. Her developing relationship with Andrew was a source of delight. She could destroy it by wishing it was more than friendship. She, of all people, knew how futile and destructive wishing could be.

A vicious pain stabbed through her leg and drove all other thoughts from her mind. She had been warned, but again, she had wished for the impossible. Her fish fell to the table, and she grabbed her thigh.

"Fiona?"

She couldn't speak. She was too proud to writhe in agony, but not disciplined enough to prevent a tortured gasp. She turned to the side and stretched her leg along the seat. Then she leaned forward and began to massage her calf. Long years of experience had taught her that this was the only hope for relief.

Stronger hands pushed hers aside. "Let me." Andrew slid into the seat and propped her foot on his lap. "I can reach it better."

"No, it's all right, I—" She gasped again. The pain was a vise, squeezing and squeezing. . . .

Andrew put his palm against the thin sole of her shoe and pushed the ball of her foot gently toward her knee. "Is that better?"

She shook her head.

He continued to hold her leg in position with one hand, but the other probed her calf through the soft corduroy of her slacks. When he seemed satisfied he had found the right spot, he began to knead it with his thumb and fingertips.

As the pain eased, she realized what he was doing and exactly what he would learn from it. There was nothing shapely about her leg. It was thin and underdeveloped, and it was rigid with scar tissue.

Humiliation filled her. She wanted to order him to stop, but as his hand eased over her knee and up toward her thigh, she knew she had no prayer of uttering the words. It felt so wonderful, so miraculous, to have him soothe away the cramp. He moved so slowly and carefully, with single-minded determination to end her suffering. She had never gotten control of the agony this quickly on her own.

She leaned against the wall, and her eyes closed against her will. Now the warmth of Andrew's hands, the gentle probing of his fingers, was more notable than the pain.

"How far does it extend?" he asked.

"You've done enough. Thank you."

"I asked you how far it goes."

She opened her eyes. His were implacable. "To my hip," she whispered.

"Ah, Fiona, why did you let it get this bad? It was all the walking, was it no'?"

She nodded.

"Why did you no' tell me?"

"All my life people have been forced to make allowances for me. I'm tired of it."

"People who care about each other make allowances. Every one of us can use a hand from time to time." *His* hands moved higher, as if to prove the point.

Her legs were turning to liquid, but of more interest was the liquid heat building inside her. Through pain and embarrassment, she was still responding to his touch. She tensed, ashamed of her own reaction, and the tension reignited the cramp. As if he could feel the newest spasm, he pressed harder, and it quickly eased.

He lifted his hands, and she felt bereft. She was afraid to look at him. "Thanks. That helped a lot."

He slid closer, stretching her thigh over his knees. Before she could stop him, one hand grasped the tender flesh at the inside of her leg and the other settled opposite it. He began to knead. "The muscle here's like stone. It will take a bit of working to make it better."

She was afraid to speak, sure that only a moan would escape her lips. She was swimming in waves of feeling, drowning in shame and resurfacing in desire. She had often yearned to be touched, but never had she guessed how powerful a thing it could be.

When he was satisfied, he pressed against the rounded curve of her hip with the heel of his hand. Once, then again. Miraculously, the pain there eased, then disappeared. At her involuntary sigh, he pressed harder. When he finally released her, her leg felt completely relaxed.

"Wiggle your toes," he ordered.

"Andrew, I'm fine." Her voice sounded exactly as she had feared it would. Dreamy. Tentative. Affected.

"Wiggle...your...toes."

"You're a tyrant, aren't you?" She wiggled, then bent her foot back and forth.

"Any more pain?"

"Not a bit." She managed to look him in the eye. There was something in the gaze he returned besides concern and determination. Something warmer flickered there.

Or was that her imagination, too?

"Do you want to try walking on it?" he asked.

"No. I can't thank you enough, but go eat your fish. It's probably cold."

"I doubt it could be. There was hardly time."

Hadn't there been? It seemed to her that he had lingered over her for years. Decades.

She struggled to sound normal. "Where did you learn to do that?"

He gently lifted her leg and slid from beneath it. Then he crossed to his own side of the booth. "I've had leg cramps myself. I used to climb, and once I got a cramp while I was hanging from the bald face of a mountain. I had to scramble up, cramp and all, or die trying."

She winced. "That's terrible."

"So I've learned what to do."

"I'm lucky."

He gazed directly at her, and the warmth she'd thought she'd seen was still present in his eyes. "Luck's a relative thing, Fiona. It might be that I was the lucky one."

* * *

Jamie Gordon hadn't drunk quite as much as his older brother Peter, and he'd been luckier for it. Just one short year ago he had decided to ease up on whisky and tighten up on his purse strings. In a moment of supreme self-knowledge he had seen the dead end on the road he was traveling, and he had decided to make something of his life.

All because of a ghost.

"Peter, would ye wake up, man?" Jamie leaned forward carefully and grabbed the toe of his brother's boot. "For God's sake, Peter, would ye please wake up?"

"Haud yer wheesht!" Peter kicked sharply, and Jamie sat back to avoid him.

Jamie didn't shut up, as requested. He knew if he did, Peter would go directly back to sleep. "We're out in the boat, Peter. Dinna make such a fuss, or the monster'll be having us for tea."

"Huh?" Peter opened his eyes. Slowly. Carefully, as if he were uncertain exactly what he might see.

"Out in the boat," Jamie repeated slowly. "On the loch. Together."

Peter stretched, but his eyes were still blank.

Jamie sighed. He was just nineteen and Peter all of twenty-one. Peter was taller by two inches, and better at soccer, shinty and rugger. There was nothing his older brother couldn't do, in fact, except think. Thinking was Jamie's job.

"I caught a fish or two while ye were sleeping," he said. He pulled his stringer out of the water and held it aloft. Two brown trout and an eel wriggled there. "Mum'll be glad, I ken, that one of us could remain sober."

"Maybe she'll give ye an extra biscuit or twa, Jamie-bairn, for being such a good wee laddie."

"Maybe I ought to stand up and pitch ye out of the boat." Jamie's eyes narrowed. "That'd sober ye."

Peter didn't stir. "Maybe ye ought to stop the girning and start the engine, Jamie-bairn." He tipped his face to the sky. "It's about to rain."

"Maybe that'd sober ye." But Jamie had to agree it was time to leave. The skies above Loch Ceo, perfectly clear an hour ago, were now fast clouding over.

"I dinna like the rain," Peter said.

Jamie knew why. A year before, Peter had nearly drowned in a freak storm. Of course, he had been warned. Jamie himself had warned his brother that the burn that trickled through Druidheachd was rising and should not be crossed.

A ghost had warned Jamie.

"Poor old Peter," he said as he pulled the cord on the engine. "Who'd have guessed such a swankie would be fair terrified o' getting wet?"

Peter made a pretense of lunging toward him, but with his coordination dulled by too much whisky, his own momentum carried him forward too fast, and he couldn't stop. He fell straight into Jamie's lap. Jamie tumbled sideways, and the cord went with him, snapping free from the engine. As Jamie watched in horror the cord sailed across the water to vanish under the rippling surface.

"Now look what ye've done, ye idjit!" Jamie shoved the sprawling Peter away and leaned over the side. "It's gone. No' a sign of it!"

"What d'ye mean, no' a sign?" Peter peered over the side with bleary eyes. "It's in there somewhere."

"Do ye want to go looking for it? I'll gladly help ye in." Jamie sat back. The sky already seemed darker, and they were a long way from shore. To make matters worse, there were no other boats in sight.

"Have we something else to use as a replacement?" Peter got down on his hands and knees and began to search the floor. It didn't take long. The boat was short and narrow, and although ordinarily neither man was neat, the boat was too limited in space for clutter. He climbed awkwardly back to his seat. "Nowt."

"I could have told ye. Nae rope, nae string..."

"Yer stringer, Jamie? How about that?"

"Too wide and stiff. But we could plait our fishing lines. That might do it. Cut them off in lengths and plait them."

Both men grabbed for their fishing rods at the same moment. Peter got to his first and triumphantly whipped it skyward, directly in the path of Jamie's jaw. The sting of the rod against his throat sent Jamie reeling backward, arms flailing. On impact from Jamie's elbow, Peter's rod went flying over the side. Peter wildly threw himself forward to retrieve it, and the boat tilted precariously. In the effort to grab his brother and keep him from sending both of them to the bottom of the loch, Jamie tossed his own rod in the general direction of the boat's floor.

"Sit still, damn ye, Peter! Ye've got nae sense today. No' a bit of it!" He held Peter tight until the boat had stopped the worst of its rocking.

"I've got to get me rod, Jamie." Peter peered into the water. He made a sound of despair. "And it looks as if ye'd better think about getting yers."

Jamie loosened his grip on Peter's collar and stared into the loch. "Bloody hell." He had missed the boat entirely. His rod floated an arm's length from his brother's, and because of the turmoil the rocking boat had created, neither was in reach. Weighted heavily to take the lines deep into the water below, they would not float for long. Even as he watched they began to sink. "Double bloody hell!"

"We'll have to row for them. Quick!"

"We have nae oars, ye idjit! Ye made me take them out. Do ye mind doing that? 'Jamie,'" he mimicked in a high voice, "'we'll have nae need of them, and they'll jist take up room!'"

"I dinna mind saying anything of the sort!"

They glared at each other, but lesson learned, neither moved a muscle.

"So, what is it yer thinking we should do?" Peter asked at last.

Jamie peered skyward again. "I'm thinking we'd better be prepared to empty the boat of water when the rain comes." As if in warning, one large raindrop splashed to his forehead and trickled down his nose. "Triple bloody hell." He sounded resigned.

"Michty! I dinna like the rain, Jamie. Ye mind what happened before?"

"There are nae ghosts out here. And what's there to warn us of, Peter? What good would it do now?"

Lightning flashed across the sky, and, as if on cue, the boat began to rock. Wind swept over the loch, and with each new gust, the boat rocked harder. "If we're lucky," Jamie shouted over the thunder, "it'll be a wee storm and quickly over. Just sit tight—and bail when ye must." He felt along the bottom of the boat for the tin he'd used for bait, emptied it over the side and handed it to his brother. He had to content himself with a smaller tin that stank of long dead herring.

Darkness descended with the storm, a nearly total darkness despite the fact that the sun should still be just above the horizon. The wind howled along the loch's surface, sending sprays of water into the boat. Jamie pulled his collar around his neck, but it was little protection. He was quickly chilled, and from the expression on his brother's face, Peter was every bit as miserable.

The little boat rode the increasingly turbulent waves as if it had been constructed for exactly that purpose. But Jamie knew that if the storm grew too violent, they would be swamped. And no one who went down in Loch Ceo lived to tell the story. The temperature was too frigid.

Fear rose inside him. What had been an irritation was now far more. Had he offended someone on high or, worse, something, some hideous, hellish creature, down below? Had he gone back one too many times on the vows he had made a year ago? He'd been to the village kirk more than once since that day beside the rising burn. He'd been so often that the minister had learned his name. Surely that was often enough for any man.

"Look! There!" Peter leaned over and rattled Jamie's knee. "Look off in the distance. Someone's coming for us!"

Was it because he still drank whisky? He rarely drank too much. The barman at the hotel had nearly *forgotten* his name.

"Jamie, have ye nae ears? There's a boat coming! A boat!"

Jamie looked up and saw his brother's arm extended over the water. He was pointing into the darkness. Jamie squinted, but he couldn't see anything. He leaned forward, hoping for a glimpse of the promised miracle.

A dark shape rose from the water, just meters away. It had a slender head with huge amber oval eyes that glinted fiercely under the glare of the next crack of lightning. Its neck was as long as the mast of a schooner. As he stared in horror, a tail arced out of the water thirty or more meters behind it and viciously slapped the waves.

Jamie screamed at exactly the same moment as Peter.

It was one of the few times in their lives that they had agreed on anything.

Chapter 6

Fiona loved pretty clothes. As a child she had been relegated to wearing neutral colors and simple, unadorned styles because her mother had believed it was best not to draw attention to a body so laced with scars. She had grown up in long-sleeved oxford cloth shirts and cotton slacks that hid the condition of her leg but didn't rub, as fashionably tight jeans might have. After she had been questioned relentlessly in high school about the scars on her neck, she had taken to wearing turtlenecks under her shirts to hide even this sign that she had been a burn victim.

She was in college before she began to question her mother's judgment. She had been burned, but she had survived. Was there an unwritten code that, as a memorial to her past, she should dress the part of a corpse? Her first independent purchase had been a coral angora sweater with a cowl neckline that nestled just under her chin. She had bought a coral-and-brown plaid skirt to wear with it, and brown boots of butter soft leather that stopped where the skirt began.

Her mother's tight-lipped assessment hadn't made the next purchase easier, but Fiona had persevered until she now possessed a wardrobe of pretty, feminine clothes that still hid the basic truth.

The basic truth, the reality of scars and damaged muscles and joints that would never work perfectly again, must have been apparent to Andrew today. Fiona knew what he had learned when he massaged her calf and thigh. The miracle was that he hadn't seemed to think it mattered. He hadn't pitied her, and he hadn't hesitated to help.

And his eyes had glowed warmly afterward, as if touching her had been a pleasure and not an act of compassion.

She carried that glow with her on their trip back to Druidheachd. Through a sudden storm that made driving slow and treacherous, she let that glow warm her. When they stopped in front of the hotel, she turned to say goodbye. Rain still fell, and the sky had grown dark, but she could see Andrew's face in the softly muted glow of the street lamps and floodlights illuminating the walkway.

"I'm glad we went. Thanks for taking me with you. And the fish and chips were great. Every bit as good as you promised."

"I plan to see Sara again next week. Would you like to go with me?"

"If it's not any trouble." She started to get out, but he put his hand on her arm and kept it there.

"Why would it be?"

She frowned at him. There was evidently more to this exchange than polite clichés. "Just that if it's out of your way to bring me, or if I slow you down too much..."

"Fiona." He shook his head. There was both exasperation and understanding in his voice. "Is that how you think of yourself? Someone who slows down the rest of us? Is that why you did no' tell *me* to slow down today when I was walking too fast? You'd prefer to suffer?"

"I'm not a masochist, Andrew."

"Did I say you were?"

"I have never preferred suffering to not suffering. Just the opposite."

"Then why did you no' tell me to slow down?"

She was embarrassed, but she knew she owed him a real explanation. He had been too good a friend for less. "I guess I don't want anybody to think of me as different." She smiled ruefully. "If I'm going to be different, I guess I'd like to be silently different."

"If you were preparing a list of words that described yourself, would *different* be at the top, do you think?"

She was caught off guard. She didn't know how to answer.

"Do you remember earlier, when you told me that the children on the burn unit are no' normal children?" He didn't wait for a reply. "I think you're correct. They've come through something the rest of us might no' be able to understand completely. I can no' minimize that. But I can tell you this, as well. None of us is normal. All of us are different in some way. And we owe it to each other to respect that. But I can no' respect you and you can no' respect me if we hide from each other."

"Is that what I was trying to do?"

"I'll make allowances for you if you make them for me."

"What could I possibly have to overlook about you?"

"I suspect you'll find all sorts of things if you look closely enough."

She found that hard to believe. Even this conversation was an example of his bone-deep warmth and compassion. "I'll be honest with you from now on. Besides, I got a taste of what happens when I'm not."

He leaned forward. Her breath caught, but she didn't close her eyes. "Good," he said. He kissed the tip of her nose, a little-sister kiss, but still strangely moving. "And I'll be honest, too."

"That means if you ever feel like I'm a burden, you won't ask me to come along out of a sense of duty?"

"A burden?" He shook his head. "Is that on the list, too?"

"Good Lord, pop psych with a Scots accent!"

"You could never be a burden. Quite the opposite."

She liked the sound of that more than she should.

She got out of the car and watched him drive away, windshield wipers slapping in random bursts and tires spraying streams of water in his wake. His car had disappeared before she opened the door and went inside.

The day had been long and tiring, and her first thought was of a warm bath followed by something simple for supper. She had warned Duncan and Mara that she probably wouldn't be back until late, so she knew they wouldn't expect her to eat with them. She had planned to rest before seeing them at all, but Duncan was in the lobby when she walked in.

"Back at last, huh?"

"Umm...." She lifted her shoulders in a stretch. "And tired. It's a long trip back and forth. But productive. We got to visit Sara, and I read to her. Andrew did the most ridiculous magic tricks. He needs lessons, but the kids ate it up."

"You were gone longer than I thought."

"We went out for lunch. I guess we stayed longer than we'd planned."

"Come have a drink with me. I want to talk to you."

"Has something happened?" She thought of her mother, completely alone in New York now that her only two children were in Scotland.

"Nothing like that. I just want to talk to you."

She raised a brow. "That's the voice you use with April, Duncan. Is it going to be one of *those* conversations?"

"No. April's a little young for this conversation."

"It's sounding worse all the time."

"Then let's get it over with."

She wanted to beg off, but she followed him toward the pub like a dutiful younger sister. Duncan had been her best friend for too long to defy him now.

The pub was almost empty, an unusual event even for such an early hour. Duncan motioned her to a seat in the corner, where they were less likely to be disturbed. She had loved the hotel pub on sight, despite its resemblance to an ancient mausoleum. With its thick stone walls and slate floors, it should have been gloomy, but she only found it remarkably old, and, like Mara, history appealed to her.

"You know, I never thought of this, but I think I like old things because anything that can survive for such a long time amazes me." She took her seat and smiled up at Duncan. "This building will be here when you and I are dust. They'll be serving beer and whisky here into eternity."

He looked down at her without smiling, and she knew what he was thinking. Survival amazed her because *she* almost hadn't survived. She shrugged. "It's a good thought, not a bad one, Duncan. Some things endure. I like that."

"Have you had anything to eat? Are you hungry?"

There were always a few meals prepared in the pub, simple fare for regular patrons. She wasn't particularly hungry, but she realized that if she ate now, she would have one less thing to do later. "Do I smell steak and kidney pie?"

"Probably."

"I'll have a little, if it's ready."

He went behind the bar and filled two glasses with beer. She had learned to drink it warm, as the locals did, and she was just as glad tonight that it was, since the pub was always chilly. She rubbed her arms to warm them. Poor circulation was a problem she would have into eternity. Like the pub, some things endured.

He returned. "What are you smiling about?"

"I'm beginning to develop a sense of humor about myself."

"Oh?" He set her glass in front of her and pulled up a chair across the table. "Your pie will be out in a moment."

"Did you eat already?"

"Yes."

She took a sip, then set her glass down. "Fire away, Duncan."

"Well, I just wondered how things are going."

She thought about that. "Fine. Are we finished?"

His smile was reluctant. "I'm coming on too strong, aren't I?"

"I think I'd rather be your friend than your heavenly assignment."

"Heavenly assignment?"

"You've always felt like you had to take care of me. You know, Duncan, the fire *wasn't* your fault, and even if you'd been at home that night, you might not have been able to do anything to help me. You might have been burned, even killed, yourself."

His eyes widened. Had he not been such a restrained man, she thought his jaw might have dropped. "What are you talking about?"

"You know darn well." She lifted her glass to him.

"So, have we reduced all my feelings for you to guilt?"

"I know you love me."

"I'm glad you haven't lost sight of it."

"But you can love me and still not feel that I'm your responsibility. I have to learn to be responsible for myself. I should have started years ago."

He sat back, but his fingers tapped a steady rhythm on the table. "You've had a lot to cope with."

"Very little of which I was allowed to cope with. Mother coped for me. You know she did, even when I wanted desperately to try coping myself. Eventually I just let her have her way. She was one obstacle I just couldn't seem to find the energy to overcome."

"How did you find the energy to come here and get away from her?"

"I'm not sure. But at least some of it was cowardice."

He frowned. "I don't understand."

Brian, the barman, came to their table and set a bowl in front of her. The inevitable chips joined it. She thanked him, and he smiled a gap-toothed salute before heading back to the bar.

"What did you mean about cowardice?" Duncan asked.

She cut open the puff pastry that sealed the bowl, and steam poured out. For the second time that day her mouth watered. "Do you know how popular the Stardust books have become?"

"I know they're selling well. I'm thrilled for you."

"My agent's been busy with subsidiary rights. Now there's a Saturday morning cartoon show in the works. Then come commercial tie-ins. They're talking about vitamins, lunch boxes, notebooks and pencils. You're the one who's a whiz in advertising, and I'm the one who's going to make a million off of it."

"That's incredible, Fiona! Why haven't you said anything before this?"

"Because that's what drove me here." She looked up from the pie. "That's what finally got me on the plane. Success. Because publicity comes with it, Duncan, and I don't want it."

"Publicity?"

"My publisher released a story about me, telling all about how I was burned as a child in Scotland and how I made up these stories during the years I was recovering. It was great press. I got so many offers for interviews." She shook her head. "Can you imagine that?"

He didn't respond. She suspected he could imagine her reaction only too well. He knew her better than anyone.

"I tried saying no. I explained that I valued my privacy above everything else, but that's like waving a red flag in front of a bull. I got more calls. Finally I just panicked. And here I am."

"Well."

"Right. Well." She started on her pie. It tasted even better than it looked.

"I'm glad you came, no matter what the reason."

"So am I." She looked up. "I really am. I was so scared. Getting on that plane was the hardest thing I've ever done. But it was the right thing to do."

"Are you still scared?"

"Sometimes. I'm so used to having other people make my decisions, the smallest thing can throw me. But I'm learning. Do you mind having me here?"

"Are you kidding?"

"You're a newlywed."

"And you're tactful to a fault. We hardly know you're around."

"Good."

"The hotel is half yours."

"I never wanted it. It was a reminder . . ."

"And now?"

"I wish I'd come back sooner. While our father was still alive."

"He wasn't an easy man."

Fiona knew that Duncan and their father Donald Sinclair had never gotten along. Duncan had been forced to visit him each summer, but the visits had never brought them closer. "I wouldn't know what kind of man he was," she said. "I wasn't invited here, and he never came to see me in New York."

"I think Mother discouraged him."

"Maybe." But Fiona knew the bitter truth. There was just no point in telling Duncan.

She was halfway through her pie when Duncan spoke again. "Look, I want to bring up something else."

"I figured you did."

"I want to talk about Andrew."

She had suspected as much, but she still felt an unpleasant shock. "Go on."

"Fiona, you don't know Andrew as well as I do."

"That's certainly true. I've hardly had the chance to know him at all."

"He and Iain are my closest friends. I'd go to hell and back for either of them."

"I doubt that will ever be required." She looked up from her dinner, which had suddenly lost its appeal. "What are you trying to say?"

"Andrew likes women."

"That's hardly an indictment."

"He and Iain both have reputations—at least, Iain used to have one before Billie. His is a thing of the past now. But Andrew's reputation isn't. I don't think there's a single woman in the Highlands whose heart doesn't beat a little faster when Andrew comes around."

She laid her fork carefully on her place mat. "Oh?"

"Andrew genuinely likes women. He enjoys their company, admires their best qualities. He knows how to make a woman like herself in return, and I think that's a huge part of his appeal."

"Why are you telling me this?"

"Because I don't want you to get hurt."

"And how could he hurt me? You've just told me that Andrew likes women, and that he's good to them and for them. He doesn't sound dangerous to my safety or well-being."

"Are you trying to misunderstand?"

She rested her forearms on the table and leaned forward. Her gaze locked with his. "Are you trying to pussyfoot around what you really want to say?"

"All right. Andrew's almost thirty, and he's never been married. He likes women, but he likes them too much to settle down with one. There, is that blunt enough?"

"No. Because I think you're trying to tell me something else. Two things, actually."

"And what are they?"

"One, that I could never hold Andrew's interest because I'm not enough of a woman for him. And two, you think I'm too immature and innocent to be able to draw my own conclusions and make my own decisions. You're taking up where Mother left off. You've appointed yourself my guardian!"

Duncan sat back. It was so unlike him to withdraw from any conflict that she knew immediately that she'd scored a point. "It never occurred to me that you weren't enough of a woman for any man," he said.

"I'm your baby sister. You still think of me that way. And when you look at me, you remember the little girl who lay in a hospital bed for months and months trying to grow new skin."

He winced, but she pushed on. "That's only a small part of who I am. I'm a lot more than that. And I'm old enough to find out about the rest of me." They were brave words. She wasn't even sure just how true they were. She just knew that they had to be said.

"Is there something wrong with my not wanting you to get hurt?"

"Yes."

Her brother was a stubborn man. Stubbornness had gotten Duncan through a difficult childhood as well as a difficult first marriage. Fiona was surprised to learn that she had a streak of stubbornness herself, but the discovery was gratifying.

"Back off," she said. "I have no reason to think that Andrew and I will ever be anything except friends. But if something else develops with any man, I'll be the one to judge how far it goes. I'm a consenting adult. And you're my brother, not my keeper."

Her courage played out, she sat quietly and watched him think, because that was the only brave thing that she could still manage.

He sighed. "Damn."

"Damn Andrew? Damn me?" Her voice cracked on the latter.

"No, damn myself. I'm sorry, Fiona."

Her eyes widened. "That's it? You're sorry?"

"I don't know what else to say."

"No! I mean, that's plenty. Great, in fact." Her smile was high-voltage. She had steeled herself for his anger, and instead she had gotten an apology. The aftermath was heady.

"Andrew told me as much."

She sobered. "You spoke to Andrew about me? I can't believe you did that."

"I didn't want to talk to you. I guess I thought I could avoid it that way."

"What did you say to him? That your sister was so innocent, so foolish, she might fall at his feet if he smiled at her?"

"Give me credit for a little sense."

She narrowed her eyes. "Why?"

This time he smiled. "If it makes you feel any better, Andrew essentially gave me the same lecture you did."

"It takes you a while to catch on, doesn't it?"

His smile tightened into something more serious. "Just be careful, Fiona. I know it's past time you made your own mistakes—" he held up his hand before she could interrupt "—*and* your own successes. Just be careful. I don't think I can stand to watch you suffer again."

"That's what it's all about, isn't it?"

"I can probably be forgiven for that, can't I?"

She reached for his hand. "Probably."

Duncan could be forgiven for not wanting her to suffer. But despite his denial, Fiona wondered if he was worried because he didn't believe she could hold any man's interest. She completely lacked a repertoire of feminine wiles. Her und of small talk teetered on the verge of bankruptcy, and ner life experience could be summed up in an incomplete phrase. And she certainly didn't have a perfect body to throw into the equation.

Long after her discussion with Duncan, she stood at the window of her suite and watched the last raindrops falling on High Street. With true Highland courtesy, an eerie mist seemed to rise from the earth to meet the rain halfway. She was exhausted, but too morose to do anything about it. She imagined Andrew's reaction to Duncan's brotherly chat, and she wondered how she could face him again.

"Fiona, are you still up?" A light knock preceded the softly spoken question.

Fiona recognized Andrew's voice, even at a whisper. It looked as if she were going to face him again immediately. She cracked the door and stared out into the hallway. "I thought you were going home to get some sleep."

"I went home. May I come in, or is it too late?"

"I haven't even changed for bed." She opened the door wider to let him through. His hair was plastered to his head, and his clothes were soaked. "Have you been out in the rain ever since you left?"

"Aye. I have. That's what I've come about."

"You don't have towels at home?"

He laughed. "I've towels aplenty. I just have no' had the opportunity to use them."

"Where have you been?"

His hazel eyes were dancing. "Rescuing a pair of yobs from the loch."

"Yobs?"

"Two good-for-nowt lads. Brothers. Peter and Jamie Gordon. Have you met our Peter and Jamie, yet?"

"I don't think so."

"Just as well. Between them they've caused more trouble in the village than the rest of our lads put together."

"Maybe you should have thought twice about rescuing them." She went into her bathroom and retrieved a fluffy white towel. She handed it to Andrew. "I'm going to make you some tea. I'd offer you whisky if I had any up here, but I'm afraid tea will have to do. Have a seat."

"I'm too wet."

"Sit on the towel, then, and I'll get you another as soon as I put the kettle on." She did just that. When she returned with another towel in tow, he was already drying himself. She watched him ruffle his hair, then stretch his head back to rub his neck. Such a simple act, but it spoke of intimacy. He passed the towel over his skin roughly but with obvious enjoyment. She had already guessed he was a man who enjoyed sensations of all kind, the feel of wind and water on his skin, the ache of tired muscles after a hard day at work, the pumping of his heart and the tingling of his flesh after a long run or the ascent of a mountain.

Her flesh tingled as she watched him.

He rubbed his shoulders, and the fabric of his shirt slid along his muscular arms. "I can only get the worst of it. I should get home, but I just had to tell you something first."

She perched in a chair. Andrew was still standing, and now he was dabbing at his chest. The square, well-defined muscles were clearly outlined by the clinging fabric, and she was hopelessly mesmerized as he pulled the shirt even tighter with each stroke of the towel. As she continued to stare, he unfastened the top three buttons to expose his skin to the towel. Rain-darkened hair gleamed with drops of moisture. She couldn't seem to turn her head or speak.

He stopped and stared pointedly at her. "Have you no curiosity?"

She found words somewhere. Her mouth had gone dry. "Was the rescue successful? Did you find your yobs?"

He grinned triumphantly. "Aye, that we did! And a blethering pair of idiots they were. They had taken their launch out to the middle of the loch to do some fishing, but they took half a bottle of whisky and twice as much beer. From what I can tell, Jamie fished and drank, and Peter drank. If they caught any fish, they had disappeared by the time we arrived."

"Were they too drunk to come in out of the rain?"

"In a manner of speaking. They could no' start their motor. All they could think to do was ride out the storm. I suppose they knew that eventually their mum would send someone to look for them. Which is what happened, of course. When I drove up to my house, there were men launching a rescue boat, and they asked me to come.'' He was drying his arms now, but his mind was definitely on the events of the evening.

She forced her mind to those events, too. ''And the Gordons were all right when you found them?''

''Now, that's relative, Fiona. They were unharmed, it's true. But were they all right?'' He shrugged and tried to look serious, but his eyes were dancing again.

''You're such a born storyteller. You know how to drag out a good thing, then drag it out some more.''

''They saw my darling.''

''What?'' She got to her feet.

''They saw my darling! In the worst part of the storm she came up right next to their boat. Shilpit laddies that they are, they nearly perished from fear on the spot.''

''You're kidding.''

''No' a bit of it. They saw her. Jamie even told us what color her eyes were. Amber, like yours, Fiona.''

No one had ever told her that her eyes were amber. Andrew's assessment left a warm place inside her. ''What else did they see?''

''A long neck, and a long body, too. Jamie says that her tail slapped the water several boat lengths behind. He was fair certain she would turn over their boat, but of course, she did no'.''

''Of course?''

''She's a shy lassie, and she does no' often show herself, but when she does, she means no harm.''

''I'm not so sure I'd count on that to protect me if I were in their shoes.''

''Jamie says that she looked straight at them before she plunged back into the depths. He claims that the waves she made as she vanished nearly upset the boat. He had to restrain Peter from jumping into the water in a panic. Peter is no' much of a thinker.''

''It doesn't sound like Jamie's ever going to win any prizes himself.''

''They're good lads, if a wee bit blate. I dinna think either of them will be drinking again for a good while.''

The kettle whistled, and she crossed to pour the boiling water into a teapot. Since Andrew clearly hadn't had dinner, she rummaged in her refrigerator. "I have the makings of a sandwich in here," she reported. "Interested?"

"No. I'll just have the tea and be going. I should be at home now, but I wanted you to hear the story from me."

She closed the door and turned to face him. "Andrew, do you believe that they really saw...something?"

He stared at her. "Believe? Of course I believe. She's there, and they saw her. What room can there be for doubt?"

"Well, you said yourself they'd been drinking. And the storm was pretty fierce for a while. They were probably scared to death to be out on the water like that, with all the lightning and thunder, and the waves getting higher and higher...."

"They saw her. I know what you're thinking, Fiona, but they saw her. I saw the fright she gave them." He shook his head. "Silly laddies, as if she'd try to harm them."

She approached him slowly. He was still dripping on her carpet, but he lowered the towel to watch as she came closer.

"You really believe, don't you?" She shook her head, amazed. "You really believe that a creature lives in Loch Ceo. It's not just a wonderful story to you."

"I believe she's there. Aye. In the same way I believe that the sun will rise tomorrow—somewhere, at least, if no' in Scotland." He smiled, and his expression beckoned her closer.

"I didn't know."

"And now you do." He dropped the towel at his feet and reached out to slide his hands down her arms. He took her hands in his and pulled her closer. "I believe she's shy, so very shy that she only comes out when she thinks that no one will be watching. I suspect she was more surprised to see the Gordon brothers than they were to see her. I believe she waits until no one is there before she rises high above the waves and glides along their ridges. She has a need to see the world around her—even, perhaps, to experience it a bit. But she's so frightened of what might happen to her...."

"I can understand that. The world wouldn't accept her. She probably knows that. She would frighten everyone who saw her."

"No' everyone. Those who love her would find her beautiful."

She was hopelessly mesmerized again, but this time by the spark kindling in his hazel eyes. "Would they?" she whispered.

"Aye." He sighed as he pulled her closer. "Aye. Very beautiful." His arms closed around her.

Fiona lifted her face to his. She wasn't surprised that he was going to kiss her. His happiness was unrestrained and undeniable. She could almost taste his joy and feel his exuberance in the way that he held her. The wet folds of his clothing clung to her as he drew her still closer, but the warmth of his body seemed to seep into her own.

His hands traveled slowly up her back, along her spine and shoulders to the nape of her neck. There were scars there, hidden from the eye, but he brushed past them to bury his hands in her hair. He tilted her head and lowered his mouth to hers. There was nothing comforting about this kiss, and nothing brotherly. His lips were demanding, and hers opened like the petals of a flower at morning's first light.

She clung to him, too astonished and too suffused with emotion to examine what was happening. His tongue teased her lips, tracing, moistening, dancing with soft velvet strokes. She responded with more hesitation than confidence. His hands dove deeper into her hair, as if the feel of it gave him pleasure. She sighed, and immediately she could feel his smile against her lips. He delved deeper, and his tongue explored with gentle, constant pressure.

Her legs seemed to grow weaker in proportion to the strength of her response. She clutched his shirt with trembling hands and held it like a lifeline. Desire bloomed inside her, a persistent, flowering yearning that swamped all other sensations. She wanted to touch him, to explore him with her hands, to feel the hard breadth of his chest, the wide span of his shoulders.

As if he knew, he lifted his head, and his eyes promised that he would not draw away if she did touch him. But her courage was gone by then, used up in the heat of that one, breathtaking, staggering kiss.

With his gaze still fixed on her face, he swept his hands over her back and finally slid them to her hips to rest there while his thumbs gently massaged her abdomen. He leaned forward again and kissed her once on each side of her mouth, swift, sweet kisses. He kissed her nose, as he had in his car, and then her eyelids.

"There are some people who, if they knew my darling, would find her the most beautiful creature in the world," he said softly.

He covered her hands and brought them to his lips to kiss each palm and seal her fingers over the kiss. Then he was gone, and the only sound in Fiona's apartment was the beating of her own heart.

Chapter 7

Fearnshader, Iain's family home, was a child's most cherished dream or terrifying nightmare—depending on the strength and direction of the child's imagination. Gargoyles loomed from parapets, and the castellated towers defining the corners held delicious promises of vampire bats and hideous cloaked phantoms.

The drive to Fearnshader from Druidheachd was pastoral and pleasant, along a rambling Scottish wynd that bordered Loch Ceo. Only when the hulking remains of ancient Ceo Castle came into view did the mood change and the turbulent history of the Highlands assert itself. Just off the loch road and past the castle, Fearnshader lent its splendidly gloomy presence to the landscape.

"Fearnshader means 'place of alders,'" Duncan told Fiona as he parked the hotel minibus beside a gatehouse at the edge of Fearnshader's vast front garden. "The alder grove between here and Ceo Castle is probably as old as the castle itself, much older than the house—which has to be older than any structure in the state of New York."

From the back seat Fiona looked out the window, content for the moment just to take in the sight of the huge manor home. "So I came here as a little girl?"

"You came here with me at least once. Lady Mary, Iain's mother, was fascinated with you. She made me bring you, and you and she had a tea party."

"I don't remember her at all, but I still have a doll that she sent me when I was in the hospital in New York, a very old and valuable doll. I think it was hers as a child." Fiona continued to stare out at Fearnshader. "That wasn't long before she died, I guess. Everything changed so quickly, didn't it?"

"Everything except Fearnshader. And Billie's changing that now."

Mara, who was sitting beside her husband, clucked her disapproval. "Billie is just refining what's already there. If Lady Mary was alive, she would be delighted that someone loved the house again and wanted to make it a home."

"Are you chastising me?" Duncan leaned over and kissed her. "I'm sure I'll love what Billie's doing. Just as soon as I get used to it."

"Your brother believes he's a thoroughly modern man. But he has no tolerance for any change that affects his boyhood memories," Mara told Fiona with a wink.

Duncan defended himself. "I've told Iain more than once that he needed to throw out half of what was here. And if I recall, you're the one who wouldn't let me paint the hotel white."

"Duncan, you wouldn't have!" Fiona was shocked.

"No, he would no' have," Mara agreed, "because it would have been the end of our marriage. But he threatened it all through the winter."

"There was no light for months. I came very close to painting the whole place egg yolk yellow with murals of palm trees and flamingos." Duncan got out of the car and came around to open doors.

Fiona was enchanted by the walkway. Peonies poked their scarlet spears through the newly cultivated earth that bordered the cobblestones, and shrub roses sporting spring's verdant first growth preened in the translucent light of a Scottish gloaming. She took her time, lingering to admire everything.

"In another month or so, the walk to the door will be a sensory feast," Duncan said. "The earliest roses will be blooming, and the peonies are nearly as fragrant. Billie promises that this is one thing she'll never change."

Billie was waiting for them at the front door. She had insisted that she was going to do the cooking for her first dinner party herself, and she had obviously stuck to her word. She balanced a bunch of fresh basil and three garlic bulbs in one hand and held the door wide with the other. "I'm so glad you're here. Somebody needs to entertain Andrew. He insists on helping in the kitchen, and the man's a menace."

"Do you *need* help?" Mara asked.

"Yours, sure. His?" She shook her head, and her short dark hair fanned out in spikes. "He claims to cook by taste alone. He's eating more than he's cooking. There'll be nothing left to serve if we don't get him out of there."

"Where's Lord Iain during all this?" Duncan asked.

"Fixing a pipe in the master bath. I know it's unlordly or something. He's supposed to be posing by the fireplace in very old tweeds, but if he doesn't stop the leak, the dining room ceiling might cave in during dinner. I'd hate to do that to you. Most of the staff is off on holiday, so there's no one to lend a hand."

"Duncan can help him, and I'll help you." Mara turned to Fiona. "Can you entertain Andrew?"

Fiona hadn't seen Andrew in a week, not since the day his darling had been spotted in the loch. She looked at Duncan, whose eyes were shuttered, but he didn't attempt to object. Whatever his feelings, he was trying not to be overprotective. "I suppose I can. If he's had enough to eat to hold him until dinner."

"The man has devoured half the contents of my cupboards," Billie said.

"That might no' do it," Mara said, "but you'd better give it a try, Fiona."

Fiona and Mara followed Billie through the expansive hallways, while Duncan took the stairs to find Iain. Fiona was fascinated by every room they passed. "This is incredible. Could I have a tour sometime?"

Billie shot her a grin. "That's a terrific idea. Get Andrew to give you one. Just don't let him show you the kitchen."

"You wouldn't mind if we prowled around?"

"Mind? You're family, aren't you? Besides, Andrew knows as much or more about the house than I do. He practically grew up here. And he won't be likely to start moving furniture at every stop."

"How is the renovation going?" Mara asked.

"It's great fun. I make a pile of things that I think we need to get rid of, Iain comes along and gives me a history of every piece and what it means to him, and eventually we're right back where we started."

"Slowly, in other words."

"Slowly and carefully. But we're moving in the right direction. Some of the rooms are actually comfortable. I'd say by summer's end, the parts of the house that we use will be really livable."

Fiona was lost already. They had only made two turns, but she was sorry she hadn't dropped bread crumbs behind her. They made one more, to a short hallway that led through an imposing wooden door temporarily propped open by a crate filled with canned goods.

"Andrew, real help's arrived. You're banished until dinnertime," Billie said.

Andrew turned. His gaze went directly to Fiona. He greeted her, then Mara, but he didn't move toward them. "You're certain? I've only begun chopping the tomatoes."

"Good, then some should still be left for the table." Billie cheerfully shooed him toward Fiona. "I've promised Fiona you'll show her the house. That should take an hour or two. Maybe that will give Iain time to figure out how to turn off the water. Duncan's on his way up there."

"I told you I could help him."

"When you arrived he was still playing Master of All He Surveys, and he would have been furious if I had sent you up. By now he should be ready for reinforcements. Desperate, in fact."

"You have a poor opinion of men."

She kissed his cheek. "I have a realistic opinion of my husband's strengths and weaknesses. Go have fun."

As he passed, he hugged Mara's shoulders and asked about April. Then he faced Fiona. "There's still enough light to see the gardens. Would you like to start there?"

A week had passed, and she had spent too much of it wondering exactly why Andrew had kissed her. In her imagination she had conjured a reunion scene filled with intimacy and subtle innuendo. Instead Andrew was looking at her as if she were a stranger.

She told herself that she should have expected this. The kiss had been exuberance, an adrenaline high, and afterward he had obviously regretted it. Now it would be her job to be pleasant while pretending the kiss hadn't meant anything to her, either. She steeled herself and found a smile. "Sure. I've already admired the gardens in the front."

He ushered her back through the doorway and into the hall. In silence they took a different set of turns until they were on a wide stone terrace that overlooked acres of what had obviously once been formal gardens. "It was very different when we were lads," Andrew said. "These were Lady Mary's pride and joy. She had a large staff of gardeners, but she did much of the work herself and all the supervision."

Fiona walked to the terrace edge and leaned against the sculpted railing. The night was surprisingly warm, and a gentle breeze caressed her cheeks. "There were roses."

"Aye. Did Duncan tell you that?"

"I don't think so. I think I remember them."

"You were far too wee to remember."

"You're right, I was. But I remember them anyway. That must have been where we had our tea party."

"Tea party?"

"Duncan tells me Lady Mary invited me for a tea party. I don't remember that. But I remember this view, I think. And roses. Not along the walkway out front. Dozens of bushes. Hundreds, maybe."

"Hundreds, aye. Behind the boxwoods to the left. They were her passion. Iain intends to restore the rose garden in her memory. Some of the roses are still there. The old ones can survive neglect. But the hybrids are all gone. They'll have to be replaced." He joined her at the railing, but he stood several feet away. "You can see the overall design

from here if you use your imagination. The boxwoods outline the different areas. There's a wee reflecting pool and
fountain beyond that stand of birches. That was the silent
garden, and we were only allowed there if we agreed to be
silent, which was seldom."

Fiona turned so that she could see him. The view was ex-
ceptional. He wore a dark tweed jacket and faded jeans that
had long ago molded themselves perfectly to his long legs.
"I can imagine the three of you playing here, romping
in and out of the boxwoods. Climbing trees, trampling
flower beds."

"Lord Ross planted a maze for us just beyond the roses.
A very intricate and complicated one. I think he rather
hoped we would never find our way out."

She laughed. "Obviously you did."

"Boxwoods grow slowly, and only now are they above eye
level. I suppose it was really a maze meant for our children."

"I bet April loves it."

"Aye. And Mara and Duncan will have more children.
Iain and Billie will have their own, as well."

"And you, of course. You'll certainly be a father someday."

"I've no thought of settling down."

She heard his message loudly, although he hadn't raised
his voice. "Well, you would have to settle down to be a father," she said lightly. "I suppose that's going to make it
tough."

"I can no' imagine having the life of a child in my hands,
having to shape and mold it." He shook his head. "I have
none of the qualities a man needs for that."

"You'd be a fantastic father. The very best kind."

"You dinna really know me, Fiona."

There was little she could say to that. From the tone of his
voice she guessed that she wasn't going to be allowed to get
to know him any better, either. "Maybe I don't know everything," she said at last, "but I've watched you with April
and Sara."

"It's easy to love a child, and the most difficult task in the
world to be a good parent." He moved away from the rail

and turned to her. "If there was enough light we could walk along the pathways, and I could show you what's left of the gardens and what Iain intends to do with the remainder. But that will have to wait. We'll have a look at the inside instead."

He was standing close to her, but he was a thousand miles away. Fiona had hoped that if she was determinedly casual, Andrew would realize that she hadn't overreacted to his kiss. Now she saw that something more overt was going to be required. "Andrew." She put her hand on his arm to stop him from moving away. "You don't have to show me anything, you know. And you have nothing to be embarrassed about, either." She was completely unused to expressing her feelings out loud. She could feel her cheeks heating from the effort.

"Embarrassed?"

She dropped her hand. "I know you regret what happened the last time you saw me. Please, don't worry about it. I understand why you kissed me. You were excited because your darling had been spotted. I know it had very little to do with me."

He stared at her for a moment. "Well, at least you did no' say it had nowt to do with you. At least you give yourself credit for having the tiniest bit to do with it."

Anger flashed through her, and she hardly recognized it. She had seldom been angry. What could anger have changed? "Look, we aren't discussing my self-esteem. We're discussing you. But if your feelings are off-limits..." She turned and started toward the house.

"Fiona." This time he stopped her. "I am no' embarrassed. Can you really believe I am?"

"You're acting like a stranger, which is your perfect right, of course. I just thought you might regret kissing me and—"

"I did no' regret it!"

She faced him. "Good."

"It was no' a good idea!"

"Then let's forget it and get on with being friends."

"Fiona, it was no' a good idea because I want to do it again."

She was stunned. She had expected anything except this. "Why? It's not an addiction. If you do it again, you're in no real danger of becoming hooked."

"Dinna you think so?" He stepped closer. "I doubt I have the power to resist anything I want badly enough."

She was mesmerized by the seductive flicker in his eyes. "Let's just assume that's true. Exactly why would you *have* to resist?" Her voice sounded shaky and unfamiliar to her own ears.

The door to the terrace opened, and Iain poked his head through it. "Bloody hell, Andrew. I've got water gushing faster than I can mop it up. Can you lend a hand? Duncan has no more idea what to do with the bloody blasted pipe than I do."

"Of course," Andrew said without taking his eyes off Fiona.

"I'm sorry, Fiona," Iain apologized. "I promise I'll give you a tour myself another time. Unless it's all under water."

"Go ahead," Fiona told Andrew. For just a moment his expression was a mixture of relief and regret. Or maybe she only imagined there was anything there at all. Just as she had imagined that she saw desire in his eyes when he talked about kissing her again.

Dinner was poached salmon with a sauce of fresh herbs from Fearnshader's conservatory and a salad from the same source. There had been enough spectacular side dishes to have everyone groaning with pleasure well before Billie served a dark chocolate torte. The groans grew louder, but no one turned down a generous slice.

Andrew had hardly looked at Fiona throughout the extended meal, but he had been completely aware of every movement she made—or didn't.

Most often she didn't move. Fiona, once a spirited, active child, had developed tranquility to an art form. Her movements were spare and infinitely more graceful because of it. She leaned slightly forward as the talk swirled around her, as if to immerse herself in it without being forced to participate. Her eyes were like depthless pools. Deep as the loch, he supposed, hinting at great mystery and an ageless serenity. They changed with the timbre of the conversation, reflecting and absorbing the emotions that others expressed.

"Andrew, you've had little to say tonight," Iain said, when they moved into the comfortably casual sitting room for coffee laced with Drambuie.

He'd had little to say because he had been so busy *not* watching Fiona. He had carefully not watched the way she smiled—a smile that barely disturbed the composure of her face but was nevertheless warm and genuine. He had carefully not watched the way her turquoise sweater softly outlined the contours of her breasts or the way her long fingers stroked the fine linen tablecloth and savored the whorls of the intricate family crest on the silverware.

He hadn't watched her lift a bright tropical blossom from the floral arrangement to brush its soft petals against her cheek and learn its exotic scent.

"I think Andrew's mentally out on the loch looking for his darling," Duncan said. "Along with half of Druidheachd."

"Only the half with boats." Restless, Andrew got up to pour himself more coffee. "Boats and the time to make a quid from our visitors."

"The hotel's been full, too," Duncan said. "But I expect it to die down soon."

"Has activity on the loch increased that much?" Fiona asked.

Andrew was aware this was the first remark she'd addressed to him since their discussion on the terrace. He faced her. "Aye. I've had my hands full, as has everyone with a boat. There've been no sightings on Loch Ness for sometime. We're taking up the slack."

"Then you think it will be temporary?"

"I suppose that depends on Nessie and my darling. They'll have to work it out between them."

"I'm sure they're in constant touch," Duncan said wryly.

Fiona hadn't turned her gaze from Andrew. "I would imagine that a lot of the people who come just want to be out on the loch. I bet they don't care if they see anything out of the ordinary. The ordinary is magnificent enough."

"Then you've been out on the water?"

"Oh, no. I've imagined it, though. It's so beautiful from the shore. It's easy to see it would be that much more beautiful gliding through the waves."

"It's particularly lovely on a clear night like this one. You should come for a cruise." Andrew realized he had excluded everyone else. "All of you," he amended. "It's rare to have a night this lovely so early in the season."

"I can't," Iain said. "There's still work to be done upstairs or there'll be permanent damage to the ceiling."

"I'd better stay and help Iain," Billie said, "or there'll be no living with him."

"We have to get back to April," Duncan said. "Or *I* do. Mara and Fiona can certainly go."

"I have to pass, as well," Mara said. "I have to be at the croft early tomorrow to help with shearing."

No regret showed on Fiona's face, but Andrew saw it in her eyes, deep where anyone who wasn't searching would miss it. "It looks like we'll have to wait," she said. "Another time, Andrew?"

Andrew could feel Duncan watching him. He had only to say aye, that they would go another time. He could make the offer again when the others weren't busy. There was nothing in Fiona's manner to indicate that she expected anything else.

But it wasn't a matter of her expectations.

"Do you have a reason no' to go tonight?" he asked.

She tilted her head. Like all her movements, this one was slight, and more effective because of it. "No, but I don't want to leave out the—"

"They've all been in my boat. You have no'."

"Aren't you tired? You've been taking people out all week."

He stared at her. The room seemed unusually still to him, as if everyone had ceased breathing. "Aye, but you're no' just people, are you?" He set down his coffee and held out his hand to her.

She didn't look around, but her cheeks delicately flushed with color. For a moment he thought she would refuse. For another, he almost wished she would. Then she stood and took his hand. "It sounds like something I'd better not miss."

Andrew turned to Duncan. "I'll bring her home afterward."

Duncan gave a curt nod. Andrew wanted to reassure him. He wanted to promise his friend that there was nothing to worry about. But even if he'd had the freedom to speak, there was nothing he could have promised. Nothing.

"Billie, Iain," he said, turning to his hosts. "I would no' abandon you so quickly, but I know you have work ahead. Is there anything else I can do before we leave?"

"Absolutely not. Shutting off the water was enough. Go and have fun," Billie said.

Andrew bent to kiss her cheek, but he held tightly to Fiona's hand so she wouldn't slip away. "Thank you for everything. It was the finest meal I've had in years."

Billie kissed him in return, and the kiss landed very near his ear. It was followed by a whisper. "I don't care if she's Duncan's sister, Andrew. Don't you dare treat Fiona like anything less than a woman tonight."

Chapter 8

Stardust yearned to be something she was not. She yearned to be tiny, with shining, rainbow scales, like the trout who had once been her friends. She yearned to be slender, with a supple body that twirled and coiled in the water like the eels who now refused to swim with her. But she was not small or slender. The lake seemed to rise as she grew, as if the weight and size of her body pushed the water higher up the beach. Now she had no one to play with except Lockjaw, the snapping turtle who preferred to sun his ancient body on a log. Lockjaw was not afraid of Stardust. He talked to her whenever she swam close enough. It was Lockjaw who told her that she was a water dragon and would never grow smaller. And it was Lockjaw who told her that far across Serenity Lake there were other dragons just like her.

Andrew's boat was neither large nor flashy. It was a cabin cruiser with comfortable seating for six. Obviously *MacDougall's Darling* had spent a long life exploring the loch and was now approaching retirement, but Andrew had kept her in such perfect condition that under the soft glow of moonlight her dark wood trim gleamed like a prized antique and her white hull was an unblemished beacon.

"She has none of the luxuries of a more modern craft. But there's no' a boat on the loch in better condition."

"And I'm sure there's not a guide who tells better stories." Fiona took Andrew's hand and let him help her aboard. The boat rocked gently under her feet.

"You'll get your sea legs before long." He didn't drop her hand. "Are you warm enough?"

"I'm fine."

"I could run inside and get you a coat."

Fiona looked beyond him to the frame cottage sitting back from the shore. *MacDougall's Darling* was anchored at the end of a short stone pier jutting out from Andrew's own property. They hadn't gone inside. She'd only glimpsed the exterior, but what she'd glimpsed was charming. "I'm fine. Really."

A high-pitched yapping carved a rift in the evening's dark tranquillity. Andrew shook his head. "I'm afraid Poppy's discovered I'm home."

Fiona already knew the story of how Duncan and Mara had rescued three breathtakingly ugly puppies wagging their tails at the gates of puppy heaven. She knew that after naming them all, April had kept Primrose, then presented Primrose's brother to Andrew. Iain had been gifted with the third look-alike, Hollyhock. The fact that the two men had never had the heart to change the dogs' names said volumes about their love for April.

"I've seen the others. Don't I get to judge this one, too?" she asked.

"He's every bit as ugly as the rest and twice as ill-mannered," Andrew warned.

"Go on and get him. Bring him along and I'll see what I think."

Andrew leapt back to the pier and disappeared into the darkness. Fiona wandered the boat, stroking the sleek vinyl cushions and the flawless woodwork. Everything was neatly in place and sparkling clean. She was peeking below at the spartan sleeping quarters when the boat began to rock. She turned just in time to brace herself before Poppy sprang.

"Down! Get down, Poppy!" Andrew leapt on board and rushed over to grab the dog who, if possible, was larger and uglier than both Primrose and Hollyhock.

"It's all right." Fiona wrapped her arms around the dog's neck and stroked his mottled fur. Poppy's eyes said "love me," while his drooling canine smile added "please?" Hooked, she murmured reassurances, which was no hardship, since his ears were at lip level.

"Get down!" Andrew pulled Poppy off Fiona and back down to all fours. "I'm sorry, Fiona. He's never been quite so poorly behaved. You would think he'd never seen a woman."

"And just how many has he seen?" She squatted to continue the dog-woman communion. Poppy was wiggling and slobbering with abandon.

"No' as many as you've probably been led to believe."

"Really? I've been told your fame extends through the Highlands."

"Fame? For what, exactly?"

Fiona looked up. Andrew's arms were crossed, and his eyes sparkled. She knew he expected her to back down, but she wasn't quite the blushing virgin he believed her to be. She shrugged carelessly. "I don't know. Every time I ask for details, the women in question just smile."

"Ah, that. They refer to my prowess at tossing the caber."

"The caber?"

"A long pole, thick and heavy." He made a circle with both hands. She whistled softly in appreciation.

"Slippery, too," he continued, "when a man's tensed to put all he has into the throw. You lift it like this." He demonstrated, bending slowly, then raising his cupped hands until they stopped just at his groin. "Then you heave it as far and as hard as you're able. I've competed throughout Scotland." He smiled seductively. "I've been declared a champion more than once."

She lifted a brow. "Now that I think about it, they all said you were a champion, although who knows how many caber tosses they've seen? But the description of . . . the caber certainly fits.''

"A man could have his head turned with such praise."

"And I bet a man could *lose* his head tossing his caber in the presence of the wrong woman."

"Oh, I'm canny whenever the occasion arises."

"And I suppose it . . . arises . . . often?"

"No' as often as you've probably been led to believe."

This time she smiled. "Isn't that where we began?"

He squatted beside her, weight resting easily on his heels. "What do you think of my Poppy?"

"I think he's spectacular."

"I will no' question that too closely." Andrew ruffled Poppy's ears, but the dog didn't turn from Fiona. "He seems to have taken a liking to you."

"He's a discriminating mutt."

"Shall we take him along, then?"

"We shall." She looked up and realized how close Andrew's face was to hers. Moonlight defined the rugged slash of his cheekbones, the square strength of his jaw, the slope of his nose. His was a Celtic face, equal parts warrior, pagan and mystic. He smiled and joked so often and easily that she suspected few saw the passion and the mystery deeply etched in his hazel eyes.

"I'm glad you came," he said. The teasing had ended. He was close enough to read her thoughts and too close to hide his own.

"Me too."

"I did no' think you would."

"Neither did I."

"I acted badly tonight."

"You have nothing to apologize for."

"Your brother warned me away from you."

Her heart began to beat faster. "I know. Is this about Duncan?"

"No. It's about my being afraid that I'll hurt you."

"You can only hurt me if I let you." Her breathing felt uneven, as if there weren't enough air in Scotland to completely fill her lungs.

He didn't speak or move. His gaze flicked to her lips, then back to her eyes. She saw caution melt into longing until there was no point where one ended and the other began. Desire was an unbroken continuum, a magnetic compulsion that held them motionless, even as both of them resisted its pull.

At last he stood. "I'll cast off."

The voice that emerged from her lips was husky and breathless, not her own. "Do you need a crew? I can do whatever you tell me."

"No' this time. I want you to sit and enjoy. It's special, when you see it the first time, our loch. Watch carefully as we pull away and you might see my darling. She's always nearby."

Fiona didn't ask how he knew or if he was teasing, since she doubted he had an answer for either question—and there were already enough unanswered questions between them. She settled herself in one of the comfortable seats at the stern and gazed out at the loch, shifting positions as the subtle purr of the engine added rhythm to the night and the boat pulled away from the pier.

Poppy jumped up on the seat to her left. Fiona kept her eyes on the water, although she wanted more than anything to watch and admire the way Andrew handled the boat. As the wind ruffled her hair she stroked the dog's velvet ears and searched the horizon for the proud lift of a water dragon's head.

Lights defined the loch's shoreline, intermittent and indistinct. She knew there were no commercial developments here except for a small, homey settlement of tourist cottages on the opposite shore that were rented each year by the same Lowland families that had rented them for decades. Fiona had explored the loch's circumference with Billie in search of an old woman who was said to tell richly embroidered stories about sea-dwelling kelpies who assumed human form—and all the poor women who had been fooled by them. Billie was working on a dissertation on local folklore, and Fiona had accompanied her on other trips into the country, as well.

"What do you see?"

The boat had slowed, but it was still moving. She hadn't expected Andrew to come up beside her. She tilted her chin to look up at him. "Everything and nothing. It's even more beautiful than I imagined."

"This is my favorite time. There's rarely anyone out here at night except the most intrepid fishermen."

"You never grow tired of it, do you?"

He lowered himself to the seat to her right so that Poppy wouldn't be displaced. "Never. Some men travel to see new sights. I come here for them."

"Then you're not a traveler?"

"I've seen the corners of the world, but I've found nowt I like better. I suppose that makes me dull and unimaginative."

"If you were making a list to describe yourself, would those adjectives be at the top?"

"A dull, unimaginative person would no' think of making a list."

"Who's steering the boat, Andrew?"

He leaned back. "She knows her own way."

Fiona knew better than to worry. The loch was his home, and she was perfectly safe. She leaned back, too, and turned just far enough to admire his profile. "Do you remember your first time out on the loch?"

"I was a babe in nappies. My father had no regular job. He was a tour guide, and he fished and sold what fish he could when no one in authority was about. He often took me with him. Iain and Duncan had their first ride on the loch in his boat."

"Those must be wonderful memories."

His voice dropped, as if her casual response had charted new depths in the conversation. "Some of them, aye. My da was a storyteller beyond compare. And he had the voice of an angel. We Scots are no' a weepy people, but when my da sang the old songs late at night at the pub, there was no' a strong man there who could stop himself from shedding a tear. He would sing, and they would buy him whisky so that he'd continue...."

There was more here, but she knew better than to pry. She searched for something safer. "Did your mother love the loch, too?"

"She hates it still. She says that Loch Ceo stole her husband."

Fiona sat forward. "Andrew, did your father drown? Is that what she meant?"

"My father died in hospital from too many dreams and too many drams."

She was at a loss for comforting words.

"He was a man no' meant to be a husband or father. A good man, nonetheless." Andrew stood and crossed to the wheel, as much, Fiona guessed, to end this portion of their conversation as to change the boat's direction. Poppy turned his head to watch, but the dog stayed where he was.

The boat picked up speed, then slowed once more. Fiona looked out at the water and watched the lights on the opposite shore grow brighter. Andrew took his seat again and pointed to the bow of the boat. "We're heading for a bonny cove where my darling was twice sighted last century, once by a doctor in Druidheachd on holiday, then again twelve years later by a wee lad and his sister. They claimed until the day they died an old man and woman that their story was true and no' combined imagination."

"How many sightings have there been?"

"Three this century that I know of. It's entirely possible there've been more, but no' everyone is willing to admit what they've seen. My father was one who did admit it. He saw my darling just hours after I was born, on his way home from the hospital."

"Wasn't your birth odd enough as it was?"

"The villagers think so. They still believe that when Duncan, Iain and I are together we have a certain power...."

Fiona remember that Billie had once said something similar, but she hadn't understood. "Power? What kind?"

"There's no attempt to define it. Iain graciously accepts it as superstition, while Dunc goes quietly mad."

"And you?"

"I think there's something to it."

"Do you? What?"

"I think that three men with a single purpose are more powerful than three hundred divided."

"Purpose?"

He leaned forward, hands on his knees; then he stood. He started around the helm to the bow, walking as skillfully on the bobbing deck as on land.

He was staring at something in the distance. She rose to follow him with Poppy at her heels and wondered if he thought he had glimpsed his darling. She didn't speak until she was beside him. There was nothing to block the wind here at the bow, and cold spray splattered her cheeks. She shivered and wished she had taken his offer of a coat. "Do you see something?"

"Aye. Over there at Gerston's Cottages. It looks as if they're tearing down the piers. It's an odd thing to do so late in the evening. There was no one working there forenoon or after."

"Maybe the owner hired men who can only work at night."

"Perhaps. Or perhaps she does no' want anyone to know what she's doing." Andrew turned to Fiona. "Or perhaps Kaye Gerston has nowt to do with this at all." He moved past her to the helm again. She followed him again and watched him take the wheel. "We'll have our look at the cove, I promise, but I think I'll investigate first. Do you mind?"

She was disappointed that the revelations about his childhood were over, but he had already given her much to ponder. She spoke as she braced herself for a faster ride. "Nope. I thrive on mysteries."

Loch Ceo was both long and wide, a small loch in comparison to Ness or Lomond, but large enough to make it impossible to view one side from the other. As they drew closer, Fiona could see what had intrigued Andrew. There were three narrow piers extending a short distance into the water, or at least there had been three narrow piers earlier that day. Now two of them looked like the bones of filleted fish, nothing but skeletal posts and crossbeams, and those were fast giving way, too.

Andrew pulled the boat up to the end of the pier that held a lone workman. "Harry Dutton, is that you?"

A blond-haired man who was kneeling at the middle of the pier ripping out boards looked up with no surprise on his face. Fiona suspected he had seen them coming. "Evening, Andrew."

"Looks like you'll soon make short work of that."

"That's what I'm being paid to do."

"Kaye's going to put some money into better piers, is she?"

"No' Kaye, I shouldn't think. It's no' her property anymore."

"Is that so?"

"Sold it, she did."

"I had no' heard."

Harry stood. Fiona saw that he was a huge man, a side of beef on thick elephant legs. "It's all going," he said. He swept his hand behind him. "Cottages and all."

"And why is that?"

Harry shrugged. "I should think to make way for something new."

"Do you know what?"

"Can't say I do."

"Is Kaye still on premises? Or has she left already?"

"Oh, she's here. Should be for a while. She's a lifetime of memories to pack."

"Aye." Andrew stood with his hands in his pockets. He had taken on the attitude of a man smoking a pipe, vigilance overlaid by endless patience. He didn't even look around, but Fiona knew he was aware of everything, the other men too far away to speak with, the darkness beyond the piers where the doomed cottages lay, the mellow light spilling from the windows of a small frame house nearer the water.

He moved at last, just a shift of weight from the balls of his feet to his heels, but she found she had been holding her breath.

"Do you know who the new owner might be, Harry?" he asked.

"There's two of them. From London. That's all I know."

"Two, you say?"

"I only saw one, a fat, bald chappie. Never heard his name."

"Martin Carlton-Jones."

"Someone you know, then?"

Fiona saw that Andrew's face had grown grim. "No," he said. "Someone I never plan to."

"I have no favorite spot on the loch, but this is *one* of my favorites." With practiced ease, Andrew dropped anchor in the middle of a deserted cove. The boat lurched a bit, then settled for lazily riding the gentle waves.

Fiona stood at his side. "One of how many?"

"A hundred." He recalculated. "Two at most."

"It's all so perfect."

He leaned against the railing and crossed his arms. Moonlight had turned her hair a soft wheat gold and her eyes the color of expensive aged whisky. "I've always been glad they could no' develop here. The shore's too steep and the land too rugged."

"Someone determined enough could find a way."

"No one has been that determined. No' yet. Perhaps the time is coming."

"It does seems odd to me that so much beauty has gone untapped in a country with limited resources. It's almost as if Druidheachd was left off the map."

"It has been left off many. Until now we've been too wee, too off the beaten path, to bother with."

"Until now?"

He had no desire to burden her. Not yet, and certainly not now. "Even Druidheachd can no' resist the march of progress forever. The day will come when we have our own McDonald's in the center of town."

"Well, maybe McDonald himself originated here. Did you think of that? Fergus *Mac*Donald of Druidheachd, a poor immigrant lad, cast away on the streets of New York with nothing in his pockets but a recipe for his old granny's minced beef sandwiches."

"Aye, you're right, of course. We should build him a memorial."

"I can see it now." She framed it with her hands. "Golden arches. Two of them intersecting."

He laughed and reached for her hand. "I've nothing against progress. I only care when it steals what's dear to us."

Her hand was cold inside his, and she looked away shyly as he eased it under the hem of his jacket. "Doesn't every kind of progress rob us of something? Before television people spent more time visiting and talking. Now they sit in their own houses and communicate with the world, but it's completely one-sided. Something was lost at the same time something was gained."

He placed her palm against his waist. He could feel each separate finger through his shirt. "I like the old ways. I dinna own a telly. There's poor reception on the loch to begin with, but I'm afraid if I had one, I'd watch it."

"That *would* be the point." She turned more fully toward him, and then she shivered. "What do you do instead?"

"You're cold." He shook his head. "I should have fetched you a coat after all." He tugged her closer. "Come here."

She came with just a hint of resistance. He tucked her under his arm and against his side. "You'll warm up in a moment."

"Tell me what you do instead of television."

There was a persistence to the question that intrigued him. He guessed it was at least partially a demand that the conversation continue just as it had, despite the fact that she was now intimately snuggled against him. The other part was intriguing, too. She seemed genuinely interested in how he spent his hours, as if she wanted to be able to visualize a portion of his life. Her life had been so sheltered and conscribed. How often had she imagined the daily activities of others and expanded her horizons through them?

He answered without admitting that in the last weeks at least some part of every day had been spent thinking of her. "I walk and I climb. I've no real passion for golf, but I play when I can. I practice my pipes more than anyone who's heard me might think."

"Pipes?"

"Bagpipes. Has Duncan no' complained to you of my playing?"

"Not a word."

"It's what I do when I need to think."

She looked up at him, cheeks kissed by the moonlight, lips soft and vulnerable. "Oh, I want to hear you play. I'd like nothing better."

"You might no' say so after you've heard me."

"I'll take my chances."

Her eyes were shining with anticipation. His heart constricted painfully in his chest before it began to speed faster. He knew better than this. He knew who and what he was, and he knew what she needed. She was the princess in the tower, badly in need of rescuing. But he was no knight. He was the son of a drunken fisherman, a Highlander with no aspirations to be anything but exactly what he was.

And what was he at that moment except a man who wanted to hold Fiona in his arms?

His own hand seemed to stray against his will, to steal up her arm to her shoulders, her neck, her hair, to burrow into the midst of the unruly strands until her face was turned to his. His thumb caressed her cheek. His thumb was calloused and her skin as soft and undefiled as spring's first wildflowers. He touched, tentatively, patiently, the corner of her mouth. He heard her breath catch and felt her body tense.

"What chances . . . will you take?" he asked.

"I don't know." Her eyes widened. "This terrifies me."

"Does it?" He stroked his thumb over her bottom lip, slowly, tenderly. "Is that all that it does, Fiona?"

"What can I offer you?" She put her hand on his cheek to stop him from shaking his head. "It's more than a lack of experience or false modesty. You only see a part of me, Andrew. There is more."

He thought of the parts of himself that no one saw. The nights when he sat alone and stared into the darkness. The days when he moved faster and faster to rid himself of black thoughts and bottomless doubts. "Have I asked you to be perfect?"

"I'm very far from perfect."

"So am I."

"Are you trying to misunderstand?"

"I understand exactly. Do you?" He leaned forward and kissed the place he had touched at the corner of her lips. Her mouth was ripe and ready for harvest, as enticing as forbidden fruit. He touched her bottom lip with his tongue, following the path of his thumb. He could feel the warmth of her breath as she sighed, but she didn't pull away. He enclosed her in his arms, a safe, warm harbor, and took her lips fully, slanting his against them. There was such sweetness, such innocent seduction, in the way that she yielded, a sigh, a gradual melting of her body into his, slowly, ever so slowly.

He had never been one to play games with women, to pressure or even to woo. Women had come to him, women with no thoughts of commitment or ownership. Women who liked his warm smile and the touch of his strong, wide hands. Women who had remained friends when they were no longer lovers.

Women so different from the one he held in his arms.

She was new to being kissed, and the teaching of it was more arousing than he could have imagined. He felt the tentative forays of her tongue in places she barely touched, places he wanted her to explore. Wanted badly. Her sweater skimmed his jacket, and as he tightened his arms around her, her breasts sank slowly against his chest. Slowly. Carefully. As if she were afraid he would find something there to disappoint him.

"Fiona," he whispered against her mouth, and once more against her cheek. From the night that he'd kissed her in the room where she had almost died, he'd had some vague idea that he could help her step over the brink into womanhood, that he could make her see that she was worth a man's attention and that any man would be luckier for it.

Now he saw how dangerous the most honorable intentions could be. But somehow, despite burgeoning fears of his own, he couldn't stop kissing her.

She stroked his cheek with her palm, then skimmed it lightly down his neck and along his shoulder. Each separate fingertip made an impression on his upper arm. He could feel each hesitant flutter of her hand as she continued her explorations. He was adrift in the scent of her hair, the silk of her skin, the pillow soft give of her breasts. Her hips nestled against his, intimately, then more intimately still. If she was frightened by what she found in return, she didn't pull away. He wondered if she understood exactly what his own arousal meant, and what proof it was of her feminine powers.

He settled his hands at her waist and urged her closer. Her sweater drifted over his hands as his thumbs traced the waistband of her skirt. At the precise moment that he touched the bare skin of her back, the sensuous spell ended.

"No." She stepped back so swiftly that she might have fallen if he hadn't had his arms around her.

His breath was erratic, but not as erratic as his heartbeat. Hands that were usually rock steady trembled badly. He had gone from control to a nearly total lack of it in mere moments. He stood very still as reality filtered through the erotic veil that had shrouded his common sense.

"Fiona, are you afraid I'll make you do something you do no' want to do?" he asked when he was certain that the voice that emerged would sound like his.

She didn't answer for a moment. She turned away from him, and he let her go. She walked to the railing and looked out over the cove. "What are we doing, Andrew? This can't go anywhere. You've made that clear, and I knew it, anyway. Of all people I should know better than to play with fire."

"Is that what we were doing?"

She faced him at last. "You wouldn't have liked what you found if you'd continued touching me."

"I know you have scars," he said bluntly.

"I *am* scars. There are places where that's all I am. It's not pretty. It's worse than that. There's no way a man could touch me and feel anything except..."

He waited, but his gaze stayed connected with hers. He waited, silently demanding that she finish.

"Except pity," she said at last. "Or compassion, which is only a slightly more enlightened version of the same. And I don't want your pity. Not yours. I couldn't stand it."

"Then you'll no' have it."

"And horror? Can you really tell me that you wouldn't find the evidence of what happened to me horrifying?"

"What happened to you *was* horrifying." He steeled himself to add more. "What's happened to you since is more so."

Her eyes widened, and she stepped back against the rail as if he'd struck her.

He pushed on. "You've determined that a man will find nowt about you to love, that no man is clever or caring enough to see past scar tissue to the woman herself. You've decided that because you're no' perfect, a man could no' be aroused by anything else about you, the softness of your breasts or the curve of your hips. Your lovely smile, the way your hair dances in the wind." He turned up his palms hopelessly. "You had the evidence pressed up against you, and you simply ignored it."

"You don't know. You can't."

"I dinna know it all, perhaps. But I know that there's nowt about you that could horrify me and much I desire."

"Have I become a mission to you?" There was no anger in her voice. If there had been, he would have walked back to the helm and started the engine. But beneath the starkness of her words he heard the cry for comfort and reassurance.

"You have become a complication," he said honestly. "I've loved you forever, Fiona. But you no longer feel like my wee sister. Perhaps once I wanted to give you confidence. Now I want to give you myself, and that could be dangerous for us both."

He knew that she didn't, couldn't, really understand what he meant. But he couldn't have explained it any better.

Her eyes glistened with unshed tears. "This is going to end badly, isn't it? You're Duncan's best friend, and Iain's, too. I could destroy that."

"Aye, if we let it come to that. But we have the power to be certain that it does no'."

"Then we ought to stay away from each other."

"That would be the coward's way out. Is that what you want?"

"What do *you* want?"

"More than I should."

"Do you have to speak in riddles?"

"All right, then. Judging from the state of my body, I want you in my bed. Scars and all, Fiona. But when you climb out of it, I want you to leave without a backward glance. I know who and what I am, and what I can offer. And I can no' offer a life you would want."

"You know that already? You know without giving me a chance to decide? Are you going to make my decisions for me, too?"

"I know who I am."

"We're a pretty pair, aren't we?"

He felt the tension that had held them in its grip crack wide open. He smiled, and suddenly the night was warm and the breeze a gentle caress. "Maybe we were put on God's green earth to be a trial to each other. Did you think of that?"

Her body softened; her shoulders slumped, and she shook her head. "You work hard at pretending you're a simple man."

He moved forward and cupped her chin in his hand. Slowly, inexorably, he turned her face to his. "Oh, I'm no' simple at all. And you're no' the sweet innocent you pretend to be. There's a woman inside you clawing her way out, Fiona. And one day soon, she will have her way."

Chapter 9

Kaye Gerston could drink a man under the table, then help him home to bed, tuck him in with a jovial flourish and leave him with the imprint of a huge smacking kiss in the center of his forehead. She was a tall woman with large bones and belly, who stood on wee Cinderella feet—which were her only vanity. Her age was indeterminate; she had always dyed her hair a flaming red, and her face had been as weather-beaten and lined during Andrew's childhood as it was now.

Kaye's face had always been open, too, as easy to read as a screaming tabloid headline, but today it was as incomprehensible as a Turkish daily.

"Do I owe you an explanation, Andrew?" she asked. "Have I given you the impression at one time or the other that I have a duty to explain myself to you?"

Andrew was an engineer, not a psychologist, but he understood guilt and fear and the ways in which they manifested themselves. Days had passed since his discovery that Kaye had sold her land, but she had avoided his phone calls and pretended not to be home when he had visited once before.

He refused to back down. "And have I given you the impression that I'm demanding something of you? I've asked for information and nowt more. Friend to friend and neighbor to neighbor."

Andrew stood just outside the door of Kaye's house and waited for an answer. She hadn't asked him in, which was unusual, too. Kaye had been a close friend of his mother, and she had always been partial to Andrew. She herself had given birth to nothing but girls, slight, fairylike creatures with graceful manners and delicate features. They might as well have been fairies, for all she'd understood them. But she had understood and appreciated Andrew, and she had always been there to cuff him soundly on the ears if he misbehaved or—more rarely—to clap him on the back if he didn't.

"My mum asks about you often," he offered at last, when she still hadn't answered.

She moved aside with an audible sigh and gestured him inside. "You may or may no' find a place to sit," she said. "It's up to you to look for one. I'm far too busy to do it for you."

Andrew stepped past her into the hallway, now a labyrinth of cartons and furniture piled into eccentric sculptures. "So it's true, you are moving."

"Aye, and glad I am of it."

He navigated the labyrinth successfully. Kaye's house had never overflowed with decorative touches, not until her husband had died and the girls had grown old enough to have their collective way. But it had always been scrupulously clean, with mismatched furniture lined up against the walls in military precision. Now all was chaos.

"I've nowt to offer you," she said bluntly when they had wound their way into a cluttered sitting room. "The coffee's lost somewhere in the kitchen, and you know how I feel about tea. More's the pity it's too early for whisky, even for me."

"I did no' come for refreshment."

She folded her arms, engulfed by a man's shirt, and tapped her sandaled, glamorously pedicured feet. "So why did you come? To say goodbye? You could have saved a trip.

I want no goodbyes. I'll be leaving soon, and that will be that."

"Is it that easy, then? You've lived here all your life. Your family's had this property for how long? Three generations? Four?"

"It matters no' at all how long they had it. Someone else has it now."

"Martin Carlton-Jones and Nigel Surrey."

Kaye narrowed her eyes. "And who were your sources for that wee slip of information?"

He touched his forehead with his forefinger.

"Mr. Carlton-Jones said that Iain Ross might cause a fuss, but he neglected to mention you," she said.

"So he told you that Iain would be unhappy?"

"And what care I?"

Andrew was sorry to be correct. Even though he had suspected the worst, he had hoped for better. Martin Carlton-Jones and Nigel Surrey were developers who specialized in holiday communities for the British upper class. For almost a year now they had made no secret of their opinion that Druidheachd could be a cozy Highlands retreat for the rich and famous. Iain had already called their hand once, but it seemed that now they were back and more insidious than ever.

The room where he stood was small and simple in design. There was a narrow window on each of three identical walls and a blackened stone fireplace on the other. The draperies had been removed, and the fireplace mantel was clear of everything but the ingrained soot of centuries. Andrew lifted a book from the carton nearest him and examined the title. "You always loved a good mystery. I still have several you've loaned me."

She batted the air disdainfully. "Keep them. I dinna need another thing to move."

"We share that, you and I. I love a good mystery, too. But I sense a real one here. Why would a woman who loves the loch as you do sell her inheritance to strangers, take the cash and move to a place she does no' love?"

"Och, it's no' so difficult, Andrew. There's no need to summon Hercule Poirot or Jane Marple. My girls dinna want this place. One's in London, one in Paris, one in Aberdeen. I've grown too old to care for the cottages alone, and why should I? So that when I die, my girls can reap the profits? No, I've sold it myself. I'm moving to Spain or Portugal, I've no' decided which. I'll sit outside in the sunshine all day if I like. And when I die, there'll still be plenty of money to divide between them. No' that any of them need it.''

He was silent. He understood everything that she'd said, but he also understood the things she hadn't. She had been forced into a corner, with too little capital to make needed improvements and too little strength to go on as she had. She had convinced herself that unlimited sunshine would make up for the loss of lifelong friends and a proud heritage. Sympathy filled him, but he knew that Kaye would hate sympathy as much as pity.

And there was still a mystery.

"Fine, then. Let's say there was no other way to do things. You woke up one morning and determined that you had to sell. Why Carlton-Jones and Surrey? Iain's made it plain to everyone that he'll buy property on the loch and beyond if it has to be sold. He's warned of strangers coming here to quietly buy up what they can until Druidheachd is no' Druidheachd any longer but a summer resort.''

"Your friend Iain has his own reasons for wanting my property.''

"And what would those be?''

"He wants it all, does he no'? It's no' enough that he's inherited most of the countryside. Now he wants it all, village, loch. . . . And what are his reasons, do you suppose?''

He forced himself to speak slowly, without passion. "I *suppose* his reason is to protect a village he loves and a way of life that needs to change slowly and carefully.''

"He's greedy, your Lord Ross! That's why he wants it all.''

Andrew held himself in check. He had known this woman all his life. "Carlton-Jones and Surrey offered you more than the property was worth, did they no', Kaye? More than Iain would have. Did you no' see that this was the way they plan to make their start? They offer more than your property's worth, and they'll offer more to the next man or woman, too. Then, when things have changed so profoundly that no one wants to live here, they'll snap up what's left at a half or a third what it's worth."

She sniffed. "They paid more than I ever thought I could get! But no' because of a plan such as the one you've outlined. They're no' that crafty, Andrew. They offered it because of the sighting. Do you no' see? They've an idea that this will be the next Loch Ness. They dinna know our creature. They dinna understand that she shows herself rarely. And by the time they do understand and the tourists are all gone again, I'll be gone, too. With their money."

He heard a plea for understanding and acceptance. He could only shake his head. "They are no' fools. They are the very men that Iain warned you about. My darling has nowt to do with their hunger for our land."

"Have you become like your friends, Andrew? Duncan Sinclair owns the only hotel in the village, and Iain Ross owns most of the property outside it. Have you become greedy, too? Do the three of you want to control all that happens here? Is that what this is about?"

For a moment he couldn't speak. Anger flared so fiercely that it threatened to consume his good judgment. Then he calmed, a millimeter at a time. "Kaye," he said at last, "you have two choices, I think. You can look into your heart and remember who Duncan, Iain and I truly are. You can remember that you've known us since the night we were born, that as weans you bounced us on your knee and dinged our wee bottoms when it was needed. Or you can forget what you know and believe the lies of two men with nowt to gain from telling the truth."

He didn't, couldn't, wait for her response. He picked his way across the floor and brushed past her without another word. Spring sunshine had brightened the sky when he first entered the house. He noted that, as he left it, dark clouds were forming.

As a young man just old enough to take his first drink, Andrew had refused, to the dismay and ridicule of his friends. He had been solidly in his twenties before he tried beer and older still before he turned to whisky. Even now he monitored his own response like a diabetic checking insulin levels. He knew exactly how much he could drink and still maintain his wits. He made certain that periodically he stopped drinking entirely, just to be sure that he still could. And daily he told himself that if the moment ever arrived when he badly craved a drink, he would never take another.

Today, after his confrontation with Kaye Gerston, he ordered whisky with his supper at the hotel pub, savoring the roar as it plunged to his empty stomach and echoed through his body. He would have liked a repeat, but instead he took his meal, cold lamb and colcannon—a puree of potatoes and turnips combined with chopped cooked cabbage—to a table in the corner. Frances Gunn, the hotel cook, made the finest colcannon in the Highlands, but today Andrew ate without tasting it.

Days had passed since he had seen Fiona. He had thought it wise to give both of them time to distance themselves from the events on his boat. Instead he had spent all his time remembering how she had felt in his arms.

He wanted to see her tonight, but he hadn't come to the hotel to find her. He knew that she wasn't upstairs, that this morning she had gone to Glasgow with Duncan. Several weeks before she had begun to make the journey with Duncan whenever he went in for meetings. Fiona visited Sara in the hospital while Duncan worked. Andrew suspected it wasn't easy for her, that each time she stepped in to the burn unit she was assaulted by memories. But she went anyway, because it did Sara and Pamela good to have her there.

"Two can stare at the wall same as one." Iain lowered himself into the chair beside Andrew and set an identical plate on the table.

Andrew hadn't heard Iain approach. He adjusted his chair so that he could see his friend. Marriage had been good to Iain. Like a feral cat who had been adopted and domesticated, he still retained his watchful demeanor and quick reflexes. But Iain was more content than Andrew had ever hoped to see him, a far more optimistic version of the man he once had been.

"Thanks for coming," Andrew said. "I did no' really expect you to get away."

"Billie's off in the country somewhere with Mara, and it's not often I get to sample Frances Gunn's cooking these days."

"Billie's every bit as good a cook."

"Absolutely true. But she doesn't cook this." Iain pointed his fork at his plate. "Or kedgeree, or boiled beef and hodgils."

"My mum made kedgeree every time you came to eat with us, you liked it so well. She always said that if you grew tall and strong, it would be her kedgeree that did it."

"How is she, Andrew? I haven't spoken to her since I told her about the wedding. Have you persuaded her yet to come back for a visit?"

"She will no' come, and I know better than to expect it. I visit her whenever I'm able. She's made friends in Fife, and she has a job she enjoys in a shop there. I think she's fair satisfied with her life."

"I plan to take Billie to meet her one day soon."

"She'd like that. She always asks about you and Duncan. She was so happy to meet Mara and April in the autumn."

Iain began slicing his meat. "You didn't ask me here to discuss old times, did you?"

Andrew considered how to begin. He had always been a direct man, never the least confused about what to say and when to say it. But his relationship with Fiona seemed to have changed all that. Now there was much he questioned and even more that he doubted. And most of all he doubted himself and his own ability to make things right.

"Kaye Gerston has sold her property on the loch to Carlton-Jones and Surrey," he said, when nothing better than the blunt truth occurred to him.

Iain took his first bite and didn't speak.

"Aye, it was a shock for me, too," Andrew acknowledged. He knew his old friend too well to be fooled.

"So, they've made a foothold at last."

Andrew pushed his own plate to one side and tilted back his chair to see Iain better. "I spoke to Kaye this morning. I spent the remainder of the day speaking to everyone who would speak in return."

"And?"

"There are several more who are considering offers. John Warren, Nancy Reed, the Coopers, who own most of the western shore and my favorite cove."

"I've spoken to each of them in the past and promised to buy their land at fair market value if they ever wanted to sell."

"Aye, each of them mentioned as much." Andrew reached for his spoon and began to drum idly on the table.

"When you do that, I know things must be worse than you've said."

"Have you done anything, Iain, that might have angered the villagers?"

"Are they angry?"

"Aye. And all had the same defense. You have more than you should. You *want* more than you should. Duncan is a greedy American and you're an arrogant laird. They've nowt bad to say about me. No' yet. But I felt a chill in the air as we spoke. I'm one of the men of midnight, for all that."

Iain carefully laid his fork on his plate. It was the equivalent of another man pounding the table with his fist. "I've been nothing less than fair to anyone here. I lease land at a rate far under that of other landlords, and I do whatever upkeep is necessary. My standards are high, my relationships with my tenants are superior—or at least they have been until now. I've sold property when I've been asked, and donated land and money whenever the cause has been just. I certainly have more than any man deserves, but I was born with it. And I've rectified that whenever I was able."

"Who is it you're trying to convince? I know who you are and the way you manage what's yours. And I know why you want to keep Carlton-Jones and Surrey from Druidheachd."

"They're vampires. They'll suck the blood from Druidheachd so quickly not even a transfusion will help. They'll take it all. Every last rock and grain of sand for miles around, and they won't rest until they've gotten what they want. It's a matter of honor now, because I threatened them. Months ago I told Martin I would use my influence, as well as all the information I have about the ways in which they've acquired land in other places, to keep them away from Druidheachd. I wasn't foolish enough to believe that I could stop them, but I expected to slow them down, perhaps enough to rethink their ambitions. Apparently even that was foolish."

"What can be done about it?"

"Does it matter what I can prove? Will anyone listen now? Martin and Nigel have obviously taken me at my word. I said that I would use my influence, and they've begun to erode that." There was nothing humorous in Iain's smile. "That's the part I didn't foresee."

"And the part that hurts?"

"Aye."

The two men stared morosely at each other until a third voice interrupted. "The two of you are looking pretty sober. Shall I get Brian over here with a bottle of our best?"

Andrew gazed up at Duncan. He was glad to see his friend, despite the strain that had developed between them since Fiona had come to Druidheachd. He silenced the internal voice that pointed out that Fiona must be back now. "Have a seat, Duncan. This concerns you, too."

Duncan grabbed a chair from another table, which wasn't difficult. The tables nearest them were suddenly vacant, which inevitably happened when the three men of midnight sat down together. "Everyone's moved away," Duncan said. "Did you see that? No one left in shouting distance."

"You make too much of it, as always," Andrew said.

"Someday I'm going to rig the lights. Then when I come over to join you, I'll have Brian shove a switch somewhere and the whole place will explode in bursts of lightning."

"And never more will another patron walk through that door."

"It might be worth it." Duncan leaned back in his chair like both of the others. "So what's going on?"

Andrew filled him in as succinctly as he could. Duncan listened, and nodded when appropriate. "Well, that explains why it's been so hard to get anyone to work for me or you, Iain."

"I've been thinking about it all day. The beauty of the scheme is this," Andrew said. "The villagers believe that Carlton-Jones and Surrey only want their land because of my darling. But the villagers also know her habits well. They believe that when time passes and she's no' sighted again, the land will no longer have value. So they want to sell while they can. Carlton-Jones and Surrey have reinforced their view. Both men are very adept at looking like fools."

"When you were making your rounds this morning, did you ask those who are considering a sale what would happen if your darling was sighted again? Wouldn't that increase the value of their land further? Shouldn't they wait to sell?" Iain asked.

"Aye, I thought of that. They responded that if my darling is sighted again, it will bring more tourists, and they're fair tired of the ones who are here already. At that point, they would want to sell anyway."

"A truly neat trap," Iain said. "Our credibility is questioned, our options narrowed. I'll do what I can to expose Martin and Nigel, but by the time I can make my case, it may be too late. If too many sell, there will be little incentive for the others to hold on." He stood and looked at his watch. "I have to get home. Billie should be back soon. Let's talk some more tomorrow."

The other men nodded. They were silent until Iain had left the pub. "Did you have a good day in Glasgow, Duncan?" Andrew asked. He couldn't resist the next question. "And did Fiona see Sara?"

Duncan didn't look at him, which was unusual. He looked just over Andrew's shoulder at nothing. "Andrew, she's still there."

For a moment Andrew was confused. "Sara?"

"Fiona. I'm afraid Sara's taken a turn for the worse. One of those infections that can complicate things in an instant. Fiona phoned while I was in a meeting. She plans to wait there all night if she has to, but she refused to leave until she got some news.''

''You left her there?''

Their gazes connected. Duncan's eyes narrowed. ''She gave me no choice. Weren't you the one who pointed out that I have to let her live her own life?''

Andrew pictured Fiona in the antiseptic waiting room at the end of the ward. He pictured tiny Sara, flushed with fever or shivering in the grip of chills. He shook his head. ''Would you have told me, Duncan, if I had no' asked?''

''I called your house the moment I got home. When you didn't answer, I came down here to see if anyone knew where you might be.''

Andrew stood. ''I'll go. I'll wait with her.'' He paused, expecting Duncan to protest.

Duncan just nodded. ''I'd feel better if you did.''

For most of her life Fiona had cultivated the art of sitting still. She had learned to wait patiently, to accept what she was given and not to expect miracles. She had woven stories in her head to pass the long, lonely hours, and when she was old enough, she had transferred them to paper.

Although she had studied art in college, Fiona had never thought herself much of an artist. No matter how hard she tried for precision, her drawings and paintings were softly focused impressions, moody visual collages that suggested a universe of emotion she had never actually been privy to. Her professors had been encouraging, but more aggressive students had garnered most of the awards and praise.

A senior class on illustration had changed that. Fiona had thrown herself into the final class project—illustrating a child's picture book—with a fervor she hadn't even known she was capable of. Instead of the required folk or fairy tale, she had illustrated one of her own stories, the birth of the water dragon Stardust in far-off Serenity Lake. Instead of the required dummy made up of preliminary pencil sketches, she had submitted exacting pen and ink drawings washed with dreamy watercolors. Her instructor had been captivated, and so had the children's book publisher who years before had been the instructor's lover.

The result had been a contract for Fiona. The patience she had spent a lifetime refining hadn't even been required. Without stamping an envelope, her career had been established.

Fiona knew how fortunate she was, and she guarded that fortune jealously. She had never expected another lucky break. She had worked tirelessly to bring that first book to fruition, and each subsequent book, too. She was a perfectionist who threw out one hundred drawings for each one that she kept. She haunted aquariums and zoos to capture the sleek, supple movements of aquatic creatures, and she sat for hours beside ponds just to understand the way that reeds rustled in the breeze and sunlight reflected off gentle waves.

She seldom went anywhere without a sketchbook. She had one with her tonight because she had brought it to entertain the children in Sara's ward. It was a trick she had discovered several weeks ago. When she had sensed that the children were tired of hearing her stories, she had asked them to write their own. She faithfully recorded their ideas; then, as they watched from their beds, she sketched their characters for them, listening attentively to their suggestions and incorporating them always.

There were more pictures today. She had steeled herself to return to the ward, even when she had discovered that Sara had been moved to a room by herself. She had forced herself to ignore the empty bed where Sara should have been and to interact with the remaining children. She had tried to be cheerful, but the children themselves were more somber than usual. Sara was a favorite, the youngest child on the ward, and everyone knew how sick she was.

Now Fiona flipped through today's sketches, as she had a dozen times already that evening. One boy's fantasy was a two-story fire-eating monster who, with one indrawn breath, could extinguish any blaze. She stared blindly at that drawing. Children were direct and uncomplicated. Had such a monster existed, the little boy wouldn't be lying in the burn ward.

Tears filled her eyes, and anger filled her heart. She closed the pad and clutched it to her chest. Long ago she had learned the futility of questioning fate. Now she simply railed against it.

"Fiona?"

For one wild instant she thought she had imagined Andrew's voice. Then she looked up and saw him standing in the doorway. She dropped the sketchbook to the seat beside her and brushed away her tears with the back of one hand. "When did you get here?"

Andrew ignored her question, walked straight over to her, lifted her from her chair and took her in his arms. She had spent days reliving the feel of his body against hers, but now she discovered that the reality was an alternate universe, so superior to fantasy that there was no resemblance.

"Is she worse?" he asked.

The words fell against her hair; his breath warmed her scalp. She clung to him, and the tears fell faster. "No, but she's not any better, either," she said on a sob.

"If she's no' worse, then that's good."

"I'm so tired of sorting through things and pretending that the bad ones are good because they could be worse." She forced a humorless laugh that sounded more like a plea.

"Shh...." He held her tighter. "I know."

"She was getting better!"

"We both knew this could happen. We'd been warned. Pamela warned me herself."

"Why didn't they protect her? They shouldn't let any visitors on that ward. People bring germs with them. They shouldn't have let *us* visit."

"The hospital does its best. I've never seen such attention to detail. And they allow us to visit because the children's spirits need healing, too."

She was sobbing harder now. He stroked her hair with steady, soothing hands. The more she tried to control herself, the more she cried. Andrew continued to hold her, to stroke her hair, and sway gently back and forth. Finally, little by little, the tears began to dry.

He pulled a huge white handkerchief from his trouser pocket and slipped it into her hand. "Now wipe your eyes."

She did. She could feel Andrew withdraw, not suddenly, but as if he were weaning her from his support. "I'm sorry," she murmured, swallowing the last of her tears. Embarrassment wormed its way through her sorrow. She felt worse with each passing second.

"Fiona." He lifted her chin so that she was gazing at him with reddened eyes. "Dinna you dare apologize. I'd like nowt better than to cry myself."

"Then why don't you?"

"I suppose I've forgotten how. You'll have to cry for us both." He took her hand, then he sat on one of the sofas and pulled her down to sit beside him. "Tell me everything you know."

She had leaned against him enough. She held herself away from him, although he didn't drop her hand. "She started running a fever this morning. That's not unusual, but it spiraled higher and higher as the morning went on. By noon they'd isolated her and started her on some heavy-duty medications."

"Is Pamela with her?"

"Yes. But she's not allowed in the room. She can watch through a glass partition, but that's all." She glanced down at her watch. "Pamela came back about an hour ago to tell me that nothing had changed. They hope to see some improvement by midnight, but it's touch and go."

"Did Pamela say that?"

"No. She's trying to be brave. But I know what I know." He didn't question that. "Have you had supper?"

"No."

"Then we'll go downstairs together. You'll eat whatever you can, then we'll come back up here and settle in until we've heard good news."

"I'm not hungry."

"Did I ask if you were?" He didn't smile. "You'll eat anyway, and when we've gotten the news we came for, we'll go back to the hotel—"

"What?"

"I'll reserve rooms at a hotel while you eat. We'll no' be driving back to Druidheachd after this. It's far too late."

She contemplated that. She'd had no plan at all, except to wait. Now she had a plan. She'd had no hope of comfort. Now comfort sat beside her.

She'd had no hope at all. But Andrew had enough hope for all of them. *Until we've heard good news.*

"I don't know what to say." She searched his face.

For a moment his resolve melted into vulnerability. Some unprotected emotion shone in his eyes. "That's just as well."

"You didn't have to come."

"Aye. I know."

She couldn't leave it at that, although it was safer. "I'm glad you did."

"I know that, too." He drew one finger along her cheekbone, as if collecting teardrops. "We'll always be glad to see each other, Fiona. No matter how much we deny it. No matter how many mistakes we make with each other. It's a blessing and a curse, and still it does no' matter. We'll always be glad to see each other, no matter what sorrow it brings."

Chapter 10

Fiona was dozing on Andrew's shoulder when Pamela arrived to tell them that Sara seemed to be responding to treatment. She had stabilized, which was the best anyone had expected so early in the crisis, and there was every hope that by tomorrow morning her fever would begin to inch back toward normal. In the meantime, the little girl was sleeping, and Pamela insisted that Fiona and Andrew do the same. She intended to use a hospital bed to get some sleep herself.

Fiona and Andrew were already heading toward the closest hotel before they exchanged more than a few words. She noted the way his strong, wide hands tensely gripped the wheel, as if he were afraid he might fall asleep if he relaxed. "You don't think they're just telling us she's better so that we'll get some sleep, do you?" she asked. "Could they just be putting a positive spin on it?"

"They could be, but I doubt it. What need have they to spare our feelings? They're far too busy to be worried about us."

"I guess you're right."

"There's nowt we can do tonight, Fiona. We'll ring first thing in the morning."

She fell silent again. Rain had fallen throughout the evening, and under the graduated glow of their headlights the street glistened like gushing oil. Just ahead a cat darted between shrubs lining the curb, but there was no other movement. Glasgow, Scotland's jittery, glittery diamond in the rough, was sleeping soundly.

Andrew pulled into a space in front of a solid and monumentally plain building. Fiona had to squint to find the sign that designated it as a hotel. "It looks like the kind of place that caters to long-term residents."

"It does, but there was room for us. I've a key to the side door."

"I imagine they'll think it odd that we're arriving without suitcases."

"I explained."

She followed him inside, up a set of stairs covered in an endearingly old-fashioned maroon carpet, past doors with cut glass knobs and walls adorned with framed lithographs of the river Clyde. He stopped in front of the last door at the end of the hall and used an ornate key in what was obviously a nineteenth century keyhole.

He ushered her inside. The room was tiny, the carpet worn. A musty smell greeted them, as if the room had been closed up for months. She ran a finger idly along the wainscoting and found it dust free. "It doesn't matter what it looks like. It has a bed."

"I thought you'd be pleased to see that."

The bed was large enough for two, visibly sagging and smothered by a chenille spread with a tartan blanket folded neatly at the foot. It gave her an odd sensation to stand there and look at it with Andrew beside her. "Where's your room?"

"At the opposite end of the hall. Will you be all right?"

She had expected to be, but something about the room gave her pause. Her skin tingled, one step from unwelcome goose bumps. She couldn't put her finger on the reason why, but she didn't feel comfortable here. She met his eyes anyway. How could she complain when he'd worked so hard to set this up? "I'm probably going to be asleep before I pull down the covers."

He handed her a small paper bag. He'd already told her that after picking up the keys he'd stopped at the chemist to buy them each a few toiletries. They would be clean tomorrow even if their clothes weren't. "Loo's down the hall," he said. "On the right. I think there's a sign."

"Thank you. For everything, Andrew. I'd be spending the night at the hospital if it weren't for you, and taking a bus home tomorrow."

As he handed her the key, he gave her a weary smile. "I'll see you in the morning, then. Shall I come for you about eight?"

"As soon as you get up." She realized she sounded like someone who was already anxious to leave. "I don't want to hold you up any longer than necessary." Her smile was a paler version of his.

He didn't touch her or even smile again. He closed the door behind him and left her standing alone in the room.

Fiona resigned herself to a long night and went down the hall to prepare for it as best she could.

Back in the room she left the door ajar as she did another visual tour. There was absolutely nothing to be frightened of here. The room was shabby but scrupulously clean; in fact, it wasn't too different from the smaller rooms at the Sinclair Hotel. The layout was nearly identical, and the double-hung window that faced the street rattled with a familiar buzz. She told herself she was being silly.

At the window she gazed below. She could just see Andrew's car and, surprisingly, Andrew. She guessed he was getting something he needed for the night. Despite a chill wind brought by the rain, she unlocked the window and tried to lift it. She preferred the wind to the musty smell, but she quickly discovered that the window wouldn't budge. It had been varnished shut.

Aware that if Andrew looked up, he would see her, she went to lock the door and turn off the light. When she returned to the window, he was nowhere in sight. She spread the draperies to let in the glow of the street lamps before she turned down the covers. She stripped off everything except her panties, then slipped back into the long-sleeved T-shirt she had been wearing. Under the covers she watched light play across the ceiling until her eyelids finally closed from their own weary weight.

There was an international conference in Glasgow that week, and not a hotel for miles around had possessed a vacant room. Andrew had snagged Fiona's through sheer good fortune. The old hotel nearest the hospital seldom had rooms to rent for the night, and therefore wasn't on lists for potential conference space. There had been just one room, rarely used and badly in need of refurbishing, that the proprietor had begrudgingly rented.

"Dinna go expecting Gleddoch House or the Copthorne," he'd said in his spiralling Glaswegian accent. "And if you decide to share it with her, tha'll be five quid more."

"I will no' be sharing it." Andrew paid the modest price.

"And where will you go?"

"I'll sleep in my car. It's no' a hardship. I've done it before."

"You'll wish you'd driven home. Cold i'll be tonight. The rain always brings it."

"I've blankets in the boot." Andrew held out his hand for Fiona's key. The proprietor shook his head, reached under the counter and came up with a key and a bottle.

He handed over both. "You'll be needing this more than me, I ken. And I've charged you enough for the room to make up for it."

Andrew grinned and took both.

Now Andrew looked at the bottle. It was by no means full, but it held the promise of a warmer night. He had made himself as comfortable as possible in the back seat of his sedan. The bench seat tilted up, so no matter how hard he tried, he was wedged against the backrest. His legs were too long to stretch out, even at an angle, and he had to make do with pulling his knees to his chest.

Propped in that position, he twisted off the bottle cap and took a swig. The whisky wasn't Scotland's finest, but it did the trick. Heat rushed through him, tingling through his limbs and warming his fingertips and toes. The prospect of the night ahead began to look less bleak.

Leaving Fiona alone in the room had been absurdly difficult. She hadn't wanted to be there by herself. She had attempted to be cheerful, but the truth had shone in her eyes. For the briefest moment he had considered telling her the truth, but in the end he had rejected it. He might have stayed if asked, and his intentions would have been the best. But he was fast learning that even the best of intentions had little effect where Fiona was concerned.

He could see her window at the building's corner. Her light had gone out some time ago, and he wondered if she was asleep yet. He wondered how she slept, on which side and how soundly. He doubted that she sprawled. She had too little confidence for that. She had spent so much time in hospital, immobilized and tortured. He doubted that she had ever learned to enjoy her body, to fling it about and claim the bed as her own.

Yet inside that body was a woman yearning to be free. She was a sensuous woman, one who loved color and images, who drank them in, then spilled them across paper in tumultuous bursts of emotion. He had been entranced years before when Duncan had shown him Fiona's first book. He had sensed the woman behind the illustrations, her loneliness, her dreams.

He still sensed her loneliness, even when they were together. But Fiona's dreams were even clearer to him, if not to anyone else. She had been imprisoned in a tormented body that longed now for solace. What had once known agony could know pleasure, as well. Yet pleasure sometimes brought greater pain, and she had endured enough of that for a lifetime.

He could not be the one to cause her more.

He unscrewed the cap from the bottle again and took another, longer drink. It wasn't a night for arbitrary limits. He was alone, in a freezing car when he could be in a warm bed beside Fiona. He imagined what it would feel like to hold her in his arms under the tartan blanket. She had such doubts about herself as a woman. She was sure that her scars would kill a man's desire. She had no idea how little they would matter to him. She had no idea how he dreamed of the swell of her breasts, the delicious narrowing of her tiny waist, the flair of her womanly hips.

What difference did scars make when it was the woman inside the body that he wanted?

He closed his eyes and tried to let the whisky carry him off to sleep. He was a large man and should have had a large man's tolerance for drink, but the moment his eyes closed, he knew he'd had too much. The darkness moved, shifting in waves inside his head. The car was parked beside the curb, yet it seemed to race beneath him. He clutched the blanket he'd taken from the boot and kneaded it with his fingertips. Finally he opened his eyes and sat up.

His head cleared almost immediately. Rain had begun again, and he listened to the soft splatter on his roof and windows. He liked rain, and like any good Scotsman had learned to ignore it when it was inconvenient. Now it emphasized the barriers between him and Fiona. As the rain fell harder, it seemed to shrink the metal frame of the car and imprison him. He was used to solitude. No matter how lively, how outgoing, he was with others, he was most comfortable alone. But he wasn't comfortable tonight. Tonight it seemed that none of the truths or the lies that he regularly told himself could make any difference.

There wasn't much left in the bottle now. He unscrewed the top once more and held it at eye level. In the glow of the rain-shrouded street lamps he could see the dim, distorted reflection of his own face. At no moment of his life had the resemblance to his father been clearer.

At first the smell of smoke was comforting. There were bonfires in the autumn in the field beside the hotel, and on the night of the Johnsmas fair fires were built on the hillsides. Her father held her on his shoulders so that she could peek over the crowds and watch the flames lick at the mists of evening. Her father had broad shoulders, and he never complained if she forgot to sit still. Her father was a strong man. He never grew tired when she sat on his shoulders, and he never scolded her.

The smoke grew stronger, and she began to cough. Just a little, at first. Not enough to wake her completely. She lay with her thumb in her mouth, sucking greedily on it after each coughing spasm. She wanted nothing more than to sleep.

The smoke thickened, and the coughing grew worse. Each indrawn breath tore at her lungs. She burrowed deeper under the covers, but even they couldn't filter the smoke. At last she opened her eyes, but the covers were pulled over her face, and only darkness greeted her.

She was awake enough to be frightened, now. She didn't like the dark. She didn't like the smoke.

"Duncan?"

She coughed again. Duncan didn't answer. "Duncan?"

She swatted the covers away, arms flailing faster and faster. She struggled to sit up. The room wasn't dark. There was a strange and terrible glow, a bonfire on the floor beside her bed. As she watched, the flames licked higher and the smoke thickened.

And then her blanket began to smoke, too.

Fiona bolted upright, the tartan blanket clutched tightly to her chest. A scream tore at her throat, but she smothered it with clamped lips. Only a moan escaped, a pitiful, horrifying moan that started deep inside her and went on and on.

She hadn't had the nightmare in years. She'd thought she had outgrown it, that the doctors who had encouraged her to talk about it had finally put the nightmare to rest.

Soft lamplight spilled through the windows, and she could see, as she forced herself to survey the room, that nothing was wrong. She sniffed, but she was greeted only by the smell of old, worn carpets and stale air. There was no smoke.

No smoke.

She was trembling. Sleep had fled, and she knew it wouldn't be back again that night. She rose on legs so weak they threatened not to hold her, turned on the bedside lamp and went to stand at the window.

The panes of hand-blown glass were so familiar, and so was the layout of the room. Even the musty smell touched a chord deep inside her. Now she knew why she hadn't felt safe here from the beginning, and why the nightmare had come back. She was alone in a room much like the one she had shared with Duncan as a child. There had been another bed, his, in the corner, and a door connecting the room to her parents'. But the room had smelled exactly like this one. Her mother had retrieved the heater and turned it on that night to drive away the chill and the smell.

She leaned a pale cheek against the glass. The street below was not the high street of Druidheachd. This was Glasgow, and she was safe. Andrew was just down the hall.

Andrew. She longed for him in that moment as she had never longed for anyone. She was no longer a child. She was a woman, but still she longed to be enclosed in his arms. Just until the trembling stopped. Just until she could remember exactly who and what she was.

She didn't know his room number. She couldn't knock on doors until she found him. She and Andrew would both be put out on the street, and rightfully so. She couldn't ask him to hold her, or to take her back to Druidheachd. She had to wait until morning when he came for her.

She had to wait and not fall asleep again.

She tried to focus on the street below, washed gently by rain as it had been earlier. Tears filled her eyes and dropped to her cheeks. She seldom cried. She had learned too early that tears were little help. Tears hadn't stopped the pain that had torn at her day and night for months after the fire. They hadn't stopped the relentless duties of doctors and nurses who hurt her terribly every time they touched her. They hadn't softened the hearts of the children who had turned away from her in horror when they glimpsed her scars. But she had cried tonight for Sara, and now she cried for herself.

There had been no fire in this room. She was not imprisoned by walls of flame. She was imprisoned by her own memories, and by a nightmare that hadn't disappeared, after all. And calling to her from somewhere over the prison walls was a man who claimed he wanted her, even as he claimed that he didn't want to hurt her.

There was movement on the street. She brushed aside her tears and turned her head. The door to Andrew's car opened, and Andrew emerged. He looked up at the window, then, head bared to the rain, he started toward the side door.

Confusion filled her, but only for a moment. The situation wasn't difficult to grasp. Andrew had only been able to find one vacant room, and he had given it to her. He hadn't told her the truth because he hadn't wanted her to worry.

He hadn't told her the truth because he couldn't imagine spending the night in the same bed with her.

She told herself that the latter couldn't be true. She was vulnerable tonight, still immersed in the darkness of her dream. Andrew wasn't disgusted by her. He treated her like a woman, not like a sideshow freak. And he hadn't seen what the fire had done to her. He could not be repulsed by what he only imagined. When he held her in his arms, there was no sign that he found her anything except desirable.

But he had begun to discover what she really was.

She remembered the day he had massaged her leg. Despite the fabric covering it, he must have noticed how extensive the scars were, how they bulged and twisted....

And he had touched her back. His fingertips had probed the skin there, skin laced so tightly with scars that there *was* no skin, not skin like other women had, at least. Her back was a patchwork quilt of scar tissue, of skin grafts that didn't have the resilience or appearance of normal skin, and sites where what skin had survived the fire had been harvested for grafts on her leg and feet.

There was a knock at her door, and nothing tentative about it. She realized that she was wearing a T-shirt and little more. She ran to the bed, scooped her pants off the floor and sat to pull them on.

He knocked again, louder this time. She nearly flew to the door to let him in. A brief look down the hallway assured her that no one had been awakened. "What are you doing here?" she whispered.

He stepped inside and pulled the door closed behind him. "I saw you at the window."

"Yes. I can see how you might have, considering that you were sleeping in your car."

"There was only one room."

"I figured that out."

"Why are you up, Fiona?"

"Why did you lie?" She stepped back to put more space between them.

"What point was there in giving you more to worry about? There was nowt to be done about it. There's no' another room available in the city. I was lucky to find this."

"It's a large bed. We could have shared it."

He didn't move, and he didn't speak. Then he turned away. "Why are you up?" He went to the window, as if checking his car.

"I just am."

He glanced at her over his shoulder. "I could no' see your face, but I had the feeling you'd been crying. I can see I was right."

Denial was absurd. She knew her eyes were red, and her cheeks were probably flushed. "I had a bad dream. That's all."

"All?" He faced her, leaning against the sill. "Do you have them often?"

"No. It was the room. It smells like . . ." She didn't want to say it.

"It smells like a room in an old hotel. Your room?"

She shrugged. "Duncan and Mara make sure that all the rooms in the Sinclair Hotel are clean. And they air them constantly."

"But it was no' always so. They've brightened things considerably."

"All right, Andrew. This room smells like the room I had as a child. And I guess that triggered my nightmare. Because I was—" She could no longer be matter-of-fact. She swallowed. "Back there." Her voice dipped dangerously. She looked away.

"Fiona." He reached her in three steps and pulled her close. His arms tightened around her.

He smelled like whisky, as well as the good clean scent of rain. She struggled to separate herself from him, but he held her tighter.

"I'm fine. You're always comforting me, and you don't need to. I'm a grown woman now."

"Since when does a grown woman no' need comfort?"

"I'm not your sister." She succeeded in pulling away. His eyes glittered strangely, almost as if he saw more than a delicately boned woman with tear-stained cheeks.

"You've nowt to fear there. I've no' thought of you as a sister since the day you stepped back on Scotland's soil."

"Then how do you think of me? Am I too pitiful to share a bed with? Did the thought of sleeping beside me upset you too much to risk it?" The words hadn't passed her lips before she regretted them. They were her worst fears, and only a tiny part of her believed them. But she was ruled by that tiny part, tossed and manipulated and horrified that it might be true. She had thought of herself as pitiful for so long that even though she had made a fragile peace with her body, she was not convinced that others ever could.

"Pitiful?" His hand shot out and cupped her chin before she could move away. He held it tight and turned her face up to his. His right hand clamped hard on her shoulder. She was immobilized. "What have I done to make you think such a thing?"

"Let go of me, Andrew."

"Tell me what I've done!"

"You've slept in your car rather than sleep in the same bed as me!"

"I slept in my car because I was afraid of what might happen if I slept with you. Shall I explain?"

Shame filled her. She had bullied him into claiming to be attracted to her. She had exposed her deepest fears and humiliated herself. And for what? How could she ever know how much truth there was in what he'd said? Andrew would never hurt her. That was the one thing she knew for certain.

"You dinna believe me." Anger sparkled in his eyes, and his mouth was a grim line. "You force me to prove myself."

"I'm not forcing you to do anything." She grabbed his wrist and pushed it away. "Look, I'll help you make a bed on the floor. Then neither of us has to worry about anything."

"You're a far different woman when you're angry." He held her by both arms so that she couldn't turn away.

"There are signs that the wee lassie who kicked my shoulders and pulled my hair is still inside you."

"I'm a grown woman!"

"Aye, that you are, Fiona. That you are." He tugged her closer. "And I'm a grown man, no' a saint."

Before she could respond, he was kissing her. He neither ravished nor punished her lips. He took them as if they belonged to him, as if *she* belonged to him and always had. He tasted like whisky and desire. She could hardly breathe, but somehow it no longer mattered. When his arms encircled her they were not a prison but a boundary within which she was nothing less than whole.

"Fiona." His voice was ragged, and his breath was warm against her cheek. "I want you. Can you doubt it?"

As if to prove his words, he pulled her hips to his. He was aroused; even a woman with no experience couldn't misunderstand. Her doubts began to dissolve. His lips were warm against her jaw, and warmer as they searched for the hollow of her throat. Her head fell back, and she moaned. He urged her hips closer, and she longed for the brush of his naked flesh against hers. Her mind filled with flashing images, forbidden and erotic, of what it would be like to take him inside her body, to merge with him, to swallow him so completely that Andrew became a part of her forever.

The images melted into reality, his hand kneading the fabric of her T-shirt, then settling against her breast. His thumb brushing slowly, achingly, over the erect nipple. She was flooded with heat, with sensations long repressed. She had abandoned hope that she would ever respond to a man this way. She had convinced herself that she had nothing to give, and that in return a man wouldn't waste his time giving her pleasure. Now she understood that what gave her pleasure also pleasured Andrew. And that when she kissed him, touched him, his satisfaction was as great as her own.

Even as she thought of touching him, she did. The top button of his shirt came free as she twisted the fabric in her hands. The hair on his chest was like silk against her palms and his skin was warm enough to singe her fingertips. He gave a guttural moan, an eruption from deep inside him, and jerked her closer. The shirt fell open as she slid her hands lower; buttons separated from buttonholes, and the fabric swung free.

His chest was rock hard and ridged with muscle. How could his skin, as firm as steel, be so sensitive to her touch? He buried his face in her hair and clenched her hips tighter. There were layers of cloth between them, but the heat of his arousal sought the moist heat inside her as surely as if they were naked.

He groaned again as she explored with hands that fluttered over him, learning the way the thick mat of hair tapered toward his belt buckle, the way that her touch dampened his skin with sweat. She could feel a tremor begin somewhere deep inside him. She had done this.

She had done this.

He kissed her again, a deep, dark kiss that reached all the way into her soul. There was nothing held back, no attempt to initiate her slowly into passion. He kissed her as if something had burst inside him, something uncontrollable and new. She shuddered with pleasure. Heat and sensation spiraled through her. She had done this. She had destroyed his caution. She was no longer a burn victim but a woman.

"Fiona." He filled his hands with her hair, tilting her head for greater access to her mouth. Then his hands traveled down her back, kneading and stroking. She was dizzy with the joy of it, dizzy and throbbing. When he lifted her shirt and touched her bare skin, she was too caught up in her own desires to realize what he was doing.

At the end of the kiss her head fell forward against his shoulder. He was touching her breast now, not through the T-shirt but flesh to flesh. She had never experienced anything like it. She bit back a moan of pleasure and squeezed her eyes shut.

And just before they closed, she glimpsed her own bare feet.

She stiffened. She tried to pull away from him, but he was beyond explanation. He murmured against her neck, her neck where a fine web of scars was hidden by her hair. He kissed her jaw, her chin and, finally, her mouth. His hand glided to her other breast.

She was torn in two. Half of her wanted to beg him to continue, and half of her wanted to cry. She splayed her hands against his bare chest and tried to push, but it only seemed to excite him.

"Fiona, come to bed." His voice was a deep rasp, a dark masculine sigh.

Fear began to fill the places where desire had been. "Andrew. Stop."

He didn't respond to her command. He hardly seemed to hear her voice. "How could you think I did no' want you? You have dreams of the fire, and I have dreams of you."

Tears sprang to her eyes, and for a moment she forgot to be afraid. He dreamed of her. He wanted her, despite what he knew of her injuries. She would not disappoint Andrew. Then she looked down again and saw the horror that was her feet, feet that had been seared by fire, feet that surgical teams had almost despaired of saving. Feet that for many years could not hold her weight. They served her proudly now, these battle-weary feet with their scars and their imperfect form, but they were a symbol of all she had endured, and all she was not.

"No!" She succeeded in backing away this time, succeeded in breaking free of his arms. "Stop it, Andrew."

He was breathing hard. His arms shot out again, and he reached for her, pulling her back to him. "You dinna mean it." He didn't give her a chance to answer. He kissed her again, as if he would find his answer there.

She was afraid, but not of him. She was afraid that he would stop kissing her when he saw what she was, that he would push her away and pity—or worse, revulsion—would finally cloud his eyes. He'd had too much to drink. She knew that now. She saw it in his loss of control. She saw it in the way he refused to listen.

He scooped her up as if she were nothing, a dust mote or dandelion down. He strode to the old bed and lowered them both to it with a flourish of masculine strength. Then he stretched out half over her. She splayed her palms against his bare chest to keep him away, but his mouth descended hungrily to hers. "Dinna think about anything but this," he murmured against her lips. "Just this and nowt more."

He covered her hands with his own and stretched them over her head. His chest brushed against her breasts. He pushed the knit fabric of her shirt higher until it was her skin, her naked breasts, that lay against him.

"No!" She twisted in panic to get away from him, twisted and fought against the strength of the hand holding hers.

"You dinna mean no." He freed her hands, but now both of his played over her skin. "You want me, and I want you. There's no shame in this, Fiona."

"No!" She twisted away, shoving him hard with her hands and her knees. She sat up, then stood on shaking legs and backed away from him. "Does *no* mean something different here than it does in America, Andrew?"

He didn't answer. He sat up slowly, almost as if he were in a dream; then he turned his back to her. She watched him lower his head to his hands.

She crumpled to the other side of the bed and did the same.

Time passed, although she couldn't have said how much. When the tension between them had stretched to a silent, shattering scream, Andrew spoke.

"Are you all right?"

She hadn't expected his first words to be a question about her well-being. She had expected fury. She deserved nothing less. She was a virgin, but she was not an adolescent drowning in her own budding sexuality. She was a woman, and she understood what it meant to lead a man on. She had asked Andrew for more than she'd allowed him to give her. There were terrible names for what she had done.

"Are *you* all right?" she asked.

"No. I dinna think I am."

She didn't know what to say. An apology seemed useless, a thing so slight that it would evaporate in the air between them.

"I would no' have forced you," he said.

"I know! Andrew, I know you wouldn't have. It's just that—"

"It's just that I lost control."

She turned a little, but she could see only the back of his head. He ran his hands through his hair, but his head was still bent.

"If you ever needed proof that I'm not worth your trouble, this was it," she said. "If you ever needed proof that I'm not enough woman for any man . . ."

"The only thing we proved tonight was that neither of us knows what we want. At least, no' deep inside, where it matters most."

"I wanted you." She heard a sob in her own voice.

"No' enough." He stood. "And why should you have?"

"Andrew—"

"I would drive us home now, but I'm no' in any shape to drive. Sleep if you can. I'll be back for you in the morning."

"Where are you going? I'm not going to let you sleep in that car."

He turned at the door. His eyes were bleak, and he shook his head. "Dinna worry yourself, Fiona. I dinna think I'll be sleeping at all."

Chapter 11

The Honourable David Gow had a useless title and a penchant for nubile young women of good family. The former had only become useless after he had indulged his addiction to the latter once too often. He had been banished from London, fired from a prestigious position at the *Times* and dispatched by his irate father to the backwaters of Scotland—where a dowager aunt kept note of his every movement.

Despite his dark good looks and clever wit, there were few nubile young women of good family available to David now. Between his aunt's eagle eye and his markedly reduced circumstances, he had settled into a life of boredom so extreme that even the harsh Scottish winter had seemed a diversion. He had learned the subtle differences between snow and more snow. He had developed a reluctant fondness for coal smoking on a soot-blackened hearth. Even his housekeeper Violet, an old woman with more cheek than teeth, had become a source of inspiration and intellectual stimulation.

Violet was the first to tell David of the creature that inhabited Loch Ceo in Druidheachd, a village so remote that few had ever heard of it. Violet had a sister who still lived in

Druidheachd, and she went there often to visit. He had paid little attention to Violet's story at first, since every loch in Scotland seemed to have a dreadful monster with glowing eyes and reptilian scales.

But when Violet told him of the most recent sighting, David's curiosity had been aroused. Time had passed since his exile, and he could assess his future. He wondered if perhaps he hadn't landed on both feet after his long fall from grace. His father was beginning to relent; David had even been invited to return to London for a short visit. Now he needed a story, a dashing, gripping story that combined scholarly insight with tabloid titillation.

One good story speeding over the international wire services could be the ticket back to his former life. The creature in Loch Ceo could buy him that ticket.

David arrived in Druidheachd on a clear, warm afternoon. He had avoided the Highlands until now, convinced that if the rest of Scotland was parochial, the Highlands were at best medieval. Despite himself, he had been charmed by the landscape and immediately caught up in its spell. There were no mountains anywhere in Europe that were quite like these. The jagged peaks seemed to rip holes in the present and send time spiraling out of sequence.

He would have to remember that line for his article.

The high street of the village was anything but busy. There were more people on foot than in cars. Neighbors chatted in front gardens of blue delphiniums and yellow primroses. An old woman who could have been Violet's twin strolled toward a low-slung building with a willow basket draped over her arm. He followed her trail, scenting gossip and information ahead.

Two hours later he was out on the loch in the launch of the very lad who had sighted the creature weeks ago. By this time David had heard the story in more detail than he, the demanding, ever-thorough journalist, had ever wished for.

"Right here it was," Jamie Gordon said. He was a pleasant looking young man, a bit gormless, but enthusiastic and open, nonetheless. "A creature so fearsome ye'd have frozen in yer tracks, too. Of course, there were nae tracks to freeze in that day. I'm thinking the creature did no' know we were there. She had nae reason to think anyone would be so gyte as to be out on the loch in a beastly storm."

"She?" David asked.

"Aye. She."

"You, umm . . . saw identifying markings?"

Jamie looked blank.

"You saw proof it was female?"

"Proof? Like tits and such?"

David kept his composure. "Yes."

"No. Nowt of the sort. But she's a lady. Andrew Mac-Dougall calls her his darling."

"Andrew MacDougall?"

"Aye, MacDougalls have always lived on this loch. Andrew's da saw her once, ye know. The night that Andrew and the other men of midnight were born. Did ye nae hear that story?"

"Men of midnight?"

"Aye. Did ye no' say ye were a reporter?" Jamie asked suspiciously. Clearly he wondered how practiced David's skills could be.

"Tell me about these men of midnight."

Jamie did so, with relish. David filed the story away in his mind. It was mildly interesting, but not of the scale he was looking for. "Can you describe the creature again, Jamie? Amber eyes, you say?"

"Aye, the color of aged whisky. I'm no' a drinking man now, but someone could show ye—if ye've never had the chance to see good malt whisky in England." He winked. "And her neck was as long as a Scotsman's . . . legs, under his kilt." He winked again.

David gave the lad points for wit. "You say you were frightened. Was it only because you weren't expecting to see the creature? Or did she threaten you?"

"Threaten? Our creature? I think no'!"

"Then she's harmless?"

"Och, she's that and more. She's as shy as a virgin. She was as surprised to see us as we were to see her. She vanished immediately, ye know. Vanished so swiftly that if Peter had no' seen her, too, I'd have wondered about my own sanity."

Evening was creeping their way. The launch rocked gently beneath them in sunset-hued waves. Soon it would be time to go back to shore. David had already taken a room in the picturesque hotel at the center of the village. He planned to stay on tomorrow, but he was already beginning to feel frustrated.

So far he had not heard or seen anything that qualified as news. There was no more to the story than had been reported—at least, nothing more that he had uncovered. There had been nearly a dozen boats on the loch when he and Jamie came out. He suspected that in the weeks since the creature's sighting, a fair number of those boats had been populated by reporters. Unless there was another sighting, the boats would dwindle, the story would be filed on the back pages of village weeklies, and he would have to find another ticket back to his town house in Kensington.

Unless there was another sighting.

"Do you suppose that your creature only comes out in a storm?" David asked.

"Nae. She comes out when she thinks that nae one is there to see her."

"That's always been the case, then?"

"Andrew MacDougall could tell ye. He knows every story there is."

David looked out over the water. The loch was a large one. From their vantage point near the middle, all shapes on the horizon were indistinct. And as night fell, his view would be obscured even more. "What do you say, Jamie. Let's stay out tonight and see if we can see your creature again."

"Stay out in the dark? Michty! I think no'. I've seen her my one time, but I'm no' one to challenge fate, Mr. Gow. I'd as soon be sleeping in my bed where there are nae creatures to be seen at all. More's the pity," he added with still another wink.

"What will you take for the boat, then? I'll take it out myself and return it as good as new in the morning."

"My boat? Och, nae. I could no' let you have it. It belongs to my brother, too, and—"

"Fifty quid," David said in his most authoritative voice. "Ye say ye'll return it in good condition?"

"That's what I said."

"Seventy-five, then, and a deposit of the same. I'll return the deposit in good condition if the boat's come to nae harm."

"Done," David said.

Jamie looked pleased with himself, but he shook his head in sympathy. "It'll be a long, cold night, Mr. Gow."

David stared at the horizon. The shore seemed to grow blurrier by the second. "I expect it to be, Jamie. But some prices have to be paid. And I'm afraid I've had enough of Scotland's winters."

At first Stardust was afraid to venture into the middle of Serenity Lake. Although her fish friends still avoided her because they were frightened by her size, it took no courage to stay close to the shore where she had been born. She was lonely, of course, and longed for a companion. Sometimes she imagined another dragon just like her, one with a neck that rose from the water like a castle's tallest tower and a body that made waves so high they gobbled up the golden sand on the farthest beach. For many months, imagining such a companion was pleasure enough.

Then one day Stardust awoke from her bed in the reeds at the lake's bottom, and she could no longer imagine another water dragon at all. She tried all that day and into the evening. But no matter how hard she concentrated, no pictures would form in her mind. Her imagination was gone. She had used it all. Stardust knew, as she fell asleep again that night, that at last she must cross the lake and find a real companion.

Sara was better. In the two weeks since the crisis she had grown stronger, until her doctors were encouraged enough to continue the program of skin grafts and therapy they had temporarily put on hold. She was back in the ward with the other children now. Fiona had seen her twice.

She hadn't seen Andrew at all.

"Andrew should be back before too long, should he no'?" Mara asked one morning. She was peering over

Fiona's shoulder at a pen and ink drawing that Fiona was adapting from one of her sketches.

"Should be." Fiona really didn't know when Andrew would be back from his final shift of the season. On the morning following their encounter at the old hotel, she and Andrew had lingered in Glasgow just long enough to hear news of Sara's recovery, then they had made the long trip back to Druidheachd in near silence. Without really looking at her, he had asked if she was all right, and she had said "of course." She had tried to apologize; he had asked her not to. And very little else had been said.

"It seems a shame that he's no' here for all the excitement." Mara didn't have to elaborate. The excitement in question was the newest sighting of Andrew's darling, several days before. A reporter from a tiny village in West Lothian had spent the night in a boat on the loch, and just before dawn his journalistic patience had been rewarded.

"I'm not sure Andrew would want to be here," Fiona said. "This place is a three-ring circus."

"Would you enjoy having Andrew to supper when he comes back? I always enjoy seeing him."

"I don't think so." Fiona searched for an excuse. Nothing occurred to her.

"Do you feel that we're throwing you together? Is that the problem?"

Fiona clutched at that. "Andrew's very kind, but I don't want him to feel he has to make something more of our friendship."

Mara touched her shoulder. "He's very kind, it's true. But never dishonest. And he's as stubborn as any Scotsman. He's nearly as stubborn as Duncan, for that matter. If Andrew felt he was being pushed, he would dig in his heels like my prize tup on shearing day."

Fiona capped her pen and faced her sister-in-law. "It's not Andrew, it's me."

Mara waited for her to go on, but Fiona couldn't.

"Are you finished for the morning?" Mara asked at last. "Or shall I leave you alone to get on with it?"

"I'm done. It's not turning out the way I wanted it to, anyway. I think I need the break."

"What's this book about, or is it bad luck to ask?"

"Stardust falls in love."

"Does she now?"

Fiona made a face. "I haven't done one drawing that I like. One water dragon per page is plenty. Two complicates things immensely."

"How true to life," Mara said wryly.

Fiona stood and stretched. She had been at her drawing board most of the morning. She had spent hours here every day since returning from the ill-fated night in Glasgow. She had hoped that hard work would put the encounter with Andrew from her mind, but she had failed. "What are your plans for the day?"

"I'm going to start on the attic. I thought you might want to help. Billie's inspired me. We've a miniature version of Fearnshader up there. Antiques and mementos from centuries. I want to get to it before it all crumbles to dust. It's your family history, after all. Yours and Duncan's, and April's, too. No' to mention my own children's."

"Are you trying to tell me something?"

Mara's laugh was like quicksilver. "I'm trying to tell you that we're trying, I suppose. For that matter, Billie and Iain are, too."

Fiona's happiness at the news was tempered by poignancy, as so much was these days. She had never dared to dream she might have children of her own, but now that fact seemed inexpressibly sad. "I'm glad I've had a chance to practice this aunt thing," she said.

"I'd say you have it mastered. April adores you."

They continued to chat on their way to the attic. Fiona couldn't remember ever having been there. It wasn't the sort of place where children would be allowed to play. Even with the lights on it was dark, and cobwebs surrounded boxes and discarded furniture like ghostly shrouds.

"It's a fire hazard," Fiona said. "I'm glad we're doing this."

"It is a wee bit of a mess. And it will take more than a day or two, I'm afraid."

"I've got time if you do."

They started with a tour, categorizing piles and scanning furniture. "If we're unclear about anything, Billie can tell us what's worth keeping," Mara said.

Fiona tried to summon enthusiasm. She needed a project of this scope to help her regain her equilibrium. "I think we should have some of the better furniture taken downstairs, to that room off the kitchen, maybe. There's nothing in there right now except a few shelves. We can get a better look at it and decide what to do."

"Let's decide what we want to have carried down."

They settled on a pair of round wooden tables, assorted chairs that had probably once graced the dining room, a love seat upholstered in tattered green velvet, and a pine cabinet that Fiona hoped to put beside her drawing table to hold art supplies.

"That's a start," Mara said. They had dragged everything except the love seat to the top of the stairwell, and both women were panting. Now Mara lowered herself to the love seat. "There are so many stories here."

Fiona looked up from a book she had found on a tall pile of volumes. It was a cookbook from the turn of the century, with hints on the proper deportment of young ladies. From the inscription she already knew that it had been a birthday gift to one of her unfortunate ancestors, a young lady named Glenda. "Stories?"

"Aye. Hundreds of them. Can you feel them, Fiona?"

Fiona imagined she held one of those stories in her hands. "I suppose. If I ever need inspiration, I'd only have to come up here and turn my imagination loose."

"The book in your hands..." Mara nodded toward it. "It belonged to a young woman with hair the color of yours. She did no' live long enough to see her hair turn gray."

Fiona stared at her. Mara shrugged sadly. "I'm sorry."

"Sorry she died, or sorry you told me?" Fiona waited, and when Mara didn't answer she nodded. "Sorry you know." She was becoming used to Mara's strange ability to know things others couldn't, and she was aware what a tremendous handicap it sometimes was.

"It's as if I were born in a world with no walls. Time seems to have no barriers." There was no self-pity in Mara's tone.

"Can you see everything as clearly as Glenda's death?"

"No, and I'm grateful for that. I only know that Glenda died young, not how or why. I dinna see the past as clearly as the future. I'm only given glimpses. This seat, for instance." Mara stroked her hand over the worn velvet. "Lovers once sat here and plotted to run away together." She smiled. "I can no' tell you when. But they made their plans right here, and executed them successfully, for all that. I'm thinking they had a long and happy marriage."

"I like that story better."

Mara stood and began to wander. The attic was huge. They had barely skimmed the surface today. "There's something of you here, Fiona."

"Something of me?" Fiona followed her.

"Aye."

"What do you mean, exactly?"

Mara turned. "Most of the time I'm frustrated that I can see so much. Just occasionally I'm frustrated that I can see so little."

"There's something of me here, but you don't know what?"

"I'm afraid that's so."

"Maybe some of my childhood mementos are stored here."

"Perhaps." Mara shook her head. "No, that's no' it. Although that may be true, as well. But I sense something...." She shook her head again in frustration. "Now, if I were no' so close to you, if I did no' love you so well..."

Fiona was filled with a warm glow. "I prefer the love to the clairvoyance."

Mara's smile was equally as warm. "And so do I."

They ended up in a corner piled high with boxes that looked newer than most of the others. Fiona dug at the tape binding the top one until she had loosened a corner, then she pulled it free. She unfolded the flap to look inside. "Look at this." She lifted out a pipe and handed it to Mara. A quick inspection showed that there was an entire collection of them, each wrapped in soft flannel.

"Some of these look to be quite old," Mara said. "But no' all of them, though I'm no expert."

"My father had a collection of pipes. I remember Duncan telling me about them when he came back from a trip here one summer. He and Andrew borrowed a pipe to smoke some old tobacco that they'd found, and my father was furious."

"Perhaps these were his."

Fiona cradled the pipe against her chest, although she wasn't aware of doing so. "I'm sure they must be. And these other boxes must be his things, too. After he died, did Duncan pack all this and carry it up here?"

"I would doubt it. Perhaps it was done for him, before he came back to stay. But he must know that it's all here."

"He and my father weren't close. Maybe Duncan just didn't have any interest in going through his things."

"Then you should," Mara said.

Fiona looked up. She was torn by emotions and memories. She remembered the young father who had doted on her, as well as the absent father who had cut her from his life. "Do you think so?"

"Aye. You wanted to help. This would be the place to begin." Mara turned away before Fiona could read her expression or respond. "It's late. Perhaps I should see if I can get Duncan or someone to start carrying down the furniture."

Fiona glanced at her watch. "You're right. But I think I'll stay here a little longer. Just to see what I've got ahead of me."

"Will we see you downstairs for supper?"

"I think I'll eat in tonight. But I'll come say good-night to April later, if that's all right."

"When has it no' been all right?" Mara paused at the stairwell. "I'll be nearby if you need me."

Fiona went through the pipes, one by one. They were beautiful examples of craftsmanship, each unusual and unique. She wondered if her father had inherited a collection, then added to it through the years. She knew almost nothing about Donald Sinclair, except that after the fire he had ceased to be a father to her at all.

And she knew the reason why.

On impulse she decided to take the box downstairs. She suspected that eventually she would find a display cabinet or shelf among her father's belongings, because she couldn't imagine that he had kept the pipes out of sight. She was too much the artist to allow such finely wrought objects to stay packed away. If Duncan didn't want them, she would find them a home elsewhere.

Halfway to the stairwell she heard the door open below. Obviously Mara had been successful in finding someone to haul down the furniture. At the top of the stairwell, she discovered whom.

With one foot on the attic floor and the other on the top step, Andrew crossed his arms and blocked her path. "Do you need help with that?"

Her hands had been perfectly steady. Now they weren't. She shook her head. "Thanks, but it's not heavy."

He didn't move to let her pass. "You're looking bonny, Fiona."

He was looking bonny, too. He wore an ivory sweater with zigzagging cables that emphasized the breadth of his chest. His jeans were faded, his shoes shined. His hair, always a bit shaggy, was boyishly rumpled by the same wind that had whipped color into his cheeks. But in the midst of that picture of good health and cheer, his hazel eyes were unutterably sad.

She wished she had changed into something more flattering than leggings and an oversize man's shirt. She tried to smile. "I think I'm just looking dusty."

"Then it becomes you."

There were a thousand things to say, and none of them could find their way past her lips. She settled for gossip over silence. "Did you hear about the newest sighting of your darling?"

"Aye. I heard. The Honourable David Gow, alone in Jamie Gordon's wee boat."

"There's been quite a stir. Druidheachd is the newest mecca for reporters and fans of the supernatural. Every room in the hotel is taken. The Wongs over at the chips shop doubled their prices, but they're still busy until midnight."

"I stopped by my house to get Poppy before I came here. There were three families from Edinburgh camping in my garden."

"Then you just got home?"

"Aye."

Her voice fell. "And you came here first thing?"

"Aye."

He had come to see her. Two weeks of doubts and fears rose up to greet Fiona, but regret was loudest of all. "Andrew..."

"You dinna have to say a thing."

"I think I do." She forced herself to meet his eyes. "I'm not worth your trouble, Andrew. I'm insecure, and I haven't lived enough to know how to make good decisions. But the one thing I'm not is stupid. And I know that throwing away our friendship because of one night when we were both unhinged is stupid."

"Our friendship is stronger than that."

"Can you forgive me?"

"I told you, Fiona, you've done nowt that merits forgiveness."

"I may be unsophisticated, but I do know what a tease is."

"And I knew your fears. Perhaps we're both guilty. You for issuing an invitation you did no' mean. Me for drinking too much and listening too little."

If he had scoffed it off, she knew that their friendship would not have survived. "I *did* mean it," she said softly. "I wanted you. I still do. But I'm not woman enough for you, Andrew."

His reply came after a telling pause. "Aye. So you think." He reached for her hand and brought it to his lips. He kissed her knuckles and held them against his cheek for a moment. Then he let her hand drop. "The games are over, Fiona. I'll no' ask you for anything again. But if *you* come asking, be absolutely certain you intend to take yes for an answer."

She didn't know what to say, and then it didn't matter anyway, because Duncan was standing on the bottom step looking up at them. Fiona wondered how much he had heard.

He spoke, and from the tone of his voice she knew he had heard it all. "Kaye Gerston called the desk, looking for you, Andrew. She wants to see you tonight, at her place."

Andrew didn't look at him. His gaze was still on Fiona. "I half expected Kaye to be gone by now. Did she say what it's about?"

"Nancy at the front desk took the call. That's all she said."

"Here's the furniture that has to go down." Fiona gestured toward the grouping to her right. "It's a good start toward getting this place cleaned up."

Andrew reached for two chairs. She stepped out of his way, and Duncan did the same when Andrew reached the bottom of the steps. In a moment he was gone.

"Are you going to help, too, Duncan, or are you going to stand there?" She started down the stairs toward him.

"Don't take out your anger at Andrew on me."

"I'm not angry at Andrew or you." She stopped on the step just above him.

"Then what was that about, or maybe I shouldn't ask."

"You shouldn't," she said firmly. There was nothing his imagination could conjure that was worse than the truth.

"Then just tell me this much. Are you okay?"

She hadn't been. She realized that now. For two weeks she definitely had not been okay. But now she was, because Andrew was back, and that revelation was frightening enough to erupt as anger. "If you really want to know, none of this is easy! I feel like Sleeping Beauty. I've been asleep for years while the rest of the world went on with its business."

"You weren't as isolated as all that."

"I might as well have been asleep for all I learned."

He didn't answer directly, but his stern mouth relaxed. "I talked to Mother this morning."

Fiona had studiously avoided conversations with their mother since her arrival. She had studiously avoided conversations *about* their mother. "I hope she's well," she said stiffly.

"She is, but she's convinced you aren't. She's threatening to come and see for herself."

"Mother on Scottish soil again? I don't think so."

"Talk to her, Fiona. Reassure her." He smiled sadly. "Keep her away."

They were eye to eye now. Equals, thanks to the steps. She saw the concern in his eyes and sighed. "I'll call her."

He didn't move aside. "Just tell me one more thing, will you? If you're Sleeping Beauty, who is Andrew, exactly?"

Fiona knew this could no longer be avoided. There was no room for secrets among the three of them. "I'm afraid that Andrew's the prince who's convinced he's not up to his role. And I'm the princess who isn't sure whether she should sleep another hundred years or awake from her spell."

He put his hand on her shoulder. One gentle hand. "You always took fairy tales too seriously."

"I have a feeling that until I take this one seriously, Duncan, the words *happily ever after* are never going to have any meaning for me again."

Chapter 12

Now that Midsummer Day was just around the corner, sunlight was a friend to be counted on. There were still hours of it remaining when Andrew readied *MacDougall's Darling* for the journey to Kaye Gerston's. He'd made himself an early supper and eaten it on his pier, where he could watch the shabby parade of boats on Loch Ceo. Rubbish floated toward him on the gentle waves, discarded soft drink cans and food wrappers. The air was perfumed with exhaust, and a stone's throw from the pier's end, a rainbow-hued film of petrol from someone's poorly maintained motor glazed the water. In the rush to profit from the sightings, the villagers fortunate enough to have boats had pressed them into service, and weekend sailors from nearby towns had busied themselves at the public launch.

Andrew climbed onto the bow and slid to the edge to check a mooring rope. It seemed sound when he tugged, but he untied it anyway, then knotted it once more to be certain, checking for defects as he did.

"I dinna know what they think they'll see," he said, gazing out at the water. "You're no' going to show yourself again, are you, darling? I suppose this means I will no' have my chance at you, either. But I'd as soon you stayed hidden now, even from me. Who knows what this mob will do if you show yourself again?''

"Hello!"

Andrew looked up but couldn't immediately locate the pleasant baritone.

"I say, over here."

Andrew spotted the man, tall and fine-boned, on the pier just behind the stern. "Just a moment. I'll be with you directly." Andrew tightened the knot to his satisfaction, tugged it three times to test it, then slid back across the bow to the deck. He vaulted over the side to the pier and faced his visitor.

"I'm surprised my dog did no' announce you." Andrew held out his hand as he introduced himself.

The man took it in a firm handshake. He was dark-haired with a particularly winning smile. "I made friends with him, I'm afraid. He won't do as a watchdog, will he? Not if prowlers know to scratch his ears. I'm David Gow."

"So you're the one who claims to have seen my darling."

"I *did* see her. Quite a sight, your darling."

"So I've been told."

"Then you've never seen her yourself?"

"Just in my dreams."

David's expression didn't change, but Andrew had the feeling that he was being examined thoroughly. "I've a favor to ask you, Mr. MacDougall."

"Andrew."

"Andrew, then. I'd like a tour of the loch in your boat."

"Have you no' already seen what you came for?"

"I suppose it might seem so. But it was a bit like putting the cart before the horse. I saw the creature before I'd had a chance to hear all the stories about her. And I'm told you tell all the best stories."

Andrew didn't respond to the flattery. "And what will you do with whatever I tell you?"

"I'm writing a series about my experiences here. I hope to include whatever I learn from you."

"And if I dinna agree?"

David Gow seemed taken aback. "I'll pay handsomely. I only want a few hours of your time."

"It's no' the money, Mr. Gow. No' all of us are willing to sell ourselves."

"It's David."

Andrew reluctantly admired the way Gow stood his ground. "What if I say no?"

"Then I may get some of my facts wrong. I doubt either of us would like that." There was no threat in Gow's tone, but he was clearly a man who was used to getting his way.

Andrew hadn't intended to take anyone out in his boat for a few days. He was weary from too little sleep, and his throat was raw from long hours on a windswept oil platform in the North Sea. He had planned to rest and recover. "When?"

"Tomorrow, if you're willing. I've just been waiting for you to return."

"Then tomorrow it is. Shall we say noon?"

"Splendid. Thank you." David paused. "Oh, one more thing…Andrew. My housekeeper came up yesterday to visit her sister. Would it be too much trouble if they came, too? It would please Violet, I know."

Andrew wanted to dislike David Gow. He didn't believe that Gow had seen his darling any more than he believed that Martin Carlton-Jones and Nigel Surrey had the best interests of Druidbheachd in mind as they sought to destroy its way of life. But this man was not exactly what Andrew had expected. "Bring them," he said gruffly.

He stepped back, turned and whistled for Poppy. The dog appeared, slinking low to the ground, as if he knew that he'd failed a major watchdog examination. Andrew motioned him into the boat; then he walked toward the bow to untie the mooring rope. Without being asked, Gow untied the one at the stern. Andrew stepped on board, and Gow tossed him the rope. "Tomorrow," he said.

Andrew grudgingly lifted a hand in farewell.

"If you see your darling, Andrew, tell her I send my greetings."

"I'll tell her you hope to make her acquaintance one day." Andrew started the motor. If David responded, the words were lost in the resulting roar.

There were no workmen at Kaye's when Andrew cut the motor and drifted the remainder of the way to the one pier still left standing. Little had been done since he had been here last, and that surprised him. He had steeled himself to see the cottages gone, the old hazel and beech trees toppled to the ground. Instead, everything was much as it had been, except that there was no sign of life, not even a light in Kaye's house.

He tied the boat and went in search of her. She wasn't in her house, as he had guessed. He found her digging in the perennial border that snaked along the drive leading to the cottages. He watched as she pounded a spade into the midst of a clump of greenery with her foot and pried her prize from the earth. She laid the contents of the spade on the grass at the border's edge; then she lifted her hand and wiped her brow.

She looked tired. For the first time Kaye Gerston truly looked old.

Andrew cleared his throat, wishing as he did that he'd chosen another method to announce himself. His throat clenched painfully, and he coughed in protest.

"Lord love us! What did ye plan to do next, Andrew? Jump up and down and skreich?" Kaye faced him.

"I'm sorry. I suppose I've picked up something I should no' have," he said hoarsely.

"Then stay away from me. I've enough problems without yours, too." She sighed. "Come inside, lad, and I'll make you something for the cough."

He followed her meekly. He'd had every intention of being forceful, and now he wanted only to sit and rest in her warm kitchen.

Kaye had no more opened the door than he realized that something was amiss. There were still boxes in the foyer, but many fewer. In the sitting room, books were neatly in place on shelves once more, and the mantel was lined with mementos. Furniture stood in disciplined ranks against the walls as it had in the days before Kaye's dainty daughters had arranged it in intimate groupings.

"I expected to see the house empty," he said.

"Then you expected wrong, did you no'?"

"I've been wrong a time or two before." He followed her into the kitchen and took the chair that she designated with a wave.

As he watched, she plugged in her kettle, then, as the water heated, she retrieved a bottle of Scotland's finest and liberally baptized an oversize cup with the contents. When the water boiled, she topped the cup and added a squeeze of lemon and a spoon of honey. "Drink it. Every bit," she commanded.

He didn't need to be told twice.

"Sometimes you remind me of Terence," she said. "He sat in this very kitchen more times than I can remember, sipping my whisky and telling me stories. You're his image."

He immediately sipped slower.

"He was a good man, your da."

Andrew was tired, and even the warmth of Kaye's toddy did little for his aching throat. He wanted to be charitable toward his father. He nearly always managed charity, if not love. But tonight he couldn't find either within him. "My father was a boozer," he said. "And if you fed him whisky, you must have seen him here often. He would take whisky wherever he could get it. Toward the end, he would take anything with alcohol in it."

"You sound bitter, lad. I've never heard you sound bitter."

"I know what he was."

"I think perhaps you may no'."

He looked up at her. Her brows were knit in a scowl. "I lived with the man, Kaye. If I dinna know, then who does?"

"Did you know that when we were in school, your da took all the prizes?" After he shook his head, she went on. "There was no one brighter than our Terence. No one who could take an ordinary day and turn it into a story that had everyone gasping for breath. And his smile . . ." She smiled herself. "He turned the heads of all the lasses in the village with that smile. Mine included. But he had no eyes for me or anyone but your mum. And Jane loved him equally as well. That's why she never left him, Andrew. Och, she had reason to. We both know she did. But when he was no' drinking, he was an angel come to earth, with a sweetness, a clarity of thought, a vision of a world the rest of us could no' see...."

Andrew felt as if someone had wrapped their fingers around his throat and was squeezing hard. "I look in the mirror sometimes, and I see him staring back at me."

"And well you should. Because you're like him, Andrew. You're what he could have been if the drink had no' got hold of him."

"*He* got hold of the drink. And the rest of us watched him drown in it."

"He loved you very much. He tried to stop drinking for you and for your mum. In the end he could no' stop for anyone. And he was afraid that you'd be bitter."

Andrew was silent as he finished his drink. It was the oddest of nights. He rarely discussed his father, and now the fingers on his throat were squeezing harder.

"I suppose you're wondering what's happened to make me ask you here," Kaye said, changing the subject.

"It's occurred to me to wonder."

"I have no' signed the final papers for the sale of this property."

"Have you no'?" he asked, with no change of expression, although his pulse sped up a beat.

"I just said so, did I no'?"

He nodded.

Kaye sighed and crossed her arms. In the light of the kitchen, Andrew could see that her red hair was turning white, one inch at a time. He wondered if that was the reason she suddenly looked so old, or if she had decided not to dye it anymore because she really was old and knew she could no longer fool herself.

"I'm dying, Andrew."

He set his cup on the table. "What do you mean?"

"I've less than a year to live. I've known for some time. I suppose I thought that if I left here I could change it somehow. Change homes, change fate." She shook her head as if she couldn't believe she'd been so foolish. "But I know better. My decision caught up with me. You're responsible, if you must know. You and your defense of Iain and Duncan. I wanted to believe differently, because it suited me. But I know those lads nearly as well as I know you, and I could no' fool myself forever. And when I began to question . . ."

"They're good men."

"Aye. So I've talked this over with my girls. They want me to stay here, where I'll be most comfortable, and for once they're right. They'll each be coming home in the next months to spend time and say goodbye."

"Are you certain you're dying?"

"Of course I'm certain! Do you think I'd be wrong about something as important as that?" She softened her words with a reluctant smile. "Ah Andrew, lad, you dinna want to believe it, that's all. I suppose I'm glad."

This time his voice was hoarse from more than encroaching illness. "I'll miss you."

For a moment, just the briefest moment, she looked sad, too. Then she shook her head. "We'll have none of that, Andrew. I'll be here a while yet. And we have to make plans."

"Do we?"

"Aye, because I've decided to leave you this land when I die."

For a moment he thought he'd heard her wrong. "Me? But why?"

"You're the only one who will no' turn it into a blasphemy."

"Your girls deserve to inherit this, Kaye."

"My girls dinna want it. And they've done well by themselves. There was more of me in each of them than I ever believed. They've good professions and strong marriages. No' a one of them needs what the sale of the land would bring. I've made a wee bonny investment or two over the years. They'll each get a good bit to remember me by."

"Is it really possible to back out at this late date? There's been work done on the property already, work ordered by Carlton-Jones, as I understand it."

"The piers had to be replaced in any case. I'll pay the men for their labor myself. But I've checked carefully, Andrew. The property is still mine until I sign the final document, and I can change my mind, like any good lass."

"Carlton-Jones and Surrey will no' sit idly by. They'll threaten..." He stopped. "Have they threatened? Have you told them?"

She smiled slyly. For a moment she looked younger, and as healthy as ever. He understood why when she spoke. "No. I've no' said a word. They're staying in Fort William for the night, and they're expecting me to deliver the final papers there in the morning. Telling them will be your task, Andrew."

Fiona sat in the hotel dining room, at a window overlooking the green, where preparations were under way for the annual Johnsmas Fair. She had intended to have supper with Mara, but early in the afternoon Mara had been called away to her shop because one of her helpers was ill. Duncan had gone to Inverness on overnight business, and April was staying with a friend. Fiona had agreed to troubleshoot if it was needed while Mara and Duncan were away, but so far—thankfully—the hotel had run smoothly. She had spent much of her life alone, and she'd developed a fondness for solitude. Now, after just six weeks in Scotland, she was sorry to be sitting by herself. She had discovered she was a social creature at heart, happiest when she was with the people she loved.

Happiest of all when she was with Andrew.

"Miss Sinclair, one of the guests is unhappy with his room, and he wants to speak with you."

Fiona had been so immersed in her thoughts that she hadn't heard Nancy approach. She was a young woman with a sweet face and congenial manner who tended the desk with the same love and care with which she tended her two young children. She was also experienced in handling difficult guests and rarely needed anyone to run interference for her.

"What's the problem?" Fiona asked.

"It's the pounding." Nancy gestured toward the window. "He says that he can no' work with the noise from the green. He's a journalist for some paper or t'other. He's the one who saw the creature, you know."

"Can't you give him a room on the other side of the hotel?"

"There's no' another room to be had. We've guests sharing as 'tis who hardly know each other."

Fiona resigned herself to a confrontation, she who had once been too shy to start a conversation. "I'll talk to him."

"I was hoping you would." The man's voice came from behind Fiona, and she turned. "I'm the guest in question," he said. "David Gow, recently from London. And you sound like an American."

"Really, Mr. Gow." Nancy said, "I expected you to wait for Miss Sinclair in the lobby."

"Fiona Sinclair." Fiona held out her hand. "It's okay," she told Nancy. She started to get up, but David waved her down.

"I don't want to interrupt your supper. I just want to join you," he said, with a smile that could recharge a battery.

She liked him immediately. "Most irregular, Mr. Gow," she said in her best imitation of an upper-class English dowager. She lifted one brow with an elegant quirk.

"I'm afraid I am most unconventional. My family despairs of me."

She gestured to the chair in front of her. "If I offer you a seat, will you agree to stop complaining about the noise?"

"Entirely possible." He took the chair and pulled it close to the table. Muttering under her breath, Nancy left them alone.

"It was all a ploy to meet you, you know," he said with another high-voltage smile. "Although now that I have, I wonder, have we met before? Your name seems familiar, although I'm certain I'd have remembered the face."

"We haven't met," she assured him.

"I've seen you around and inquired a bit."

"A detective in our midst. Why did you want to meet me? Are you doing a piece on hotels for your paper?"

"Only a very intimate piece on beautiful hotel owners."

She saw he was serious—as serious as an obvious philanderer like David Gow could ever be. Six weeks ago his admiration might have puzzled her. It certainly would have dismayed her. Now she was simply intrigued. "What do you find beautiful about me?" she asked.

He cocked his head, like a portrait artist assessing his newest model. The server arrived with Fiona's tatties and mash, and David ordered a drink. He waited until they were alone again before he answered.

"Some women are beautiful because of a feature or two. Lush, kissable lips, startling eyes." He shrugged. "Some have no outstanding features, but their face is a perfect blend, a designer masterpiece. And some women, like you, Fiona, aren't technically beautiful. No lips or eyes to build a temple to, no boring, vacuous symmetry of features. Just a strength of character and a feminine grace that transcends the ordinary."

"You are very good at this." David's words had given Fiona a warm glow. As practiced as they obviously were, they seemed to have been recited with sincerity.

"Better than almost anyone." He lifted his drink to her.

She leaned forward. "Am I supposed to crumple at your feet now, or much later down the road?" She really wanted to know.

"It would save us both a great deal of time if you crumpled immediately."

"I'm afraid I've never crumpled. I warn you, I might get it wrong."

His eyes sparkled seductively. "I would be pleased to assist in every way."

She laughed. She would never have believed that flirting with a man could be such fun. David Gow was handsome and charming, a lethal combination for a woman with no confidence. But Fiona had grown beyond that woman. She had unfurled her feminine wings, and even if she wasn't confident enough to fly, she could flutter her wings provocatively.

"You're not taking this at all seriously, are you?" he asked.

"Not one bit. But you're a terrific ego boost."

"I'm pleased to be of service. *Any* service."

"Fiona."

Fiona turned at the sound of another voice. She watched Andrew approach from the rear of the dining room. The warm glow inside her ignited into something more exotic. "Well, hi. What are you doing here?"

He nodded curtly at David, as if they had already met. "I'm looking for Duncan."

"He went to Inverness this afternoon, and he won't be back until tomorrow." She searched Andrew's face. He looked tired, more tired than she had ever seen him. His hair was rumpled, and stubble carpeted his cheeks. Concern filled her, replacing the excitement she had felt at his arrival. "Are you all right?"

He brushed off the question with a wave of his hand. "I'll be going, then." He nodded toward David and started out of the dining room.

"Would you excuse me?" she asked David. She tossed her napkin on the table, and before he could answer, she started after Andrew.

She caught up with him in the lobby. "Andrew!" She put her hand on his arm. "What's going on?"

"I dinna want to interrupt your supper, Fiona." There was no smile to soften the words.

Despite the curtness of his tone she didn't drop her hand. "It doesn't matter. Is something wrong?"

"I wanted to see Duncan, that's all."

"Well, I'm in charge until he gets back. Can I help?"

He looked more exhausted by the second. When his voice emerged, it was one decibel stronger than a rasp. "It's been a night for good news and bad. And I wanted Duncan to help me deliver some of it."

She nodded, as if she understood, even though she didn't. She felt emboldened by her concern and by the sheer pleasure of being in his presence again. "Well, will I do instead?"

He opened his mouth as if to refuse. Then he clamped it shut. He stared at her for a moment. "You've left Gow sitting in the dining room."

She shrugged. She had already forgotten about David Gow. "I'll apologize. No doubt he'll attach himself to someone."

"What about your supper?"

"You look like you could use some company. I'll take it back to the kitchen and have Frances save it for me. I'm not even hungry."

"It's a long drive."

She laughed. He was making excuses for her, but she was in no mood to accept them. "Good grief! I'll take an apple."

He seemed torn. She touched his stubbly cheek. She tried to make her fingertips convey what her lips could only hint at. "It would give me the greatest pleasure to be able to do something for you for a change. May I do this?"

"What about the hotel?"

"Mara's due back any moment. It will be fine."

"Come on, then," he said, turning away from her. "I'll wait for you in my car."

His task to break the news to Carlton-Jones and Surrey. And *his* task to spend the evening with Fiona beside him. There was an incomparable sweetness to each, particularly the latter. Fiona sat in the seat next to his, her hair the same brash gold as the twilight horizon, and Andrew felt as if the sun had come to bide awhile beside him.

He had been unaccountably upset to find her talking to Gow. He had nowt against the man—except that he was an obvious liar—but he wondered if Fiona realized that men like Gow devoured women for the sheer pleasure of it. She was a bairn when it came to men. She had no idea how voracious, how self-indulgent, they could be.

Despite repeated evidence, she had no idea how much Andrew ached to indulge himself at her expense.

"I haven't been to Fort William before." It was Fiona's fourth try at conversation. Unsure what to say and confused by his own feelings, he had hardly responded to the other three. She seemed undaunted.

"I've nowt against Fort William. It's pleasant enough."

"But?"

"There was no 'but.'"

"You don't sound enthused. Andrew, are you ill?"

He probably was. Andrew was beginning to realize that his throat was not just raw from exposure. He had to struggle to make himself heard. "I suppose my mind's on what I'm about to do."

Fiona turned to watch him. He didn't have to see to know. He could feel the subtle shifting of her body, hear the rustle of her clothing. The soft swish of fabric against upholstery, the soft whisper of one leg rubbing against the other.

"Why don't you tell me what's happening?" she said.

He did, because it was easier than just sitting beside her, imagining each breath she took, each move she made. He planned just to give her the briefest overview, but she asked questions, and he elaborated. When he got to the part about Kaye's intentions to will him her property, Fiona whistled softly.

"Andrew, what an incredible gift."

"I still dinna understand." He was surprised to find he had relaxed considerably. Just the sound of Fiona's voice was healing.

"What don't you understand? She wants you to have it. She knows that you won't put up condos or build a shopping mall. It's her way of preserving something that's meant the world to her."

"But Iain would have bought the property from her at a fair price, and he would no' have abused it."

"She wanted *you* to have it. Let's face it, Iain owns most of the countryside. And Duncan has the largest and most valuable piece of the village proper."

"Duncan *and* you."

"The loch belongs to you, Andrew, and Kaye understands that. It's your home and your heart."

He was silent, mulling over the things she had said. "Odd, is it no', that the three of us—" He allowed himself one careful glance.

"The infamous men of midnight," she said with a grin.

That grin, so unabashed and exuberant, touched something deep inside him. "Aye. The three of us, the ridiculous men of midnight, have so much of the village and beyond in our possession now."

"But not a one of you feels you really own it. It's almost a sacred trust to each of you. Even Duncan. I know he had a chance to sell the hotel last year, but he held on to it, even though he swore he would never live in Scotland. It's crazy, but it's as if it was meant to happen this way."

"What about you, Fiona?"

"Me?"

"What are your plans? It seems as if Duncan will be staying here now. He and Mara are going to build a home. She has plans for her school...."

She was silent for a long time. "I like it here," she said at last.

His breath rasped painfully in his chest. He let it out slowly. "Do you?"

"Why wouldn't I?"

She seemed genuinely puzzled and perhaps a little hurt. He couldn't answer. He couldn't ask her if she planned to stay awhile, a decade, forever. The answer mattered too much.

She snuggled down in her seat and closed her eyes. He felt that, too, as if the air in the car had changed somehow, as if molecules had been permanently rearranged. He swore he could hear her breathing slow, and in his mind's eye he could see her breasts rise and fall in a deeper cadence.

To distract his thoughts, he turned on a tape of Celtic folk songs and they passed the rest of the trip in silence.

It was only much later when he finally pulled up in front of the luxurious old hotel where Martin Carlton-Jones and Nigel Surrey were staying that she opened her eyes.

"We're here?"

"Aye." He did what he had forbidden himself to do earlier. He turned to watch her. Her cheeks were ivory, as if sleep had robbed them of color, but as she stirred, they deepened to a pale apricot. He could not have prevented his next movement, not with the thought and planning of centuries. He touched her hair, which was a paler gold in the moonlight. Her eyes were slumberous cat's eyes. She was still not quite awake but far from asleep.

"Why do we always deny ourselves the things we want most, Andrew?"

His heart missed a beat. "Do we?"

"Yes. I think so. We spend all our lives learning to live without what we cherish most, and we call it self-discipline or moderation in all things."

"Exactly what are you referring to?"

"I was thinking of the property you're going to inherit. You don't feel worthy of such a large gift, but you want it. I know you do."

He leaned closer. "Is that all you meant?"

She didn't answer for a moment. He could see her come more fully awake. He wondered what it would be like to hold her tightly against him in the mornings as her eyes slowly opened. To listen to the soft sound of her breathing and feel her body respond without inhibition to his.

"No, that's not all I meant," she said softly.

"What have you denied yourself, Fiona?"

"I waited too long to fly. I've never wanted anything more than to be a normal woman with a normal life. But I let fear strangle me."

"And now?"

She smiled, a sleepy, wanton smile as old as woman. "Maybe someday I'll find the courage to pursue what I most cherish."

He wanted to kiss her. Her mouth was soft and ripe for kissing. He had only to lean closer and take her lips with his. But he forced himself to turn instead to open his door. "Do you want to wait in the lobby? Or do you want to come with me? A bonny scene it will no' be. Carlton-Jones and Surrey are no' used to being thwarted."

"Oh, I want to be there. I wouldn't miss this for the world."

Her answer surprised him. "You're certain?"

"Absolutely. Carlton-Jones and Surrey are greedy through and through. They don't cherish Mrs. Gerston's land, they merely desire it. You cherish it, Andrew. The days are gone when Highland men defended what was theirs with dirk and claymore. I'll have to be content with this."

He turned back to her and gazed on what he cherished most. She believed in him in a way he didn't believe in himself. And he believed in her. They were held captive by their own bonds, yet they strained toward each other, yearning....

He knew better than to kiss Fiona again, but when had a MacDougall put reality before his dreams? He gave a harsh sigh and bent his head. She wove her fingers in his hair as his mouth sought hers. Her thumb traced his cheekbone. Her lips were eager and pliant, and she gave him everything he asked for.

When he finally lifted his head, her eyes were shining. "And with that, I send you into battle," she whispered. "May the best man win, my brave Highland warrior."

Chapter 13

Fiona got up just after dawn, did the exercises she was required to do every day, then dressed for a breakfast picnic beside the loch. She brought her sketchbook and two of Frances Gunn's famous scones, along with a jug of hot tea flavored with thick, fresh cream. She needed inspiration for a drawing, and now that the loch had been "discovered" it was only quiet during the morning's earliest hours. She wanted to capture the way that waterbugs skimmed the shallows and gulls spread their wings before they dove to feast on minnows.

She was discouraged by her lack of progress on the next Stardust book. Her editor was nudging her to submit what she had finished, but Fiona wasn't satisfied enough with her work to submit anything yet. Images eluded her, images of two water dragons dancing in the water together. The book was for children, yet she knew that she couldn't tell the story properly without conveying the water dragons' joy, even exuberance, at finding each other. Until she could, she had no book.

Primrose followed Fiona to her favorite cove. He was disgruntled that April had left him for the night, and he needed coddling and reassurance. She gave both dutifully, and after she'd spread her blanket on the ground, he spread his long body along one end and closed his eyes, satisfied.

Fiona stared out at the water. She was still staring an hour later, no closer to putting pencil to paper than she had been before coming. But the loch had changed in that time. There were boats now, just a few, but a harbinger of things to come as the day progressed. It seemed that everyone in the British Isles planned to come and search for Andrew's darling. On the way back from Fort William last night she and Andrew had passed a farm not far from the village. Overnight it had become a caravan site. Tents and caravans now lined fields that should have been planted with oats or wheat. The wily farmer had found a more lucrative crop.

Kaye Gerston had decided not to sell, and now that prime piece of property on the loch would be Andrew's someday. But who else would succumb to the offers of Martin Carlton-Jones and Nigel Surrey or men just like them? How long before Druidheachd became a place to visit instead of a place to live?

Fiona turned her head in the direction of Andrew's house. She couldn't see the little cottage from here, but she thought she could make out the end of his pier. It had been late when they'd left Fort William, and neither of them had said much on the long trip home. The meeting with Carlton-Jones and Surrey had been a different matter. Plenty had been said there. She had disliked the two men on sight and would have disliked them even if she hadn't known what they were up to.

Martin Carlton-Jones was overweight and bald. Nigel Surrey was only bald. He had come down to the lobby dressed in a shiny polyester warm-up suit, as if Fiona and Andrew had interrupted his hopeless quest for physical perfection. Both men had been affable at first, as if there were no reason to be on guard against two inconsequential Druidheachd residents.

"You have Kaye Gerston's final papers?" Nigel had asked, mopping hard-earned sweat off his forehead as he spoke. "That's why you're here?"

"No. There will be no final papers. Mrs. Gerston's changed her mind. She'll no' be selling to you or anyone."

Martin stepped forward. He seemed perplexed. "What do you mean?"

"She's decided to keep the property."

"But she can't do that."

"Can she no'?" Andrew's smile was lethal. "That will surprise her, since her solicitor has assured her she's perfectly within the law."

Martin's expression changed. It was a subtle change, as if he wanted to continue to appear a bit dim-witted. But Fiona suspected that his mind was working at Concorde speed. "Why are *you* here, MacDougall?" he asked.

"As a favor to Mrs. Gerston. She's not well. You've preyed on an old, sick woman, and I'm here to be certain it will no' happen again."

"You made the trip all this way just to tell us she changed her mind, when she could have had her solicitor call? There must have been something in it for you," Nigel said.

"Aye. The greatest satisfaction in the world." Andrew took a step closer. He towered over both men in every way. "And I have my own message to deliver. You'll no' find it easy to buy up our village, our loch or our countryside. You've already had dealings with Duncan Sinclair and Iain Ross. Now you'll have to deal with me, too. We'll stand together, with everyone else who feels as we do, and we'll protect what's ours. I'd tell you to look elsewhere for your land and your village, but I would no' wish you or your kind on any community. Go back where you came from and be content with what you have. Because you will never have what's ours."

Martin Carlton-Jones, obviously taken back, turned to Fiona, as if hoping to find a victim to make him feel better.

"I'll be standing beside them," she said, before he could address her. "And so will every woman in the village who values what she has. I'll be sure of it."

Afterward Andrew had dropped her back at the hotel with a fleeting smile and a squeeze of her hand. He had thanked her for going with him, but now she wondered if her presence had really made any difference to him. She felt immature and foolish. A man like Andrew needed someone who could stand at his side in every instance and in every way. She was nothing but a poor substitute. Her fantasies of a full and satisfying life were persistent but absurd. She hadn't even been courageous enough to give him one night of pleasure.

And perhaps, even if she had found the courage, he would have found no pleasure anyway.

Resigned to another unproductive morning, she started to pack up. There was no inspiration to be found here, only black thoughts and the remnants of dreams. Routed from comfort, Primrose wandered down to the water while she folded the blanket. Then he began to bark.

She looked out over the water again and saw a boat coming closer. Shading her eyes, she stared into the glare of the sun and saw that the boat was *MacDougall's Darling* with Andrew at the helm. He drew closer until he was drifting toward the shore.

She waved, determined not to flaunt her self-doubts. "Ahoy, Captain!"

He nosed the boat forward until the bow was touching the bank where the water was deep enough to keep from scraping bottom. He motioned for her to come on board. She was dubious, but he stepped out on the bow and held a hand toward her. She crawled on to the bow and took his hand. In a moment she was on the deck beside him.

"Out for a morning sail?" she asked.

"Aye." The voice that emerged was more nearly a croak.

"Andrew? Are you all right?"

He shook his head. His forehead was furrowed in a frown so fierce that his eyebrows were nearly a straight line.

"You can't talk?"

"No."

That was now perfectly evident. "You poor thing." She felt his cheeks. They were cool, and so was his forehead. "Is anything hurting?"

He shook his head. He didn't mention his pride, but she suspected it was gravely wounded.

"Your throat's not sore? Chest? Head?" She watched him shake his head in answer to each question.

"Woke feeling fit, then went to call Poppy," he croaked.

"Lord, don't talk anymore. You'll lose what little voice you have left."

"Going to hotel. Got to tell Gow can no' take him out."

Fiona knew that Andrew had agreed to take David Gow out for the afternoon, along with his housekeeper Violet Higgins and her sister Muriel. Last night she had sensed Andrew's lack of enthusiasm, but now she sensed no satisfaction at canceling the trip.

"You didn't really want to take him out anyway, did you?"

"Want to get rid of the man."

She laughed. He scowled.

"Then why don't you take him? You can croak a story or two and take his money. You might feel better about everything after that."

"You've no sympathy." The croak was fast becoming a whisper.

She laughed again. "Andrew..." She rose on tiptoe to kiss his cheek. "I've got sympathy coming out my pores. But you're not sick, you know. You're just losing your voice." She rested a finger against his lips. "Shh... It'll be completely gone if you say much more."

He took her hands in his and clasped them to his chest, but he didn't speak.

"This is kind of fun," she said. "You can't argue with me. A woman could get used to this." She laughed as he narrowed his eyes. "Look, I've got an idea. Why don't you take me with you this afternoon?" She ignored the savage shake of his head. "I'm serious. I'll tell all the stories David Gow could ever digest. Maybe they won't be the same ones you'd tell, but I do remember some of your stories, you know. And I can make up what I don't remember. I'm pretty good at that, after all."

He shook his head again, but she ignored it once more. "Why? Are you afraid I'm a better storyteller than you are? Or is it just that you don't want me on the same boat with David Gow? The man does have a way about him, doesn't he?"

He didn't try to answer; he tried to stare her down. She would not be thwarted. "Come on, Andrew. You've been such a good friend to me, and it will be days before your voice is back to normal. Let me do this for you. Then we can kiss David Gow goodbye.'' She smiled as his eyes blazed. ''Not literally, of course.''

He sighed. That, at least, was clear. Finally he gave a gruff nod.

''Good. We'll meet you at the public launch then?''

He managed a final croak. ''Noon.''

He'd drunk a gallon of hot tea with lemon and honey, and swallowed every medication in his house that related to throats. And still his voice emerged only with the most vicious prodding. Andrew watched Fiona charm his guests, both female and male alike, and wondered—grudgingly—if some good might come from his illness after all. This was one more thing that Fiona was proving she could do.

''Our creature's said to live at the very bottom of the loch,'' Fiona told the guests, ''in a cave so well hidden that even if the loch were dry, she couldn't be found.''

''Once there was talk of draining the loch,'' Violet said. ''When my mum was a wee girlie. A scientist from Edinburgh nearly prodded the village into it. Wanted to find the creature, he did, wanted it so badly he did no' mind killing her. And where would they have put all that water, I'm thinking?''

''There was talk once, when we were lassies, of dragging the loch with nets,'' Muriel said, peering over the side. ''I believe it was tried.''

''It was,'' Fiona said. ''With no luck, of course. The loch is so deep in places—deeper than Loch Ness, in fact—that there's no hope of a net long or large enough. There was also talk of poisoning the water with quick lime and of charging it with electricity, to see what died and floated to the top. Luckily neither was ever tried.''

Violet straightened with difficulty. She was younger than her sister, who looked to be nearly seventy, but the two women were much alike in appearance, with lively blue eyes just visible under gray Prince Valiant bangs. ''Where were you when you saw the creature?'' she asked Gow.

"Over there." Gow pointed in the direction they were heading.

"Now that's unusual," Fiona said. "Most of the sightings haven't been on that side of the loch. I wonder why you were so favored?"

He smiled the engaging smile that set Andrew's teeth on edge. "I've never had a problem with the ladies."

Violet snorted. "You've had your share of problems, I'm thinking. Is that no' why you're in Scotland, lad?"

Gow laughed. "Tell us about the sightings, Fiona."

Fiona launched into one of the most preposterous stories that Andrew had ever heard.

"Once there was a young man named Alan Mac-Dougall," she said, in her musical voice, "and he was the very first to see the creature. It happened so long ago that we've lost track of the date, of course. Some think it was more than five centuries ago, but still the story lives on."

"I'm riveted to the spot," Gow said. "Tell us more."

"Well, poor Alan was dying for love. His sweetheart was betrothed to another, and as far as she was concerned, Alan didn't even exist. He was a scrawny lad. The dashing, brawny MacDougalls came much later." She flashed Andrew a smile. "Poor Alan was always getting beaten when the village lads took sides against each other. He was small, and his eyesight was poor. He was pockmarked, and one arm was too short. They even say he walked like a turkey—"

"Fiona!" Andrew croaked.

She raised one brow. "Wasn't I supposed to tell them that part?" She shrugged. "I'm sorry. Like every MacDougall to come along since, he walked like a man twice his size. Is that better?"

Andrew glared at her.

"Anyway, one day Alan saw the woman he loved—her name was Verity—on the road to her castle. Did I mention that she was the daughter of a rich man? Well, Verity turned her head when he passed, and after that he heard her giggling with her maids. Alan realized at last that Verity only saw him as an object of ridicule. So he decided that he would drown himself that night in the loch. He waited until dark so he wouldn't get caught, then he stole a boat that was tied up on the shore and rowed it out to the middle. I'm afraid he wasn't a very brave young man. The stalwart, courageous MacDougalls came much later." This time she winked at Andrew.

"Was this Alan really one of your ancestors, Andrew?" Gow asked.

Andrew tried to imagine David Gow with his legs where his arms normally hung. The picture so delighted him that a grin came naturally.

Gow turned back to Fiona. "Well?"

"Alan stole the boat instead of merely jumping off a bank. He was afraid he'd chicken out once he was in the water and climb right back on shore. The problem is that our Alan wasn't very strong."

"The strong MacDougalls came much later," Gow said.

"You've heard this before?" Fiona asked with a straight face.

"I'm beginning to think I'll never hear it all."

"Well, because Alan wasn't very strong, it took him most of the night to row the boat to the middle of the loch. I believe I forgot to mention that he had no sense of direction, didn't I?"

"The MacDougalls with a sense of direction came much later," Muriel said with a cackling laugh.

"No, I don't believe they ever did. Did they Andrew?"

Andrew wanted to haul her below deck and kiss the impudent smile off her soft, sweet lips. She was transforming herself before his eyes again. He knew that he was seeing the Fiona she had been destined to become before the fire that had robbed her of her courage.

"Anyway, Alan finally made it to the middle, but by then it was almost dawn. He'd hoped to rest a bit before he killed himself—although I find it hard to imagine why. But because the sky was growing lighter and the sun was about to appear, he realized he was going to have to make a quick job of it, tired or not. So he stood up, pinched his nostrils together—although I find that hard to imagine, too—and jumped overboard."

"I thought this story was about the loch monster," Gow said.

"Ah, it is. You see, just at the moment that Alan jumped, the creature rose from the depths of the loch, and Alan landed on her back."

Gow groaned. So did Andrew, although less obtrusively.

Fiona continued. "So there he was, riding the back of a terrible water creature like a medieval rodeo cowboy. Now, drowning had appealed to poor Alan. He'd imagined his own bloated body washing up on the shore to the weeping and wailing of the village women. He'd even thought that perhaps he'd look better bloated a bit, and that maybe Verity might feel a little remorse for the way that she'd treated him. But he couldn't imagine that even *he* would look any better if he was chewed into a million teensy pieces. In fact, he doubted that anyone would take the time to put his remains back together again and identify him. So Alan did the only thing he knew to do. He screamed."

"And well he should have," Violet said with a sniff.

"MacDougall's darling is a very gentle creature. She wouldn't hurt anyone, of course. She feeds on the reeds and rushes at the loch bottom, and even the fish are her friends. But Alan, being the first MacDougall to see her, didn't know this. The smart MacDougalls—"

"Came much later," the three guests chorused in unison.

"Exactly. So meanwhile, poor Alan screamed out his puny lungs. The creature, frightened herself now, gave a mighty buck. Alan soared through the air and landed smack dab in the middle of the boat. At first, of course, he was dazed. He couldn't believe he'd been so lucky. Then the creature rose from the water and put her face right up against his...."

"And?" Gow prompted.

"And Alan realized that the creature was far more lovely, far kinder and more charming than Verity had ever been. Right that minute, Alan fell madly in love with her. And although she descended into the water and he never saw her again, he adored her until the day he died."

"The MacDougalls with good taste came much later?" Gow asked.

"Oh no, Alan was the *first* MacDougall with good taste.
And all the others who've come after Alan have loved her,
too. Unreservedly."

"Is any of this true, Andrew?" Gow asked.

Andrew looked straight at Fiona. "Every bit," he said.
"Although some of us have loved a woman just as well."
His voice emerged as a whisper, but he knew she had heard
him. Her expression softened like honeycomb in the sun.

"That truly was a ludicrous saga," David told Fiona.
"I've never heard such a succession of outrageous stories.
Tall tales, isn't that what you Americans call them?"

Fiona stretched lazily in the warmth of the afternoon sun.
MacDougall's Darling was cruising back toward shore after an extended tour. Muriel and Violet were at the helm
getting a boating lesson from Andrew, and David had just
come back to join her. "Exactly what did you expect?"

"Nothing quite so colorful. You're quite good at this. I'd
almost think you'd had practice."

Fiona heard more than casual praise in his voice. "Oh?"

"In fact, I'd say you are very nearly a professional."

"I'm honored."

"You're famous."

She turned in her chair so that she could see his face.
"Famous?"

"I have a niece. I buy her storybooks."

"Oh, I see."

"I thought your name was familiar when we were introduced. I think I said as much."

"Writers can generally escape into obscurity, particularly writers of children's books."

"And that's what you wanted to do?"

Fiona suspected that was now an impossibility. "That's
what I hoped to do."

"And well you might have, if you hadn't made up those
absurd stories today. Tell me, is Loch Ceo the Serenity Lake
in your books? And is Stardust its creature?"

"You not only buy my books, you read them?"

"They are lovely stories. Brilliant. I feel I know them by
heart. They're the only books my niece will let me read her."

"She's a very discriminating young lady."

"Is Loch Ceo Serenity Lake?"

Fiona considered what to tell him. David was a reporter, and she wasn't foolish enough to believe that this would not be mentioned in his next missive from Druidheachd. "I was born here, and I heard stories about the creature as a little girl. But I left Scotland when I was only three."

"Then it's just a coincidence?"

She couldn't deny the place of those stories in her life. "No. I remembered them, even though I was very young. I had a lot of time to think and imagine as a child. My fantasies were more palatable than reality." She saw the question in his eyes. "I was badly burned as a little girl, and I was in and out of hospitals for much of my childhood. It was my way of escaping."

He didn't express pity. He certainly didn't seem revolted. He just nodded. "It's odd, isn't it, how one's worst misfortune can become a remarkable gift to the world?"

"What a lovely way to put it."

"So you remembered the stories you'd heard, and you changed and embroidered them and they became the Stardust books."

"David, I came back to Scotland because I wanted to avoid publicity."

"I'm afraid this is a cliché. But there is no corner of the world so remote that we can run away from who we are."

"You're going to write about this, aren't you?"

"Not if you forbid me."

"You would agree not to?"

"Yes, I think I might. But I hope I won't have to."

Fiona realized that this moment had become a crossroads. She could continue to hide, as she had hidden all her life. Or she could come forward now and tell the world a little about herself. Surely there were other people like her, people who had been scarred by fire or by other tragedies, who would draw courage from her story. A picture of tiny Sara flashed through her mind, Sara, who, as she grew, would have to cope with the same sorrows that Fiona had. There was so little she could do for Sara or the other children on the burn ward. If someday Sara and others like her could draw courage from her experiences . . .

"I won't ask you not to," she said. "You'll be fair and kind. I trust you, David."

"Never, ever think that I can be trusted, Fiona." He leaned forward and kissed her. He was smiling when he withdrew. "I believe that at this moment your Andrew would like to throw me to his darling. The MacDougalls who aren't possessive of their women have yet to be created, I'm afraid."

He stood and strolled to the side.

Fiona glanced toward Andrew, but he turned away. Whatever was in his eyes was lost to her.

At last they docked, and she stood beside Andrew as he gravely shook hands with their passengers. "We'll talk again," David said, as he took her hand. "We'll have to go over details."

"You'll be around for a while, then?"

"For a bit. Circulation at the paper has increased noticeably since my stories of the creature have been running. I'd be hard-pressed to leave now."

"Before you saw my darling, did it occur to you that circulation might increase?" Andrew croaked.

"It certainly did," David said. "Surprising how things work out, isn't it?" He stepped on to the pier and held out his hand to Violet, then Muriel. With a wave they were gone.

"Well, it went well, don't you think?" Fiona asked Andrew.

"You certainly seemed to enjoy yourself."

"Wasn't I supposed to?"

He ignored her and started back to the helm. She followed at his heels. "Andrew, David knows about my books. He figured it out."

He shrugged.

"He's going to write about me. I guess I can't hide forever."

"Why should you?"

She suspected that the gruffness of his voice wasn't due to laryngitis alone. "Why are you angry at me?"

"I'm no' angry."

"You sound angry. And I don't think I've done anything."

"I'm no' angry."

She watched him polish the controls with a soft rag and tidy the immaculate helm. She wondered if his house was the same and guessed it wouldn't be. She suspected that the boat was Andrew's real home. "I told David how I remembered stories about your darling when I went to America."

He grunted, and she went on. "It's funny, isn't it? A seed is planted, then it grows in the strangest ways. I remembered stories about the loch. Some of them were probably yours. But some of them were my father's. Now people will read and remember my stories. I wonder what my father thought about that? I wonder if he even knew about the Stardust books before he died?"

Andrew looked up. "He never said?"

"No."

"He was no' an easy man."

"So I've been told. I wouldn't know, myself."

He looked puzzled.

She wished she hadn't started this. She didn't know how the conversation had led to this point so quickly. "Look, you shouldn't be talking. I'm sorry. I should go and leave you alone."

He took her arm as she turned to go. "Donald Sinclair was a hard man, but he loved you," he rasped. "Do you no' believe it?"

"Loved me?" She stared at him. "Oh, I think not, Andrew. He never called me or wrote me, not once after the accident. And he never came to America to see me."

"You never came here, either. You refused to come."

"Do you think that was the way I wanted it?" She shook her head. His hand fell to his side, and she turned to leave again.

"Was it no'?" he asked.

"No."

"Then why did you stay away?"

"It doesn't matter now."

"It does."

She realized he wasn't going to drop this. "I wrote my father when I was ten. I asked him if I could come with Duncan to Druidheachd that summer. I didn't tell my mother. I was afraid she would forbid me to come if I did. I thought she was the one who was keeping my father away."

She stared out at the loch and didn't face him. Her father's rejection was so old that she hadn't expected it to hurt anymore. Now she found it still did. "He never answered my letter, and Duncan went off to Scotland without me. My mother found me crying one day, and she finally persuaded me to tell her what I'd done. And then she told me why my father never wrote or called, and why he refused to see me."

She turned back to him. "He couldn't stand the sight of me, Andrew. Oh, Mother didn't put it quite that way. She tried to protect me by telling me that it was just the way he was, that he had always expected everything and everyone to be perfect, and that it wasn't my fault that I wasn't perfect anymore. But I knew what she really meant. I wasn't just imperfect. I was ugly. Hideous. And my father couldn't ever stand to look at me again."

"Fiona..."

She managed a smile. "You know what? It was his loss."

His eyes said everything his battered voice couldn't.

She looked away, because compassion was the gateway to tears, and she didn't want to cry. "I don't know why I told you this." But the moment she said the words she did know. She had told him because he deserved an explanation for why she was so frightened to let him see her scars. He deserved to know where her worst fears about herself had come from.

"I dinna believe it."

"You don't believe what I've told you?"

"I dinna believe your father stopped loving you."

"There are twenty-two years of silence to prove it."

"A dead man can no' defend himself, Fiona."

She touched his hand. Her gaze followed because she still couldn't look him in the eye. "Yes, he's dead, but you're alive. Can a living man forgive a woman who's afraid that he'll find her as imperfect as her own father did?"

He wove his fingers through hers. "Aye, he can, if the woman someday stops hiding behind her fears."

Chapter 14

Duncan and Iain were already waiting when Andrew arrived at the pub. After docking the boat he had napped well into the evening, and on waking, his voice, although not completely restored, was strong enough for conversation. He didn't have to be forceful with his old friends. He merely needed to be heard.

Andrew greeted them and took his chair. Duncan signaled Brian, and a generous dram was placed in front of him. There was no need to shout over the rowdy good cheer of the crowd. As soon as he had joined his friends, the closest tables mysteriously emptied. As always, the men of midnight were given wide berth.

"You sound god-awful," Duncan said. "Are you all right?"

"Nowt wrong that this will no' cure." Andrew held up what was now an empty glass.

"I'm hearing rumors about Gerston's Cottages," Iain said.

Andrew quickly filled them in while Brian came back and filled his glass again.

Duncan gave a long, low whistle. "So the lines are drawn for all to see."

Andrew gestured to the patrons on the other side of the pub. "Carlton-Jones and Surrey have lost their foothold, but they may well gain another. There's an air of discontent in the village and beyond. Some residents talk of selling to escape the tourists pouring in to look for my darling. Some talk of selling because the time is right—they think they'll no' have a chance to sell at this price again."

"Do you remember Margaret Henley's predictions when we were born?" Iain asked. Margaret Henley, long since passed on, had been the village seer, a woman gifted with extraordinary second sight.

"Aye. We were no' to be separated. We were to grow up in each other's shadows, to strengthen the bonds that began at our birth," Andrew said.

Duncan finished the prediction. "Because a black cloud would descend over the village someday, and the three of us would have to stand together against it."

Andrew sat forward. "Surely you dinna think this is what old Margaret meant?"

"Were you expecting something more spectacular? A war? Famine? Plague?" Iain asked. "Greed is far more insidious. If Carlton-Jones and Surrey or men like them move into Druidheachd, the village will exist no longer. There'll be nothing left but a name and a fading history, and few who care about either."

"I feel more equipped for full-scale war," Andrew said. "Greed is invisible, an enemy without form or substance."

"As difficult to pin down as a black cloud," Iain said.

They fell silent. Andrew finished his second whisky, but he felt no better. He signaled for a third.

"I feel helpless," Iain said. "I overplayed my hand with Martin and Nigel months ago, and now they've effectively neutralized me. Because of all I have, when I speak out against greed, I'm perceived as greedy myself."

"And I'm the American interloper," Duncan said. "More than a few people think I object to Druidheachd expanding its tourist base because more hotels will be built and I'll have competition."

"At least there are no fingers pointing at me," Andrew said, holding up his glass for Brian to refill.

"Then perhaps you'll have to be the one to finish the battle," Iain said.

Andrew considered that. He had never thought of himself as the guardian of all that was good in Druidheachd or anywhere. He was simply Andrew MacDougall, everybody's friend, the peasant in the odd play that had cast Iain as the lord and Duncan as the clever merchant. "What can I do?"

"I think it's time to make our fears public," Iain said. "I think we have to call a meeting and bring all of this out in the open."

"At the kirk," Duncan said. "I can talk to the minister and ask for use of it."

"And who's to run this meeting?" Andrew asked.

Both men looked squarely at him. He shook his head, but their expressions didn't change. "We'll be there," Iain said. "But we've come to the final act in this drama, Andrew, and I'm afraid you're destined to be the star."

"Surely you dinna believe that this is what we were born for? You've become as superstitious as the villagers who once believed that Mara was a ghost or a fairy."

"Sometimes I'm not completely convinced that they were wrong." Duncan didn't smile. "There are things that happen here..."

"Aye," Iain said. "That there are."

Andrew stared at the two men who were closer to him than brothers. Their lives had been entwined since birth, yet he wondered if he had ever seen them this clearly before. He had been content all his days to let his friends be the things he was not. Iain was the undisputed leader. Born to privilege—as well as tragedy—he had easily mastered the world he had been bequeathed, ordering his personal life and the lives of those who were dependent on him with aristocratic compassion and precision.

Duncan had been the most aggressive of the three. He had charged into the world at the earliest opportunity and carved out his own personal kingdom with skill and intelligence. Even now, when his roles as husband and father were more important to him than financial success, he was still effectively setting the hotel on its financial feet and launching a new business on the side.

Andrew had always known exactly who he was. He was Terence MacDougall's son, with an abundance of charm and good nature to see him through his life. Yet he realized now that even with all their own strengths, Iain and Duncan had always seen more in him than he had seen in himself.

As if he had read Andrew's mind, Duncan spoke. "You might have fooled the rest of the world, but you never fooled us. We know exactly what you're capable of, Andrew. Iain and I have done all we can. I stood up to Martin and Nigel when they tried to buy the hotel. Iain stood up to them when they wanted his land. Now it's time for you to step forward. You have the confidence of the villagers in a way we never will."

Andrew stared at his empty glass. Three whiskies and he wanted another. Did he want it because he hoped to silence the voice inside him whispering that his friends were wrong? Did he want it because he had always known that at heart he was no different from his father and that someday he would end up exactly like him? Or did he want yet another mind-deadening dram because deep inside he was afraid to take his rightful place beside Iain and Duncan, to be someone more than he had ever believed he could be?

Just like Fiona.

For the first time he truly understood Fiona's fears. For the first time he realized how insidious his own had become.

"A week from Sunday, at seven, if we can get the kirk," he said at last. "Post a notice in the lobby, Duncan, and one here. I'll put up something at Cameron's, and I'll speak with the old men and women who have nowt better to do than gossip. That way we'll be certain that everyone will know."

He stood and looked down at his friends. "I suppose that it does no' matter if this is what we were born for or just an obstacle that's been put in our paths. We'll see this through, and I'll be thankful you're standing beside me." For a moment his voice seemed to fail him once more. It fell to a lower octave. "There are no finer friends anywhere in the universe," he said gruffly.

He had always been the most sentimental of the three men. But Iain and Duncan rose to their feet as if they were one body and flung their arms around his shoulders in fierce, male hugs.

The lights in the pub flickered and died. For a long moment complete, astonished silence reigned.

Then Andrew began to laugh.

Fiona had been watching dark clouds roll in over the village all evening, so the power outage didn't surprise her. Somewhere in the far distance, where the storm was raging, a line was probably down.

She sat at one of the windows in her suite and gazed over the green. The street lamps were dark, and not a glimmer could be seen from any building. She'd been given candles for such an event, but she preferred not to light them. She wasn't afraid of the dark, but later, the smell of lingering smoke might trigger another nightmare.

When the knock sounded on her door, she felt her way across the room to answer it. She expected Mara, but it was Andrew who was standing there. Andrew, smelling of whisky, who was nothing more than a dark, imposing outline of a man. Before she could speak he put his hands on her shoulders. "You're all right, Fiona?"

"Sure. Why shouldn't I be?"

"I thought you might be frightened."

"No. Darkness has never bothered me."

"I nearly killed myself climbing the stairs."

"Then I think you'd better come in and make yourself at home until the lights come back on. Climbing down the stairs might be even worse." She stood aside to let him enter. When she had closed the door, she groped for his hand. "I'll lead you across the room. Take it slow."

Safely across the room they fell on her sofa together. "You sound a lot better," she said. "Your powers of recovery are amazing."

"I think no'."

"Then you're still feeling bad?"

He was silent. He had dropped her hand upon reaching the sofa, and it was too dark here to see him. Still, she experienced his presence in the oddest way, as if there were a space in her life that was filled now, when before it had been empty.

"I'm well, Fiona," he said finally. "But I'm only just beginning to understand how little I've recovered."

"I don't understand."

"Neither did I until tonight."

She waited for him to go on, but the silence fell again. When he did speak, she thought he had changed the subject.

"Do you remember my father, Fiona?"

"Not at all."

"Did you know he was enchanted with you? Whenever he encountered you in the village he treated you like a bonny dolly. For your third birthday he carved you a wee walking stick with a dragon head, and you used it to bash my legs whenever I refused to do what you wanted."

She laughed. "Really, I don't know why you still speak to me."

"There was another side to my father."

She turned so that she was facing in his direction. She could just make out his shape against the white wall. "Was there?"

"He was an alcoholic."

She had never heard him use that word. "Yes, I know."

"On my climb up the stairs, I remembered a night much like this one. When I was a lad we were often without power, most often because my da had no money to pay our bill. We were less often without food, although that happened from time to time. My mother had a large vegetable garden, and when my da was sober he fished. At the end of winter, when there was no food left in our cupboard, my granny was there to help."

Fiona hadn't realized that Andrew's childhood had been so bleak. He was not a man to complain. "What happened that night?"

"That night there was neither power nor food. Our telephone had been disconnected, and our car had no' run for weeks. It was too cold to walk to my granny's, and by the end of the evening, we had run out of peat. My mother gave me a piece of bread with honey she had scraped from the bottom of a jar, then she put me to bed, under a thick layer of blankets. But I was still too cold and hungry to fall sleep. I lay there and listened to my parents fighting."

"And you remember it still?"

"Aye. I remember hearing my da cry, then my mother cry, too. He told her that he had no choice, you see. He was exactly the man God had made him, a weak and foolish man at that. He wanted to be different, but he could no' be anything but what he was. That was his excuse for all his failings, and I suppose it was a way of denying all his strengths, too. Because if he was just as God made him and had no control over his life, then nowt he did, no' good or bad, was his to claim. That's how he lived his life, a puppet to any force that pulled his strings."

Fiona's heart ached for Andrew, but considerably less so for the man who had fathered him, Terence MacDougall, who had allowed his own child to go hungry. "Did you believe him? Did you believe it wasn't his fault?"

"I was only a wee laddie. My choice was to call my own father a liar or to believe that he truly had no choice, that he could no' help what he was. So for years, that's what I told myself."

"And now?"

Andrew was silent. Fiona wanted to touch him, to reassure him somehow, but she didn't know what to say. She still didn't understand exactly why he had told her this, although she was more than touched that he had.

The silence extended. Outside she could hear the storm approaching, the light sprinkle of rain at its border tapping against the old slate roof. On the street below there was a scurry of feet and a shout as someone ran for shelter. She felt and heard Andrew stand. She stood, too, and she was in his arms. He didn't kiss her; he just held her against him and stroked her hair. He lifted one curl and brushed it against his cheek; then he stepped away. "There's something I must do," he said.

"Would you like me to come with you?"

"No. I'll do this alone."

"Be careful outside. There's thunder in the distance."

"Aye."

Fiona heard his footsteps. She yearned to call him back, to offer herself as solace, but her devils were as relentless as his. The door opened, then closed again, and she was alone.

The full bottle of whisky that Andrew had bought from Brian felt almost warm under his anorak, mostly, he supposed, because it was dry and nothing else that was touching his skin was. The heavens had opened, and it was difficult to tell where the rain ended and the loch began.

Beneath his feet *MacDougall's Darling* cruised slowly forward. Her lights swept the water, but nothing except mist and rain was illuminated. Only a fool would be out on the water tonight, a fool or a man who had experienced an epiphany.

The rain had long since washed away the whisky he'd had at the pub, completely sobering him. Some whispering voice deep inside him begged for more, for something to dull the pain of his revelations, for something to persuade him that the course he had set for himself could be altered.

But the bottle stayed against his skin and his hands stayed steady on the wheel. He was piloting the boat by feel, sensing both his location and destination.

He knew exactly where he wanted to go. Iain had traveled this path before him. Iain, too, had been haunted by his past and his destiny. Months ago he had drowned both in the deepest part of the loch, and it was to that spot that Andrew headed now.

Lightning split the sky, and he thought about the night he had rescued Jamie and Peter Gordon. It would be like his darling to show herself tonight, but he wasn't here to find her.

He was here to find himself.

Minutes passed, and the rain fell harder. He reduced his speed once, then again, until he was barely moving. The boat rocked harder under his feet, and he grasped the wheel until his knuckles turned white. Satisfied at last, he switched off the engine, and then, holding fast to the railing, he felt his way toward the stern.

Drenching rain sluiced over his brow and down his neck. Water sloshed over his shoes, and icy waves crashed over the sides. Once he nearly lost his balance, but he clung stubbornly to the railing, afraid that if he fell the bottle would shatter.

He reached the stern at last and wedged himself between a seat and the side. He knew the danger of being swept overboard. Almost no one bathed in frigid Loch Ceo and lived to tell about it.

Safe for the moment, he unzipped his anorak and pulled out the bottle. It was Brian's recommendation, the pub's finest whisky.

Andrew had wanted nothing but the best.

Rain streaked the glass almost immediately, and the bottle slid through his hands. He was cold, and his fingers weren't steady. It took him nearly a minute to get a good grip and unscrew the cap. It gave with a reassuring sigh, almost as if the whisky had a mind or a life of its own. That seemed entirely appropriate to him.

"A life for a life," he said.

Unaccountably, he thought of a night much like this one when Terence had taken him fishing. He had been an adolescent, both vulnerable and hostile, and above all certain of his own immortality, as only a boy that age can be. But there had been whisky on that cruise, too, and they had very nearly not made it home alive. By the time Andrew had fought the boat in to shore with his father passed out on the deck, his mother, waiting on the pier, had been as pale as a corpse. She had clasped his struggling adolescent body against hers, and she had made him promise that he would never go out in the boat with his father again.

Terence had died six months later.

But Andrew did not have to die young. He did not have to wonder the rest of his days if in this, too, he would someday be like his father. Like Terence, he was exactly the man God had created him to be. And that man, like all men everywhere, had been given choices.

He unscrewed the cap all the way, then he leaned forward. The boat bobbed dangerously beneath him, but he hardly noticed. He turned over the bottle and watched as the pub's most expensive whisky poured into the water.

He was not an alcoholic. Not yet, and perhaps, even if he continued to drink, not ever. But now he would never have to face that possibility. He would never have to wonder if someday, like his father, he would walk too far along the whisky road to ever find his way back.

He had been given a choice. He had made his.

He thought then of Fiona. From the beginning he had thought himself unworthy of her. He had never believed he had the potential to be a loving husband and responsible father. He had seen the best and the worst in Terence, and he had believed himself to be the same.

He was not.

He stood drenched and shivering, staring at the water. Eventually the storm blew over, the waves calmed, the last raindrops fell. Still he stood there.

At last Andrew went down to the cabin, but he wasn't ready to leave. Instead he pulled out his bagpipe, stowed in the safest, driest place on board because he often played for his guests. He breathed air into the bag through the blowpipe, tuned the drones to the chanter and blew a short passage. When he was satisfied he went to the stern and lifted the blowpipe to his lips again.

And he began to play.

Chapter 15

Even though more than a week had passed since the night of the storm, the haunting wail of a lone bagpipe still seemed to drift through Fiona's window. She didn't know what trick of the wind had carried the music straight to her room that night, or even why she was so certain that Andrew had been the piper. She only knew that she had never heard anything so poignant or wrenching, and that if she lived to be a hundred, she never would again.

Now she stood at the window and gazed at the darkening sky. Even after the pipes had grown silent, the music had played on in her mind, like a background score for the unfolding events of her life.

"Fiona?" Mara pushed open the door, which Fiona had left ajar. "Am I disturbing you? I brought you some soup. It's Frances's cock-a-leekie. I know you like it."

"You're so thoughtful." Fiona crossed the room and took the small tureen from Mara's hands. "I was just about to make a sandwich."

"Soup's perfect on a night like this one." Mara followed Fiona inside. "It may be summer, but the air's far too damp and cold for my taste. And another storm's brewing."

The past week had seen nothing but storms. Dark clouds had hovered over the village, spilling rain at regular intervals and never quite dissipating. Fiona still hadn't grown used to the persistent chill. "Will you share some soup with me?" she asked.

"I ate earlier with April, when you were out. Andrew stopped by, and we fed him, as well."

"I'm surprised there's anything left for me." Fiona kept her voice light, although trying to fool Mara was futile. Not only was Mara gifted with second sight, she was one of the most astute people Fiona had ever met.

"He asked about you."

"He's a considerate man. I suspect he also wanted to know how April was doing in school, how your yarn is selling at the shop, and whether you've broken ground for your new house."

"Aye, but no' with the same amount of interest. I told him you'd gone with Duncan to visit Sara."

Fiona jumped on the new subject. "It's hard to believe Sara's on her way home to England right now." That morning, just hours before the little girl's discharge from the hospital, Fiona had visited one final time. She had missed not having Andrew at the hospital with her, but he had made the trip earlier in the week to say his own goodbyes.

The farewell had been every bit as hard as Fiona had expected. She had presented Sara with an original watercolor of Stardust, framed and ready to put on the wall of her new bedroom. Then, as the little girl blew kisses, Fiona had stripped off her hospital mask and gown and gone downstairs to meet Duncan for the ride back to Druidheachd.

"You'll miss her," Mara said. It wasn't a question. Mara had little need to check out her observations.

"A lot." After the goodbyes Fiona had been filled with sharply contrasting emotions. She was glad that Sara was finally well enough to leave the hospital, but she wasn't glad that she wouldn't be seeing her regularly.

She set down the tureen and toyed with the lid. "You know, on the way home it occurred to me that there are still ways I can help her. She's going to have questions as she grows up, questions that only another burn survivor can really answer. I think I'll visit once she settles in and keep in touch after that. Her grandmother invited me, and I think her aunt and uncle will be grateful for help.''

"It's only just beginning to occur to you that you're needed, isn't it?''

Fiona looked up and smiled a little. "I'll be going back to the burn unit, too, as a volunteer. The sister in charge asked if I would. She says that the children ask for me when I'm not there. And do you know why? Not because of my stories or my drawings, although they like those well enough. But because I tell them that I was burned, too. When they see me, they start to believe that maybe someday they'll be whole again, like me.''

"Are the children right, Fiona? Are you whole?''

It was a strange question, but Fiona understood perfectly. "Almost.''

"You have things to face, yet. But you've come so far, so fast.''

Fiona thought of Andrew. All roads led back to him. In the past week she had seen him from a distance twice, and once he had stopped her in the lobby for a casual conversation. But there had been no further moments of intimacy. At an early age she had adapted herself to solitude; now she was discovering all over again what it meant to be lonely.

"One thing I have to face is the fact that this book may never be finished," she said, guiding the subject in a less personal direction. "I wish my editor was better at math. If she calls once more in the middle of the night because she can't master the time change, I may blurt out the truth.''

"And the truth is?''

"I've done over a hundred sketches for the last part of the book, and not one of them is right.''

"It will come.'' Mara took Fiona's hand and squeezed it. "Have some soup now. You have tomorrow to try again.'' She crossed the room, and the door closed soundlessly behind her.

As she dished up and ate the soup, Fiona thought about Mara's news. Andrew had been at the hotel tonight. She wondered if he had known that she was in Glasgow. Perhaps he had chosen a time to visit when he was sure he wouldn't have to confront her.

Or perhaps he hadn't given any thought to her at all. More likely his mind had been on other things. He had been extraordinarily busy.

The village buzzed with news of the upcoming meeting to discuss the future of Druidheachd. Andrew had worked nonstop to be certain that everyone in the village intended to come. After the confrontation in Fort William, Carlton-Jones and Surrey had begun to twist the arms of property owners who had showed interest in their offers. Their attempts to collect signatures on the dotted line had met with dubious success. There was a deep-seated distrust in the Highlands of undue haste and bullies. So although several owners of small cottages had succumbed, those with larger properties had dug in their heels to wait.

So much rode on Sunday night.

She finished the soup and cleaned up, then she began to restlessly wander the room. She had just finished a book, and television held no interest. Fiona had learned her housekeeping skills from a mother determined to keep all germs away, so her rooms were already spotless. Only one thing was out of place.

The last box she had brought down from the attic sat in the corner beside the door. Since the day that Mara had piqued her interest, Fiona had spent hours sorting through her father's belongings. Most had gone straight to charity. Others she and Duncan had divided between them. The collection of pipes now resided in Duncan's office, a sign, she supposed, that Duncan still had some feeling for the man who had sired him, no matter how inadequate their relationship had been while Donald Sinclair was still alive.

The box was filled with papers. She had already sorted through the top third, and so far she'd only found miscellaneous bills of sale and receipts from years before. She had started a pile for Duncan to check over, although she suspected that everything was too old to be relevant. Donald Sinclair had been organized to a fault. Duncan had told her that the files in the hotel office had been compulsively current.

Now, with nothing better to do, she lifted a new stack of papers from the box and settled herself on the sofa to continue her work. As she had expected, she found more outdated documents. She could almost visualize her father filing bills and forms until they were no longer useful, then carefully storing them in boxes for that one chance in a million that they might be needed again. She pictured a man with an obsessive need to maintain order.

A man who demanded perfection in everything and everyone.

She scanned the next neatly typed paper, which looked like a budget or a list of expenses from two decades ago. She started to stack it with the others, when her own name caught her eye.

She was the sixth item on the list. "Miscellaneous medical expenses for Fiona." There was a notation in pen beside it. "Question Melissa."

Her hands faltered, and what was left of the pile drifted to her lap. From the beginning she had hoped to find some clue to her own past in her father's things, the tiniest scrap of evidence that he hadn't forsaken his imperfect daughter. But until this moment there hadn't been even a mention of her name.

Now she understood why. Twenty years ago or more she had been reduced to an annoying expense in Donald Sinclair's budget. She had been put from his sight as coldly and meticulously as the outdated hotel records. Somewhere in this box or another there was undoubtedly a file folder containing every bill he'd been forced to pay for her care.

She pictured the words on the file guide. Sinclair, Fiona. Formerly beloved daughter.

The tone of her inner voice was as bitter as that image. Anger burst into flames inside her, and for a moment she was so filled with it that it screened out everything else. Until the day her father died, she had held fast to a secret hope that he would come to her and beg for forgiveness. Even after his death, she still had searched relentlessly for proof that she'd mattered even a little. Now the fantasy was over.

Since childhood she had convinced herself that she needed her father's approval and love. With Donald Sinclair's guidance she might step out into the world, instead of hiding in the safe, stultifying prison that her mother had created to shelter her.

It had all been a lie. Just as her mother had told her, Donald Sinclair had abandoned his daughter because she was no longer a perfect child.

But she had told herself an even worse lie. She had believed that she needed him to become whole and perfect again.

She did not.

The question Mara had asked earlier came back to her. *Are the children right, Fiona? Are you whole?*

And she had answered: *Almost.*

Almost, but not quite.

Now Fiona realized that all her life she had used her own imperfections and her father's abandonment as a shield to keep the world away. She was not at fault for his desertion. She was only at fault for letting it matter so much.

Through the years, one decision at a time, she had let cowardice become a way of life. But there were no excuses now.

Almost.

She had never needed her parents' approval or even their strength to become the woman she was meant to be. They had been far from perfect, too. Yet despite everything, she realized that she loved them still. And if she could fondly remember the young father who had carried his little girl so contentedly on his shoulders, despite the rejection that had come after, then she was living proof. Perfection was not the key to love or freedom.

She had yearned to be free all her life, when all she'd ever had to do was spread her wings and fly. She had learned that in her weeks in Druidheachd. She'd learned that she had everything she needed inside her. She always had.

She got to her feet, and the papers fluttered to the floor. She stooped to scoop them up, but her mind was somewhere else. She carried the papers to the corner and set them on the carpet beside the box. She would have to go through them again, since they were out of order. But that could wait for another time. There was already too much to think about.

She straightened and started to turn, but a letter on the top caught her eye. She frowned and leaned closer; then she dropped to her knees and held it at arm's length.

"Fiona dearest . . ."

And once again her world spun out of orbit.

* * *

He was a Scotsman, bred to ignore the weather, a Highlander who took storms and fog and chilling winds in his stride.

He was heartily sick of evil black clouds, of days that resembled night, and nights so damp that the fire on his hearth sputtered in a perpetual death throe.

Andrew threw another stick on the impotent flames and turned away. He had lived in this cottage all his life; he had nearly been born here. The cottage had never seemed so small or smothering, and he had never wanted more to leave it.

But where could he go? Until he was utterly secure in his decision not to drink again, he did not need the enticements of the pub. He didn't yearn for his old ways, but he knew better than to tempt fate.

He would be welcome in Duncan or Iain's homes, but he was loath to inflict himself on his friends or their wives. These days he wasn't good company. The man who could retreat easily behind wit and a broad smile was a man he no longer knew. He was only just beginning to know the real Andrew MacDougall.

He could go to Fiona.

Andrew had considered that often enough over the past week. Once he had driven halfway to the hotel before he turned back home. He had yearned to share his discovery, his revelations, with her. But what would he have gained? Until she could share with him, until she could give herself, there were barriers between them that made true communication impossible.

Poppy rose from his place in front of the fire and cocked his head. Then he sprang forward, hurtling toward the door like a greyhound on his final lap. At the last possible moment he slid to a stop, rammed his head against the door and began to bark.

Andrew crossed the room, pushed the dog to one side and opened the door to peer out into the evening gloom. Rain had begun again, cold, penetrating rain, and at first he saw nothing. Then a woman in a long mackintosh materialized in the shadows of the beech trees that lined his walk.

"Fiona?" He shouted a few stern words to Poppy, who was yapping joyfully.

She came to a stop under the shelter of his entryway. "I wasn't sure you'd be home."

"Come in. You'll catch your death of cold out in this."

She stepped inside but refused to stand by the fire until she had taken off her coat. He hung it on a peg, then turned back to examine her. "It's no' a night for a walk."

"It was the right night for this one."

He saw that she was clutching something to her chest. In the flicker of his fire, he read strong emotions on her face, but he couldn't identify them. "What do you have there?"

"My past." She held her bundle tighter.

"Did you come to share it?" he asked gently.

"Yes. I . . . Andrew, do you want me to leave?"

He had never wanted anything as much as her presence. But he only shook his head. "No."

"I should have called. Only, I thought if I did, you might say no. And I couldn't have stood that."

"I would have said yes and come to get you."

"I've never been inside your house."

"There's little to it. You've missed nowt." Her hair was wet, a mass of corkscrew curls dangling over her forehead and neck. Raindrops sparkled on her lashes, and color suffused her cheeks. He thought she had never looked bonnier.

"I think it's the coziest house in the world." She made her way into the center of the room, her dark denim skirt swirling around her calves as she moved. He watched as she drank in every detail. The wide plank floors that glowed like miser's gold in the firelight. The fireplace he had built himself from stones carried from Bein Domhain, the mountain where Mara had her croft.

He found himself telling her about it. "I built the fireplace two years ago. There was a wee worthless one there when I was young."

"It's wonderful." Still clutching the bundle to her chest, she ran one fingertip along the edge of the mantel. It was a beam of solid cherry, painstakingly chiseled and sanded, then rubbed with six coats of oil during the long winter just past. "You've put so much love into it."

Love? Andrew wasn't certain of that. He thought of all the hours he'd spent here throughout the years, lonely hours when his worst fears had hovered unseen in this lochside monument to his childhood. He had changed things slowly and carefully, built a new fireplace to replace the old one—which far too often during his boyhood had been as cold and empty as the worst winter night. He had sanded and varnished floors where his father had often sprawled, too dizzy some nights to make his way to bed. He'd painted walls and replaced furniture, built shelves and partitions to change the cottage into something new.

When all he had ever needed to do was change himself.

"You're smiling." Fiona smiled, too. "Did I say something funny?"

He shook his head. "The very funniest stories are the ones that take the longest to understand."

She tilted her head in question.

"I'm glad you like my cottage. I like it, as well. There are only good memories here now."

She moved closer, in the same manner that she always did. A step at a time, with long pauses punctuating each movement, as if she weren't certain she had any right to propel herself through space. "I brought something to show you," she said, when she was so close that he could read the subtle nuances in her whisky-colored eyes.

He wondered if whisky eyes were an addiction he would be forced to forsake, too. She held out her bundle. As he watched, she unwrapped a layer of plastic, then another of brown paper. She had taken no chances on the rain.

"Take them," she said.

He took what appeared to be a stack of old letters. "Do you mind if I sit?"

"Please."

He moved to the settee that was closest and made himself comfortable. She sat on the far end, perched as if for flight.

Andrew snapped on the reading lamp.

He was halfway through the first letter before he began to understand. He looked up. Fiona was watching him intently, but he couldn't read her expression. "Finish them all before you say anything," she said.

He read on, although it wasn't an easy thing to do. Somewhere, halfway through the pile or beyond, his eyes began to blur.

He felt Fiona sit forward, waiting for him to finish. Gamely he finished the letters, although by then, there was no need to read them all.

"He loved me," Fiona said, when he had finished.

Her simple statement summed up everything. More than twenty years of pain and guilt. A father's confessions to a daughter he had never been able to face. The pathetic withdrawal of a man who had once been filled with life and love.

"He believed the fire was his fault," she said. There were tears in her voice as well as her eyes. Andrew saw them through his own.

He cleared his throat. "So he was the one who placed the heater in the closet."

"Yes. Apparently he'd noticed that the cord was frayed, and he'd planned to take it to be repaired. I remember Duncan saying once that our father wasn't a man to throw away anything. So he put the heater away, but he forgot to tell my mother. The hotel was full that week, and he was busier than usual. He didn't think of it again. Until it was too late."

"He never forgave himself."

Fiona shook her head. "That's the hardest part. He wrote me these letters, Andrew, one on each of my birthdays. He didn't miss a year. And they're all the same. I think his guilt grew worse as time passed. He loved me. He's made that part so clear. But he was terrified to face me, to see what his own carelessness had caused. So he poured out his heart on paper once a year, and the rest of the time he grew sterner and stiffer, until even his son couldn't love him anymore. I think that was the way he felt it should be. He was so ashamed that he couldn't even allow Duncan to love him."

"And he never mailed the letters."

"No. Don't you see? If he had mailed them, I might have forgiven him. And he was sure that he didn't deserve forgiveness. He punished himself until he died."

"He was a poor, sad man."

"My mother was right about him, Andrew. That's the most terrible thing of all. He was exactly what she said, a man who couldn't tolerate imperfections. But it was never my imperfections that made him abandon me. It was his own."

He placed the letters on the lamp table. She was still at the end of the settee, too far away to touch or comfort. As he watched, she moved closer. He didn't reach out for her, only sat very still. His breath burned in his chest, but he was afraid to release it.

"I'm very much like him," she said softly. "I despise the parts of myself that are less than perfect. I use them as excuses to wall myself away from the things I want most."

She was beside him now. One heartbeat away. He lifted his hand and captured a teardrop at the side of her nose. His hand wasn't quite steady. "And what is it that you want, Fiona?"

"I don't know. I'm still afraid."

His hand fell to his side.

"To be held by you," she said, even more softly. "I want to be held by you."

"Do you? And the things that come after holding? Do you want them, too?"

"I want to feel. I want to feel you."

He knew better than to take her like this. She was at her most vulnerable and still unsure of what she had to give. She needed time to assimilate all that she'd learned. But even as he opened his mouth to tell her so, he knew that he wouldn't find the words.

She needed him tonight, and, God help him, he needed her just as much.

Despite everything, he still might have found the strength to move away if she hadn't cupped his face in her hands. "I want to feel you inside me, Andrew."

He groaned and pulled her closer. His fingers threaded through her wet curls, and he brought her lips to his. She tasted like raindrops and tears, like the dark sweetness of twilight and the bright sunrise of hope. The kiss was a shared joy, an exchange. Perhaps she wanted to be held, but she wanted to hold, as well. Her hands moved along his neck and shoulders as they kissed, exploring and giving pleasure. He kissed the corner of her mouth, brushed his lips along her jawline and moved lower to find the racing jolt of her pulse.

She moaned, a soft, womanly purr that resonated through his body. He captured the sound against his lips. "Ah, Fiona, do that again."

She sighed, and the sound was just as sensuous. His lips moved still lower, to the hollow of her throat. He heard her breath catch as he kissed her there. One hand crept to her waist, and he anchored his thumb in the waistband of her skirt, splaying his fingers over her denim-clad hips.

His lips captured hers once more, and hers parted instinctively. This time the moan was his. He was lost in the pleasure of her surrender. The kiss deepened, and her arms circled him tighter, almost as if she were afraid he would leave her. He lay back against the cushions and brought her to rest against him. He could feel the soft give of her breasts against his chest and the curve of her hip against his thigh. One leg lay between his, a sorceress's weapon of torture. Each time she moved he could feel his body's transfiguration. They were only moments into their lovemaking, and he was moving toward fulfillment.

Both hands were at her waist now. He felt a button against his fingertips and made short work of it. He tugged her blouse away from the waistband and rested his palms against her bare skin. Her breath caught, just for a moment, but she didn't protest. Her flesh was warm and not entirely smooth. His heart beat faster at the intimacy of this contact. His fingertips sought and found the bottom edge of her bra, tracing the line of elastic back and forth as he kissed her.

She didn't protest when he moved to her sides. The skin there wasn't perfectly smooth, either, but the small flaws took nothing away from the experience of caressing her. This was Fiona, warm and sweet and aching to be touched. His Fiona, who was so much more than the sum of her scars.

She murmured something when he unsnapped her bra. He kissed her again, lingering over her lips as his hands lingered at her back. Then gently, more gently than he knew he could, he stroked the sides of her breasts with his thumbs.

"You feel like velvet," he whispered against her cheek. "Like everything that's soft and new. And you're so very warm."

"Do I really please you?"

He took the time to prove it to her, although he was reluctant to abandon the provocative pleasure of her breasts. He found her hand and guided it to his lap, to the place where pretense could never flourish. He groaned as her fingers curled around him. "There's no finer barometer of my pleasure or lack of it."

"Andrew..." She stroked him, inexpertly, innocently, and with such success that he had to cover her hand and lock his fingers tightly with hers.

"Do more of that, and the night will end before it's begun."

"It's begun," she whispered. "It's more than begun, Andrew."

She was right, and they were still before the fire. The evening had begun here, but clearly it needed to end elsewhere. He grasped her hips and moved her away; then, before she could ask why, he stood and pulled her to her feet.

He swung her up into his arms, laughing roughly as she gasped. "You're a wee bitty thing, Fiona. An armful and no more."

Her face was just inches from his. Her eyes gleamed in the firelight. "I intend to be more than an armful."

The cottage was small, his room only a few strides away. His bed loomed in the corner, lit only by the dubious cloud-covered moon and the lamp glowing faintly in the sitting room. He lowered her to the floor. There was no laughter now. He was suddenly aware of the commitment they both had made. "I could no' live with myself if I hurt you." He cupped her chin and tilted her head so that she was gazing at him, although it was too dark to read what was in her eyes. "It's no' too late to say no."

"And still early enough to say yes."

He wanted to tell her all that he was feeling, who he was and who he intended to be for the remainder of his life. He wanted to offer her everything inside him, his past and his future, the memories of the man he had been and the hopes of the man he had become.

But despite her brave words, he knew she was frightened. She wanted him, but she was still so afraid to reveal all that she was. He could not overwhelm her. She had come to him tonight.

And that had to be enough.

He touched the top button of her blouse. "I've dreamed of this."

She stood very still. "Have you?"

He pulled the button through its hole. He traced the deeper opening with one finger. "Aye. Shall I tell you what I dreamed?"

"I think so. Yes."

"I dreamed that we were together, just this way. And that when I undressed you, you became a swallow and soared high in the sky above me."

"That's a sad dream, Andrew."

He unbuttoned the second button, and the third. His thumb dipped deeper, lightly brushing her flesh. Back and forth, as gently as a whisper. "Then, just as I had given you up and bowed my head to mourn, you came back to earth and lighted on my shoulder. And when I looked down at you, you were a woman again. My woman."

"Ah..."

He spread open her blouse. Her bra was a strip of gleaming white, but the darkness hid her well. He pushed the blouse from her shoulders, and it floated to the floor behind her. "Dinna fly away from me, Fiona."

"And if I do, will you wait for me?"

He felt the question deep inside him, and he feared that she wasn't ready for this. But he couldn't make himself stop. He didn't know how. "I'll wait always." He forced his hands to his sides, but he couldn't force himself to move away.

She nodded. He could see the outline of her head against his window. Then she reached up and touched her bra, and when she lowered her hand, the bra came with it.

He could just see a beautifully feminine outline, the ripe curves of her breasts, the narrow nip of her waist. He moved forward, and she stood her ground. He touched her breast, and he was lost. She was as soft as he had imagined. What scars his fingers could discover had stretched and thinned as she'd grown until they were only spiderwebs crisscrossing the sweetly rounded flesh. "You're all I dreamed."

"I'm no one's dream, Andrew." Her voice trembled. "But tonight I'm your reality, if you'll have me."

He showed her that he would. He scooped her closer and discovered the reality of a back that was textured with both smooth and coarse skin. He felt her hold her breath as he explored her, as if she were waiting for him to push her away. He murmured reassurances and kissed her chin, her cheeks and finally her lips. She melted against him, and he felt the age-old thrill of conquest. Nothing he had discovered had lessened his desire. She was Fiona, and the rest was immaterial.

He found the strength and self-control to undress her slowly and then to let her undress him. They had the night, and he found the patience. Her skirt pooled at her feet, then her slip. For a woman so convinced she could never seduce a man, her underthings were a revelation. He felt silk so fine that it must have been transparent, and the tantalizingly delicate froth of lace. She wore a satin garter belt to hold up her stockings, a sensuous and welcome surprise that was easily smoothed over her hips. He silently vowed to undress her again someday in brightest sunlight, and the thought made it harder, and yet more rewarding, to be patient.

When it was his turn to submit, her hands, sometimes tentative but more often eager, were almost his undoing, but he didn't rush her. When she faltered, he helped. When she didn't falter, he stood in quiet, blissful agony.

The room was cold, and he felt her shiver as she leaned against him to slide down his trousers. Only then did he take matters into his own hands, kicking off his shoes and making quick work of the remainder of his clothes. He drew back the covers, but she stood beside the bed. He couldn't read her expression, but he could read her thoughts.

"It's no' too late," he said. His voice protested, cracking strangely on the last word.

She sat on the bed and extended her hand, and he was lost again.

Beside her and under the covers, stretched leg to leg, hip to hip, he thought he would go mad. Her scent was everywhere. Her hair brushed his cheeks; her breasts brushed his chest. He could feel her moist heat drawing him closer. He knew how slow he must go, how careful he must be. He forced his hands to linger, his lips to seduce, not plunder. He had never lost himself so quickly, had never been forced to fight for even a semblance of control.

Her flesh seemed to soften against his, and she sighed her pleasure as he kissed the crook of her shoulder, the nape of her neck. She moaned as he sucked at her earlobe, and when his thumb stroked her nipple, she shuddered against him.

He knew what it was to give a woman pleasure. Now he discovered what it was to give his woman, the one woman in the universe who had been created for him, pleasure and more. Because Andrew knew as he touched her skin, the precious, scarred skin that had defeated the hungers of a raging fire, that he was helping her defeat the doubts that had been with her for so many years.

And how could she doubt herself now? How could she have any doubts when his body was taut with desire and her hands were caressing the evidence?

At last he shifted her beneath him, slowly, carefully. He already knew she was ready for him. His own caresses had grown intimate, and he knew she was moist, that he wouldn't hurt her any more than necessary if he made love to her now. He had taken a moment to prepare himself, because pregnancy was unthinkable when so much was unsettled between them. But now the thought of hurting her deterred him again. He hesitated.

In that moment, she was more courageous than he. She drew him closer and instinctively lifted herself to him. He felt her stretch slowly to accommodate him. He was a large man, and she was a small woman, but that barrier could not defeat them.

Time moved as slowly as he did. It seemed a new day when he lifted her in his arms and rested against her. "Fiona?"

"I love you, Andrew."

His throat tightened, and blood roared in his ears. "Fiona. Darling." He began to move again, carefully as before, but never so slowly again. She gasped and began to move with him. All thoughts of patience, of teaching her about love, vanished.

She was teaching him.

The sounds she made deep in her throat were the sweetest he had ever heard. She arched against him, and any semblance of sanity fled. He held her tighter and thrust harder. She moved with him, warm as sunshine and velvet soft. He could only see the outline of her head on the pillowcase, but he thought he saw the gleam of tears in her eyes.

He called her name as she gasped his.

And in that moment, time stood still.

* * *

The first thing Fiona felt as she awoke was wonder. Wonder that her body could feel so replete, wonder that she had slept so soundly, wonder that a bed could feel so warm and comfortable.

And then she remembered.

Andrew.

In a flood of sensation she recalled what had happened last night. She had come to Andrew's home, and he had patiently and expertly taken her virginity. He had wanted her.

Andrew had wanted her.

She could feel a smile on her lips as she relived what she could of those moments. He had been tender and passionate, an unlikely, stunning combination that had carried her to some place well outside herself. And Andrew had been there to guide her back.

She opened her eyes and saw her arm, then her hand, with long, relaxed fingers curled around the edge of a cream-colored duvet. Light filtered in from a window not far away, highlighting the contrast between the pale purity of the fabric and the patchwork quilt of skin once touched by fire. She always slept in shirts that covered her to her wrists. For a moment the sight of her own arm was as shocking as a woman's first glimpse of a naked man.

And then her smile died.

It was morning, and the sky was growing lighter. Andrew was sleeping soundly beside her, the warmth of his breath gently tickling the nape of her neck. His arm lay across her waist, and his hand rested possessively against her abdomen.

And soon *he* would awaken, too.

She did her best to stem the tide, but panic flooded her. Her gaze was fixed on her arm, on the only part of her body that she could see. Andrew would see it, too, see what he had touched in darkness, see what he had so gently, thoroughly loved.

She told herself to be calm. She told herself that love was not about perfection in form or spirit. She had never, never in her wildest imagination, believed that lovemaking could be as powerful, as exquisite, as what had passed between them last night. She had prepared herself for pain, for shyness and whatever residue of pleasure could seep through those formidable barriers. She had expected that residue to be enough.

She had expected so little and gotten so much.

Andrew shifted slightly, and she went stiff with apprehension. She imagined the pity in his eyes when he saw her body for the first time. He could not have discovered by touch alone just how damaged she was. Last night had been heaven, but this morning would be hell.

And suddenly, she knew she couldn't submit to it.

The sky was growing lighter, although it appeared to be another gloomy day. Had the sun been shining, the room would be flooded with light, and she would be completely visible when she stood. As it was, if she moved now, she could dress quickly. Even if Andrew woke up as she did, the light was dim enough to provide protection.

She didn't have time to question her decision. She moved on impulse, on information learned as a child and later as an adolescent. Every taunt, every whispered word of pity, was loud in her ears. She couldn't bear to taint the memory of last night with that.

She couldn't bear for Andrew to know how scarred she was still. Both outside and in.

He mumbled something as she inched out from under his arm, but when she dared a glance at him, his eyes were still closed. She sat up carefully, praying he wouldn't awaken. The room seemed to grow lighter by the moment. She eased herself off the bed and wished she could wrap herself in a sheet, but there was only the duvet, far too heavy, and covering him, as well. If she tried to remove that, he would know.

As she moved across the wood floor her bare feet sounded like gunshots, despite the care she took to step quietly. She couldn't remember exactly where Andrew had undressed her. The memory of the *way* he had, with such tender care and something almost like awe, was crystal clear. For a moment she paused, filled with the achingly sweet memory. There had been nothing of pity in the way he had made love to her last night. He had wanted her; he had wanted to give her pleasure.

She wanted to crawl back into bed with him and forget her own superficial pride.

But she couldn't.

She found her clothes on the floor at the foot of the bed. Her hands were trembling by then, and she fumbled with each piece, making long work of something that should have been easy. She didn't dare glance at Andrew. Once begun, her mission was best accomplished in haste. And she didn't want to stop dressing halfway through. She didn't want him to see her like this. Not the naked body or the naked fears.

She finished at last, pulling her dark stockings high and snapping them into place. She wondered what Andrew had thought of the absurdly feminine underwear, if he had found it an odd choice for someone with so little feminine appeal. She turned, as if to find the answer on his slumbering face.

And she saw that he was watching her.

For a moment she stood completely still. She wondered how long he had been staring at her, and exactly what he had seen.

"Very little," he said, as if he had read her mind. He didn't smile. "You've hidden yourself well, Fiona."

She considered lying. She could tell him that she had to get back to the hotel right away because she was afraid Duncan or Mara would look for her this morning and become concerned. She could say that she had wanted to make him breakfast, and the cottage was too cold for naked flesh.

But this was Andrew, and he deserved better. She said nothing.

"Did last night mean nowt?" He sat up. The duvet lay carelessly over his lap, but his chest was broader and more powerful than her hands had told her. He was magnificent.

"Last night meant everything," she said.

"I think no'." He shook his head, and his eyes were sad. "Who was it that I made love to last night? I remember the feel of her. She was soft and pliable, as womanly as a man's fondest dream. But today she's gone, as surely as if she were that dream, and a dream only."

"Andrew..."

"Come back to bed. Take off your clothes and come back to bed."

She yearned to do it. She yearned to believe that it would change nothing, that he would be as eager to love her once

he'd seen her as he had been last night in the darkness. Her
hand went to the top button of her blouse.

And froze.

He didn't make it easier. His gaze was steady and un-
blinking. "Until you trust me," he said, "until you trust me
to know who it is you really are, then we've nowt to say to
each other."

For a moment she couldn't believe she'd heard him right.
He had always understood her fears. Andrew, more than
anyone in the world, had understood.

"I understand, but I will no' accept this from you," he
said, as if, once again, he had read her thoughts.

Anger erupted somewhere deep inside her, like lava
spewing from a long-dormant volcano. "And who are you
to decide what I will and will not do!"

He stared at her until the silence had a sound of its own.
Then he spoke. "I'm the man who will love you, Fiona. The
moment that you truly begin to love yourself."

Chapter 16

On a warm summer morning Stardust began her journey to the other side of Serenity Lake. She said goodbye to Lockjaw, who wished her a safe trip. The trout were too frightened to say farewell, but they flapped their fins from a safe distance. The eels spelled out Good Luck with their nimble bodies. Stardust quickly reached the drop off where the water grew deeper. She had never come this far before, and for a moment she almost turned back. Then she thought about how lonely she was. Even her imagination had failed her. Stardust knew that she had to cross the lake, even if Lockjaw was wrong and there were no other water dragons waiting for her. The water was deep and dark, but she had to try.

"It's a nice little church, but I'm in danger of becoming a sun worshiper. If the sun ever shines again." Duncan strolled down the center aisle of the village kirk with Iain at his side.

Andrew was already at the front, arranging the lectern that would be used for the meeting. He hadn't felt comfortable using the pulpit, and the minister, a sympathetic man who was concerned about the fate of his parishioners, had brought in a simple wooden stand from his own study.

"No sermons, Andrew?" Iain nodded at the old walnut pulpit looming in the corner. "And I'd so looked forward to hearing you preach."

"I suspect before the night is finished you'll hear more preaching than you'd ever wished." Andrew joined them just in front of the first pew.

"Do you think we'll have a good turnout?" Iain asked.

"I think everyone who matters will come. Those who plan to sell and those who are on the fence. Those who have no stake in it will stay at home."

"Then everyone should be here," Duncan said. "Everyone has a stake."

Iain set the papers he'd been carrying on the lectern. "Have you prepared a speech?" he asked Andrew.

"I think that would be unwise. If I'm too formal, they'll feel I'm trying to manipulate them. I'm just going to state my concerns. They'll have the papers you've prepared that show what Carlton-Jones and Surrey have done in other places and what's happened as a result. But in the long run, it will no' be what I say or what they read that matters. It will be how determined they are to help each other. If each thinks only of himself, we'll be lost. But if they're willing to act for the greater good..."

The other two men were silent. All of them knew how difficult this was going to be.

"Kaye Gerston was planning to come and speak out," Andrew said, "but she's in hospital in Inverness."

"Since when?" Duncan asked.

"Yesterday." Andrew had driven her there himself, just hours after Fiona had walked out of his life, perhaps forever. It looked as if Kaye would recover enough to be released early tomorrow morning. He wasn't sure that he would recover at all.

"She would have been a powerful influence," Iain said.

"Aye, but there will be others who'll speak out for what's right."

"It looks like people are beginning to arrive," Duncan said. "It would be best if we didn't sit together."

"Is Mara coming?" Andrew hesitated. "And Fiona?"

"Yes. One of the local teenagers is watching April, but I think there'll be a number of children here. For their sake, you're going to have to douse any fireworks before they go off."

Andrew watched his friends take seats in different aisles. The church was old, and it carried the musty smell of centuries of prayer and worship. It's architects had carefully eschewed the sentimental or emotional, preferring stern gray stone and a design as rigid as a Calvinist's spine. But the emotion and sentiment were hidden here. They were impregnated in the air, worn into pews that had held both the newborn and the dying. Centuries of men and women had mourned in this place, even if they had managed it with Scottish stoicism and dispatch. Young people had committed themselves to each other and to God on the very place where he stood.

And now Andrew was asking for a different kind of commitment. He was not a particularly religious man and not a superstitious one. But he was glad that they had chosen the kirk as their meeting place. It seemed only right.

The villagers filed in slowly at first; then the tempo picked up, until people were sliding to the center of the pews to make room for newcomers. There was an air of suppressed excitement. Children, scrubbed within an inch of their lives, bounced on pews and signaled each other across the room. Old women leaning on canes and old men moved slowly down the aisles to find seats. He tried to greet them all and thank them for coming, but the task grew too large as the time neared to start.

Andrew glanced at his watch. It was almost seven. Mara still hadn't arrived, although Billie had come in to sit beside Iain.

Fiona was nowhere to be seen.

Andrew wondered what he would do when she did arrive. He hadn't seen her since she'd left his house two mornings ago. He didn't know what she'd thought or felt. He had been harsh, so harsh that his own words still rang in his head. But he couldn't take them back, because they were true. Until Fiona believed in him and in herself, they had no future together.

All too well he understood self-doubt and the terrible price is exacted.

He looked toward the door, but it wasn't Fiona who strolled into the kirk. David Gow, looking as if he belonged in a glossy magazine advertisement, took a seat halfway into the room.

Andrew had no doubt why Gow was here. Next week this meeting would be portrayed in Gow's newspaper as a quaint attempt by the village of Druidheachd to keep progress at bay. Gow was a brother in spirit to men like Carlton-Jones and Surrey. He used whatever was at his disposal to better his own lot.

The question now was how many of the villagers were like him?

Andrew shook another hand or two, then started toward the front. The room grew quiet. He was undisputably the moderator. The meeting was about to begin.

Normally he wore his kilt for formal occasions, but he hadn't wanted to be accused of even a hint of drama tonight. Instead he was wearing a suit pulled from the back of his closet. The suit was a dark tweed prison and the tie a silk hangman's noose. But he was willing to endure the worst punishment to set the right tone.

At the front he resisted yanking at his starched white collar. He waited until the room fell silent. Then he stepped over to the lectern.

At that precise moment, Mara and Fiona walked in.

He didn't begin, as if, like a good host, he was waiting for his newest guests to be seated. But the truth was that he couldn't speak. His mouth was as dry as a stale scone, and his throat felt as if the scone was lodged there. He had expected to feel some sense of detachment, some sense that he had been right to risk their relationship in order to make his point clearly and finally. Instead, all he felt was fear. Because as he faced Fiona in the crowded church, he realized just how much he loved her and what his life would be worth if she turned away from him forever.

She was seated now, a pale-faced waif with her chin held absurdly high. He wanted to lope down the aisle, toss her over his shoulder and flee Druidheachd forever. He wanted to forget what was right and settle for what was safe.

Instead, he cleared his throat and began.

"For those of you who dinna know, my name is Andrew MacDougall, and with the support of the minister of this kirk, I've called this meeting to discuss the events of the past months."

At first he spoke slowly and carefully, searching for the right words. These were not people who would be convinced easily. Many of them were the descendants of stubborn men and women who, in the early nineteenth century, had avoided the wholesale exile of Highlanders known as the Clearances.

The people sitting in this kirk were wary as well as astute. They made decisions with the same skill and care with which they made their livings. Scots had an international reputation for parsimony, but Andrew knew the truth about that. Scotland was a harsh land, and throughout history it had been a poor one. For centuries the Highlands had been poorest of all. After the Clearances, those who had remained had not survived through luck. They had learned to husband their resources, trade on their own unique talents and make careful, considered decisions. The old ways were important in Druidheachd, because the old ways had stood the test of time.

He tried to present his concerns without emotion, but when he spoke about what the village and the land meant to him, the emotion crept in. He had tried not to glance at Fiona, but against his will, his eyes sought her then. *Her* eyes were luminous, and despite everything else that was between them, he knew she supported him in this.

Just as he had expected, the debate began the moment he finished. A stranger, a man in a costly gray suit, rose to his feet. "I would like to speak, if I may. I represent Mr. Carlton-Jones and Mr. Surrey. And I would like to address this." He held aloft the sheet of facts and figures that each person had received at the door.

Iain had prepared the document carefully. There was nothing in it that couldn't be verified. It was an indictment of the business practices of the men in question and an unvoiced prediction of what would happen to Druidheachd if enough villagers sold their property.

Iain stood, too, and Andrew held up his hand to silence the man in gray. "You'll be welcome to speak in due time," he said. "But this is a meeting for the citizens of this village and the surrounding countryside, and until they've had a chance to be heard, I'll have to ask you to be seated."

The man protested. Andrew stood his ground. A murmur swept the room, but no one spoke in defense of the man's rights.

"Iain," Andrew said, "have you something to say?"

Iain came to the front. The murmur grew louder, then died.

"There are many ways for a man to attain what he most wants," Iain said. "One of them is to spread rumors that belittle anyone who stands in his way." He let his words sink in before he continued. "I could do that as well as any man, but I've chosen instead to fight this issue with facts. You have those facts before you. Now, if you have any questions for me, I'll answer every one of them."

There were questions, and some of them were overtly hostile. Andrew had expected as much. Iain handled them all with aplomb. He explained in clear language what had happened to the towns that had fallen prey to developments such as the one Carlton-Jones and Surrey envisioned. With figures and examples he backed up his claims that Carlton-Jones and Surrey's developments were among the most destructive. "It comes down to the simplest of values," he said at last, when there were no more questions. "Each of you must separate what is truly important from what, in the long run, is inconsequential."

"Easy for you to say, isn't it, Iain Ross?" A matronly woman in the second row lumbered to her feet. Andrew recognized her as Darla MacBride, a local busybody with the tongue of a viper and the disposition of a hedgehog. Compared to others sitting in the pews, Darla's family was relatively new to the village. Only two generations of MacBrides resided in the kirkyard.

"None of this has been easy for me to say, Mrs. MacBride," Iain said evenly. "I'm deeply concerned about what's happening here."

"And why is that? Is it because those English gentlemen can pay more for our land than you can? Everybody here knows that you want it for yourself!"

"Everybody here doesn't know that," said another female voice. "Iain Ross and his father before him have managed their land wisely and well. He's a fair and intelligent landlord, and I'll not have you malign him this way!"

Darla sat down, making disgusted noises that carried to the last pew.

"I have no wish to own so much as one more blade of grass," Iain said. "In fact this is as good a time as any to announce that I've just donated Ceo Castle and the land surrounding it to Historic Scotland, to be managed as a national historical site."

"Couldn't pay the taxes, I suppose," Darla said.

"If I couldn't pay the taxes on property that's belonged to my family for centuries, why would I try to buy property in the village? Have I need of it for another home, perhaps?"

There was no response from Darla, but another rumble of voices ensued.

Iain took his seat. Andrew waited for the next speakers to emerge. They did, in fast succession. One woman's voice trembled audibly as she tried to explain why she had just sold her family's property to Carlton-Jones and Surrey. A man stood up to announce that he hadn't sold and didn't intend to. The debate raged on.

Andrew lost his patience in the midst of a particularly virulent speech by a man he'd often drunk with at the pub. The man was defending his right to do anything he bloody well pleased.

"Of course you've the right," Andrew said. "You've also the right to bray like a blethering jackass any time you choose! Just pardon the rest of us for no' going along with you. Some of us are more interested in what happens to our friends and neighbors than whether we'll have enough quid to bet on the soccer matches!"

Had anyone been foolish enough to drop a pin, it would have sounded like a bomb. Andrew's eyes swept to Fiona again. He expected to see censure. Instead, her eyes were dancing. She lifted her hands and began to applaud. Fully half the room joined in.

Duncan was the eighth speaker. Mara leaned over to whisper in Fiona's ear as he strolled to the front. The stroll was high drama. Except for Iain, everyone else had spoken from their seats.

"Does he no' look bonny tonight, our Duncan?"

"You think he looks bonny all the time, Mara."

"Aye, I suppose. And will his son be as bonny, do you think?"

Fiona turned and searched Mara's face. Despite the serious nature of this meeting, she looked completely serene. "Are you pregnant? Is that what you're telling me?"

"Aye. Duncan does no' know, of course. I knew better than to tell him while the clouds hung heavy over Druidheachd."

"Mara, that's great!" But even in the midst of her congratulations, Fiona pondered Mara's last statement. "You know more than you're saying, don't you? Everything's going to turn out right, isn't it?"

"That depends. In a moment the men of midnight will have done all they can, just as it was predicted they would. But there's one here who's yet to speak. One whose destiny is tied up in the village now that her past has been resolved. One who needs to explain to these good people exactly what Druidheachd is, and what it means."

"You can't mean me!"

"Aye. And you've known you must speak since you walked through the door. For my son and for the daughter Billie carries. And for your own weans, Fiona."

Duncan began, and Mara turned away to watch him. Fiona hardly heard a word he said as she sorted wildly through Mara's revelations. A son for the Sinclairs and a daughter for the Rosses. She wondered if Mara was sure. She wondered if Billie knew.

And then there was *her* part in this. Her own part, and one she was terrified to play out.

She had ached to speak almost from the first. No one had talked about the mysterious, mystical appeal of Druidheachd, of its history, its secrets. No one had painted pictures of the mist-shrouded peaks of Bein Domhain, of Cumhann Moor with its eerie landscape and its ghosts of lovers long dead. No one had spoken of Andrew's darling, not even Andrew. They had talked of taxes and property values, of duties to neighbors.

But no one had talked of the things that set this one tiny village apart from hundreds of other Highland clachans.

There was a spattering of applause, and she realized that Duncan had finished. But before he could be seated, Darla

MacBride began to shout. "You're not even one of us, Duncan Sinclair! You were raised in America. You've no right to speak here."

Duncan began a response, but he stopped when Fiona stood and started down the center aisle. "Fiona?"

She was halfway to the front before she knew she was on her feet. Anger had carried her forward, as well as the knowledge that, for once, she knew her own destiny as well as Mara did.

"I'd like to answer Mrs. MacBride, if I may." She reached Duncan's side. He didn't sit down. He nodded curtly, but he stayed beside her as if he expected her to collapse. She turned to him. "I'm all right. Go on."

He looked apprehensive. She touched his hand. "Go on," she said. He shrugged and started down the aisle. Only when he was seated did she turn to face the audience.

There were so many of them. For a moment she faltered.

"She's got no right to speak here, either," Darla MacBride said loudly.

It was all the courage Fiona needed. "Don't you think so?" She forced herself to look out over the audience again, and her fear evaporated. She was shaking with anger, yet for all their faults, these people were hers. She had grown up without them, but they belonged to her and she belonged to them in a way that she would never belong to anyone else.

She moved slowly toward the first pew. The room had grown still again. Even the babies had quieted, and the little children watched her with their mouths open.

She lifted a hand and touched the opposite cuff of her blouse, a cuff that neatly hid the truth about what she had endured. She fingered the double thickness of fabric, and strangely, it gave her courage. She had endured. Like this wonderful old village, she had endured. And the fire and its aftermath had given her a clearer vision of Druidheachd's future than she might have had without it. She, of all people, knew what it meant to lose roots, family, history.

"Duncan was born here. I was born here," she said. Her voice was clear and strong. She was sure it had reached the back pews.

"So what if you were," Darla said. "That means nowt to me!"

For the first time since she'd walked to the front, Fiona looked at Andrew. He wanted her to sit down; she knew he did. He didn't want her to suffer, not for this, not for him. But he couldn't know that she wasn't suffering.

She was never going to suffer again.

She turned her gaze to Darla. "I almost died here, Mrs. MacBride. And that matters, don't you think? That gives me the right to speak as one of you. I was meant to grow up here, but I wasn't given that chance. This village and everyone in it was erased from my life, just as it's about to be erased from yours. Well, I'm back, and now I know exactly why I am. To tell you exactly what you'll lose if you continue this madness."

Even Darla MacBride fell silent.

Fiona began to paint the picture she saw in her mind, but with words. She described what it had been like to leave as a small child and come home as an adult. She talked about her first glimpse of Bein Domhain, her first ride on the loch. She talked about the majesty of the old buildings, the music of the tiny burn, the way that the clouds met the earth and cleansed everything in their path.

"There's magic here," she said. She walked over to stand directly in front of Darla. "Magic that not everyone can see. The measure of whether someone deserves to speak at this meeting is not how long they've lived here but how much of that magic they've touched."

Darla drew an audible breath.

Fiona turned away from her and smiled at Mara. "There are ghosts here, and fairies. There's a mysterious creature in our loch who far too rarely blesses us with her presence. But there's something even more important. There's tradition, and kindness and a wealth of memories. And there's history that will be destroyed if we let Druidheachd change too quickly."

She was almost finished. She had only one thing left to say. She gazed around the room. "Whatever you decide, someday you'll have to explain your position to your children and grandchildren, your nieces and nephews. Will you tell them that magic died one summer, and you sold the remnants for a few pieces of silver? Or will you tell them that the magic is still here, and that they have only to reach out their hands to find it?"

Her cheeks were flushed; she could feel their heat. But she had never felt better or stronger. She hadn't intended to look at Andrew again, but her traitorous eyes sought his for one quick glance.

His expression was inscrutable, but his hazel eyes blazed fiercely with pride.

Chapter 17

No sunshine in the world was more beautiful than Scotland's. From the moment the sun rose on Monday morning the village was bathed in a golden glow that gilded the gray stone houses and plucked rainbow hues from the lovingly tended cottage gardens. Hollyhocks swayed in the sun-warmed breeze, and roses cascaded over austere iron fences, as if to point out that there was nothing in life that couldn't be changed with enough love and care.

Nothing that couldn't be changed.

In the late afternoon Billie strolled through the hotel attic with Fiona and Mara at her side, lifting dusty items and scrutinizing them carefully. In less than a minute she had discarded three lamps and a radio that Fiona had hoped was an antique.

Billie picked up a stack of crocheted doilies that were crumbling from age and neglect. She shook her head and relegated them to the discard pile. "I think there are enough people who'll stand firm to keep Carlton-Jones and Surrey from having what they want."

Last night's meeting had been the topic of discussion since Billie's arrival. "I want to believe you're right," Fiona said.

"She is." Mara lifted a chipped crystal bowl from the top of a cardboard carton and handed it to Billie. "Worth a repair?"

Billie held it up to the light. "Nope. But Martha Stewart would use it for flowers. She'd put sweet peas or drooping ferns over the chipped part."

"What did you mean, Billie's right?" Fiona asked Mara. "Do you know something we don't?"

Billie grimaced. "She always knows something we don't."

"Do I know exactly what the result of last night's meeting will be?" Mara shrugged. "No. Do I know that we'll raise our children here, and that life will be good?" She smiled.

"Does that mean yes?"

"It's never as clear as all that. But I felt the black clouds drifting away last night, and when I awoke this morning, the village was ablaze in sunshine."

Billie lifted an old cribbage board from a box and ran her thumb over the holes. "Speaking of children . . ."

Fiona exchanged glances with Mara.

"I'm pregnant," Billie said. "At least, I think I am." She looked up, and her eyes narrowed. "Darn, you're no fun at all. You already knew, didn't you?"

"I had a wee suspicion." Mara embraced her. "So am I."

Billie hugged her back, the cribbage board temporarily forgotten in one hand. "Does Duncan know?"

"Aye. I told him last night. But I told Fiona first." Mara stretched out her arm to include Fiona in their embrace. "And it's largely due to her, I think, that I could tell Duncan today. I think we owe the future of the village to our Fiona."

Fiona tried to protest, but Billie shushed her. "You were magnificent," she said, hugging Fiona hard. "If Carlton-Jones and Surrey abandon their plans, it will be as much because of what you said as anything else."

"The men of midnight had a bit to do with it," Fiona said.

"Aye, a bit," Mara said. "But they needed you, Fiona. We all did. And we always will."

Fiona thought about what she planned to do in a few minutes. She had left the meeting last night without speaking to Andrew, who had been surrounded by people. She hadn't seen him today, either, but she knew from Duncan that Andrew had driven into Inverness early in the morning to bring Kaye Gerston home from the hospital.

He should be home soon.

"Can the two of you finish this without me?" She back-handed the air ineffectually.

"You go on. Andrew needs you more than we do," Mara said.

Fiona met her eyes. "What else do you know?"

"If you go to him now, you'll find out for yourself."

"I thought you couldn't see the destiny of people you loved?"

"She doesn't need second sight to know what's between you and Andrew," Billie said. "Plain old eyesight is plenty good enough."

Andrew crossed the pub threshold but was blocked immediately by friends who wanted to have a word with him about last night. He had turned down half a dozen drams by the time he arrived at the bar, and he shook his head as Brian raised a bottle high. "Just water."

"Am I hearing you right? Water?"

"You are, and that's all I'll be having from now on," Andrew said. "Even if I have to pay for it, I will."

"Water, Andrew?"

Andrew looked up to find Iain beside him. "That's what I'm drinking, aye."

"Well, I've heard it said the stuff's not so bad. Make mine water, too, Brian."

Brian grumbled under his breath.

Andrew turned and leaned against the bar. "You can drink whatever you choose, Iain. I'll no' grab the glass from your hand."

Iain lifted the water that Brian put down in front of him. "*Slainte mhah.* To your health, Andrew. To the best of health forever."

Andrew lifted his own in response. He hadn't looked forward to explaining his decision to stop drinking to his friends, but he should have known that Iain wouldn't need an explanation.

"Give me whatever you gave them," Duncan said, crossing the room to join them.

"It will no' be to your liking," Brian grumbled. He slid Duncan a glass of water from a full ten feet away.

Duncan looked at his water, then he looked at Andrew. He gave one of his rare smiles. "I like it fine."

"We're alone again," Andrew said, and it was true. As always, the other patrons had taken tables in the far corners of the room. "I thought after last night the villagers might have determined that we're only men. With no special power among us."

"Did you think that would be the result?" Iain asked. "Then you weren't at the same meeting I attended. There was enough power in that room to light up Druidheachd for years."

"Aye, but we have no more power than any three men who come together for something they believe in. That's what the people here have never understood. We're no different from any of them. They've given us a name, and a reputation, but we're only men."

Duncan had given similar speeches more times than Andrew could count. Now he shook his head. "I think you're wrong."

"Do you?"

"I think there's a special significance to being born at midnight. It's neither day nor night, one day or the next. It's a moment that hovers alone in time, poised on the brink of change. And that's exactly where Druidheachd has been. Poised at midnight, waiting for the next part of its history to begin. And I think that next part began last night. I just hope it unfolds the way we know it should."

"Fiona is no' the only one in the Sinclair family capable of poetry."

Duncan watched Andrew thoughtfully. "I think Fiona turned the tide of the meeting last night."

Andrew couldn't even think about what Fiona had done without feeling his throat tighten. "Aye."

"She's always been my little sister. It's been my job from the beginning to protect her."

"I know."

"I guess she proved last night that she doesn't need my protection."

"That she did."

"I'm sorry," Duncan said gruffly.

Andrew didn't have to ask what Duncan was apologizing for. He was giving Andrew a clear go-ahead. Andrew just didn't know how to tell his friend he had no idea how he should proceed with Fiona. He cleared his throat. "I dinna know why we were born at the same moment. I've no notion if it was fate or coincidence or someone's idea of a joke. I'm just glad that it happened that way."

Duncan clapped him on the back. "And do you suppose that now, since we may very well have served out our cosmic purpose, life will settle down for all of us? We'll move into middle age worrying about mortgages and high blood pressure and where to take our next vacation, instead of curses and ghosts and creatures in the loch?"

They gazed thoughtfully at each other. "Not bloody likely," Iain said with a wry smile. And as one, the three men lifted their water glasses in silent toast.

"Fiona?"

Four feet from the hotel's front door, Fiona recognized David Gow's cultured accent. Reluctantly she turned to wait for him to cross the lobby and join her. "I'm afraid I'm on my way out," she apologized. "If it's another problem with your room, you'd do better to speak with Nancy."

"It's not a problem at all. I'm leaving town in a few minutes, and I wanted to say goodbye."

"Well, we'll miss you." She extended her hand. "I hope you found your stay... enlightening?"

"Quite so." He favored her with one of his thousand-watt smiles, along with the handshake. "I have something for you." He extended a file folder.

She took it and held it to her chest.

"No, go on and look at it now. Please."

She was on her way to Andrew's, and she really didn't want a delay, but her curiosity got the better of her. She opened the folder and found a neatly typed article, probably his submission for the next issue of his paper. She looked up.

"If you'd take a moment and read it, I'd be grateful."

She nodded reluctantly. She scanned the article at first, then she found herself backing up to read every word. When she had finished, she didn't know what to say. "David..."

"My farewell present."

"You've as much as admitted that you didn't really see our creature, that it was a trick of the waves and light."

"Not quite. I've said that it could have been."

The article was beautifully written. Despite herself, Fiona was enormously impressed with his abilities. She had never read a more moving testament to the powers of myth and legend and one man's desire to believe in both. No one could fault David for what he had claimed, but neither would anyone with an ounce of skepticism believe that a creature really existed in Loch Ceo. Fiona could almost hear the village's tourist revenue trickling away.

"You've gotten yourself off the hook nicely." She looked up. "And you've defused the tourist bomb here. Now maybe Druidheachd has a chance of getting back to normal."

"More than a chance. I'm a better reporter than you might think, with better sources."

"What do you mean?"

"Well, I know for a fact that the gent who was representing Carlton-Jones and Surrey at the meeting last night has recommended that they abandon this project. He doesn't think the company has a prayer of getting all the land they need. He indicated to me that they've reluctantly agreed."

"You're sure?"

He smiled again. "As sure as I am that the royal family will have another crisis in the next six months."

"That's as good as it gets." She handed him the folder, and he tucked it under his arm.

He reached for her hand and held it for a moment. "You were wonderful last night, Fiona. I'm planning to do an article on you and the Stardust books when the rest of this dies down. I hope you'll agree."

"On one condition."

"Anything."

"You tell me right here and now that you never saw Andrew's darling."

"I think I'm looking at Andrew's darling."

"David..."

He lifted her hand to his lips and kissed it. Then he released it. "I can't tell you that."

"Are you afraid I'll tell someone? I won't. You've done more than anyone could have expected to make things right."

"I can't tell you I never saw her, Fiona, because it's not true. I had every intention of lying when I set out that night. I made myself as comfortable as I could and settled in to get some asleep. And in the hour just before dawn, I woke up and saw Andrew's darling no more than twenty feet away, stretching her magnificent neck toward the stars. She turned and saw me, and for a moment she did nothing at all. Then she flipped her tail and arched her back and dove gracefully back into the water."

Fiona was silent, imagining that sight.

"Do you believe me?" he asked.

She nodded.

"I won't say it changed my life." His smile belied his words.

"Thank you for telling me."

"You can tell Andrew, although I doubt he'll believe it."

"I don't know. Of all people, Andrew believes in miracles."

"I'll be in touch in a month or so." David opened the door for her and lifted his hand in farewell.

Outside the sun was still shining brightly, although it was past six o'clock. Fiona crossed the village green and wound her way toward the loch. Andrew's house was a good distance by foot, but she knew better than to hurry. She couldn't risk a cramp, and she didn't want to be exhausted when she arrived.

The air smelled of summer, of wild dog roses and freshly mowed grass. The loch had its own distinct smell, a clean, elemental fragrance, like the moments just before a rainstorm. She stopped more than once to gaze out over it when the road took her close enough for a good view.

Finally she turned off on the narrow wynd that led to Andrew's cottage and the ones much farther beyond. She hadn't called, because she hadn't wanted to risk a rejection. Now she hoped that the long walk hadn't been for nothing.

She was relieved to see Andrew's sedan parked beside a cluster of larch trees. His lights were on, and his windows were thrown open to the fresh breeze. From inside the house she heard Poppy's yapping, then, more faintly, Andrew's voice.

"No, you'll no' be going out with me this time, lad. I'm in no mood for your company tonight."

Fiona didn't have to calculate where Andrew might be going. He was going where he always did when he needed to think and plan. He was going out on the loch to commune with his darling.

And she was going with him.

She was waiting when he stepped aboard minutes later, waiting at the cruiser's starboard side and gazing out over the water. She turned when she knew he had seen her.

"Hello, Andrew."

"Fiona . . ."

"Isn't it a wonderful evening? It's still so light."

"Aye."

"I heard you talking to Poppy. I knew you'd be coming out. May I come with you?"

He answered by turning aside to cast off. She settled herself at the stern, and as she did, she remembered the night he had brought her out on the loch for the first time. He had told her then that there was a woman inside her, clawing her way free.

He had been right.

The motor rumbled, and the boat began to move away from the pier. He guided it with skill until they were free of the shore and past the only other boat in sight. Then he opened the throttle and started across the water.

She had expected him to come and sit with her, as he had that first time. Since they were virtually alone on the loch, she doubted it was necessary to stand rigidly at the helm, but that was what he did.

She contented herself with admiring the view. The sun was sinking slowly, and the light was growing softer. Sunset was still an hour or more away, and even then, the sky would stay light for a time. Winter days were cruelly brief and summer days unending, but nothing in Scotland was mundane or ordinary. It was a land given to excesses, a land she would be happy to live in forever.

Time ceased to have any meaning. Tonight the loch was a blue so dark it seemed to dispense with color entirely. Except for the wake of the boat, the surface was still. She imagined Andrew's darling somewhere far below them.

The motor purred a softer cadence, and the boat began to slow. Fiona realized they were approaching the sheltered cove where Andrew had brought her the first time.

They were completely alone when he turned off the motor. For a moment the silence was as loud as a roar. She got to her feet. Andrew hadn't moved toward her, so she covered the space between them instead. "I'm glad you chose this place. It has nice memories connected to it."

"Aye."

"I don't think anyone will be developing this cove for a long time."

"We can hope that's the case."

"I think it will be." She told him what David had said about Carlton-Jones and Surrey. "Druidheachd is bound to change, but it looks as if maybe it will change slowly. And now that everyone's been alerted to what could happen, maybe there'll be more safeguards established. That's the next thing we have to work on."

"We, Fiona? Do you plan to stay here, then?"

"I'm not going anywhere. This is my home now."

"Fiona..."

She saw anguish in his eyes and something very close to guilt. She stepped forward and put a finger to his lips. "You have nothing to apologize for, Andrew. You were right about me. I was hiding from you. I guess I've been a little like your darling in that way. I've been more afraid of exposure than anything. I've only risked a glance or two at the real world when I was sure that no one was there to see me."

He took her hand. "I had no right to try to force you to be something you're no'."

"You didn't force me. You told me the truth about myself, and you told me what it was doing to you."

He tightened his grip. "You've no need to let me off so easily. I've regretted what I did every moment since. I want you any way I can have you."

"You can have me the way I am, Andrew. The scars, the fears, the insecurities. And you can have the rest, too. The better parts of me, and the best." She stepped back, and she smiled as she unfastened the top button of her blouse. "I love you, Andrew."

He covered her hands. "You dinna have to do this."

"I want you to see who I am. It's taken me too many years to realize that this is a body to be proud of. I survived a fire, and every scar I have is a miracle. Maybe the scars aren't pretty, but I'm alive because of them. And I'm very, very glad I am."

He gathered her hands to his chest. "Then let's go down to the cabin," he said hoarsely.

"No. I want you to see me here, where the light is stronger." She pulled away from him. She was determined, and she was just discovering that she could be every bit as stubborn as her beloved Scotsman.

She had dressed carefully for this moment, and undressing posed no difficulties. She neither sped through it nor lingered. She undressed with the same lack of fanfare that she did each night before bed. When she was finished, she stood before him, her clothes spread out at her feet.

She knew what he saw. And she knew the love that filtered his gaze. She was not perfect, but neither was he.

"This is who I am," she said.

He clasped her close; then he lifted her into his arms. She didn't protest as he took the few stairs to the cabin. There was light here, too, enough to let her feast her eyes as he pulled off his shirt and pants and joined her on the narrow bed.

This time there was no fear and no shame as he explored her body. She offered herself proudly, and in return she took everything he offered her with the same fierce pride. When they were one at last, she held him close, basking in his desire for her.

"I love you," he said gruffly. "You know it, do you no'?"

"Aye."

"And you'll marry me, and have my children?"

"Aye," she said again. "God willing, we'll do it in that order."

He laughed and clasped her closer. And then there was no laughter, only unflagging joy.

He was sleeping soundly when she finally could bear to part from him. The tiny cabin had filled with glorious tinted light, and she knew the sun was setting. She wanted to see it, but she couldn't wake Andrew. He looked entirely too happy to disturb.

She pulled on his shirt, which fell nearly to her knees, and climbed the steps, checking at the top to be sure they were still alone. Then she strolled out on deck, gathering her clothes as she went.

The sky was ablaze with colors she never could have duplicated in a thousand years. She felt as if they were inside her, too. They were the colors of hope and of dreams come true. She stood at the side and looked over the glistening water. When she drew the final illustrations for her book, she would try to capture this moment.

"It's our loch," Andrew said from behind her. His arms came around her, and she leaned against him. She could feel his belt buckle press against her back, but his arms were bare.

"I never want to miss a sunset again," she said.

"Then we will no'."

They stood quietly and watched the loch absorb the colors of the sky. Orange and mauve painted the surface, and lavender washed in from the farthest shore.

Fiona felt Andrew shift behind her, and then his arm lifted and he was pointing to their left. She followed his finger with her gaze.

A ripple disturbed the water not more than ten feet away, a ripple that grew steadily wider as she watched. She drew a breath that seemed to go on and on, and just as she was sure her lungs would burst, a head rose, a narrow, magnificent head with oval amber eyes.

Fiona's eyes filled. She couldn't move or exhale. She stood transfixed.

Another head broke the surface, with a neck that was longer and thicker. The first swung around, and for a moment the two water dragons stared at each other. Then their heads began to sway.

The water dragons danced, gliding through the water together, as if they had been lovers, always.

They descended under the water at last. When there was no sign they had ever been there, Fiona slumped against Andrew and his arms tightened like metal bands. She turned and lifted her face to his. "They knew we were here."

''We'll send our children to this cove someday to see them.''

She tasted the salt of tears when he kissed her. And she didn't know whose tears they were.

* * * * *

COMING NEXT MONTH

MILLION DOLLAR SWEEPSTAKES (III)

No purchase necessary. To enter, follow the directions published. Method of entry may vary. For eligibility, entries must be received no later than March 31, 1996. No liability is assumed for printing errors, lost, late or misdirected entries. Odds of winning are determined by the number of eligible entries distributed and received. Prizewinners will be determined no later than June 30, 1996.

Sweepstakes open to residents of the U.S. (except Puerto Rico), Canada, Europe and Taiwan who are 18 years of age or older. All applicable laws and regulations apply. Sweepstakes offer void wherever prohibited by law. Values of all prizes are in U.S. currency. This sweepstakes is presented by Torstar Corp., its subsidiaries and affiliates, in conjunction with book, merchandise and/or product offerings. For a copy of the Official Rules send a self-addressed, stamped envelope (WA residents need not affix return postage) to: MILLION DOLLAR SWEEPSTAKES (III) Rules, P.O. Box 4573, Blair, NE 68009, USA.

EXTRA BONUS PRIZE DRAWING

No purchase necessary. The Extra Bonus Prize will be awarded in a random drawing to be conducted no later than 5/30/96 from among all entries received. To qualify, entries must be received by 3/31/96 and comply with published directions. Drawing open to residents of the U.S. (except Puerto Rico), Canada, Europe and Taiwan who are 18 years of age or older. All applicable laws and regulations apply; offer void wherever prohibited by law. Odds of winning are dependent upon number of eligibile entries received. Prize is valued in U.S. currency. The offer is presented by Torstar Corp., its subsidiaries and affiliates in conjunction with book, merchandise and/or product offering. For a copy of the Official Rules governing this sweepstakes, send a self-addressed, stamped envelope (WA residents need not affix return postage) to: Extra Bonus Prize Drawing Rules, P.O. Box 4590, Blair, NE 68009, USA.

SWP-S895

Can an invitation to a bachelor auction, a personal ad or a kiss-off bouquet be the beginning of true love?

Find out in Silhouette's sexy, sassy new series beginning in August

WANTED: PERFECT PARTNER
by Debbie Macomber

LISTEN UP, LOVER
by Lori Herter

Because we know just how busy you really are, we're offering you a FREE personal organizer (retail value $19.99). With the purchase of WANTED: PERFECT PARTNER or LISTEN UP, LOVER, you can send in for a FREE personal organizer! Perfect for your hustle-'n-bustle life-style. Look in the back pages of the August *Yours Truly*™ titles for more details.

And in September and October, *Yours Truly*™ offers you not one but TWO proofs of purchase toward your Pages & Privileges gifts and benefits.

So act now to receive your FREE personal organizer and pencil in a visit to your favorite retail outlet and pick up your copies of *Yours Truly*™.

Love—when you least expect it!

YTT2